A Madman's Song

JIM MARTIN

DEDICATION

To Melissa, for your invaluable feedback during the writing process and for always making sure I was giving my best. It's been a long journey but, with your help, I finally made it to the finish line.

To Suzanne, Lindsay and Chasidy – for your encouragement, support, and unending patience over the past couple of years.

ACKNOWLEDGMENTS

To Shannon Kreps and Connie Heinberg for their generous assistance with the publication of this book.

CHAPTER 1

May 6, 1950

The tide of season's change had arrived the week before, ushering in the first lazy days of summer with a steady shower of rain. But on this particular pleasant Saturday morning, warm rays of sunshine were blossoming over the horizon, stretching across the sky and chasing away the last remnants of cloud and precipitation. By all accounts, it was a day like any other in the quiet little town of Millford Springs, Texas.

The downtown streets were bustling by mid-afternoon with the usual weekend activities: boutiques filled with shoppers, women caught up on the latest gossip at the hair salon, and teenagers lined the sidewalk in front of the Centennial Cinema for the matinee. Some were looking forward to the film itself, while others, sweethearts in tow, were more eager to hold hands and sneak a kiss or two in the darkened auditorium.

Boys and girls stood in wide-eyed wonder outside Mr. Ellis's candy store, begging their moms for a nickel's worth of salt water taffy or any number of other brightly colored confections, while, next door at the Springs Diner, patrons were treated to a slice of pie and, as the sign in the window touted, *The Best Cup of Coffee in Texas.*

On the surface, it appeared to be just another sleepy summer afternoon; the kind that often ended with neighbors and backyard barbecues, children running about catching fireflies in glass jars, and idle moments sipping glasses of iced tea on the front porch while listening to cicadas fill the night with song.

But today was not as it seemed. Nearby, a great darkness was unfolding. A darkness which would soon culminate in an unspeakable act of violence. An event so unfathomable and horrific in nature, that it would shatter the innocence of this idyllic town forever.

....

Thirteen-year-old Charlie Peterson had just settled down on the front porch steps with his new issue of **Kid Colt-Outlaw**. Legs stretched out, and back against the banister, he glanced over the cover, to find the line that had attracted him: *52 big pages of mile-a-minute Western thrills!*

Anticipating the adventures within, he flipped open to the first page. But before he could read a single line, the creaking of a screen door caught his attention. Stepping out of the house across the street, wearing a short-sleeved white blouse and long pink skirt, was Ellie Carmichael. Her blond hair was pulled back in a ponytail and tied with a ribbon that matched her skirt.

Normally, nothing distracted Charlie while he was reading his comics. But, if there was one thing he liked even more than Kid Colt, it was Ellie. He would often lie awake at night, dreaming that he was a cowboy saving her from all manner of peril – the runaway trains, wild animals, and vile scoundrels - of which there was no end. She probably required rescuing far more often than the average twelve-year-old girl, and Charlie was sure that most young men would have given up, citing her as just too much trouble. He didn't mind however, for in the end he was always her hero.

In the real world, the only time he'd ever come close to a rescue had been a couple weeks earlier, when Ellie had fallen off of her bike while coming home from school. Suffering from scraped elbows, a cut knee, and a considerable limp, she'd found it difficult to continue on without a good deal of pain. Charlie had scooped her up in his arms and carried her the remaining two blocks to her house.

The next day, he stopped and picked a bunch of honeysuckle, which grew along the fence outside the town library. He knew how much Ellie liked it because, each time they passed that way, she would stop to breathe in the sweet perfumed air. *'Don't you just love it?'* she would always ask, to which he would smile and say he did.

When he'd handed her the tangled mass of vines and flowers that day, she'd said it was the nicest thing anyone had ever done for her. And, after he mentioned that he'd been stung twice by bees while retrieving the flowers, she took a step forward, raised up on her bare toes, and touched her lips to his, lingering a second or two.

"I love you, Charlie Peterson," she'd whispered in his ear.

He had been kissed before; once, by Eleanor Bainbridge, when she chased him down on the playground and cornered him inside the monkey bars, and then again last Christmas, when his Aunt Beatrice slobbered all over him, remarking on how much he'd grown in the past year. Neither experience had been a pleasurable one. As a matter of fact, he'd considered them downright gross.

But this time was different. While Ellie had already inspired a myriad of new emotions unlike anything he'd ever experienced in his life, nothing compared to the warm euphoria that flooded over him when he felt the softness of her lips against his own. In that moment, he knew without a doubt that his heart belonged to her.

"Hey, cowboy," Ellie said now as she walked across the street towards him. "You want to go into town with me? It's a good day for ice cream."

Charlie cocked his head to the side and looked up towards the sky, as if the question required deep thought. "Well," he said, giving her a playful smile, "I don't think so. I'm not a big fan of ice cream."

"That's too bad," she replied, placing her hands on her hips and rocking to the side. She gave him a shrug, feigning disinterest. "Guess I'll just have to ask Joey Maxwell instead."

At that, Charlie was on his feet. "You wouldn't! Would you?"

Ellie threw her head back and laughed. When she looked at him again, delicate strands of long blonde hair spilled across her face, framing a set of blue eyes that possessed a smile all their own. "Gotcha!" she exclaimed.

Charlie blushed and couldn't help but smile. She had called his bluff, clearly much better at this game than he was.

"You already knew I wouldn't say no to you."

"True," she said. "But I've also seen how fast you can devour a cup of Rocky Road."

....

Rather than taking the streets all the way into town, they decided to cut through the wooded area behind the neighborhood. A creek ran parallel with the town there, then curved southeast and past the county line. They followed the creek bed until they came to the bend, then continued walking straight, which would take them past the cemetery and into the western corner of town.

Charlie suggested taking a shortcut through the cemetery, but Ellie wasn't particularly fond of the idea, especially with the stories of the widow Willoughby, who, it was said, walked the graveyard in search of her lost husband.

Bernard Willoughby had become a casualty of the First World War when the dugout he was in took a direct hit from heavy artillery, turning everyone inside into indistinguishable bits of flesh and bone. There had been no body to send home and Martha Willoughby, his young wife, had therefore refused to accept his death, losing her grasp on reality and becoming more reclusive with each passing year. Then, one morning in 1924, she was found hanging by a cord of leather in the garage behind the house.

Charlie's older brother, Paul, claimed to have seen the widow the previous September while walking home from a high school football game. He said the woman rose right up out of the ground, glowing as brightly as the moon, and with outstretched arms, beckoned him to come closer. He turned and ran, not looking back, but swore he had felt her cold dead hand on his shoulder more than once on the way home.

Charlie knew that this was a load of bull, because had it happened, Paul would have without a doubt shit his pants right then and there and never spoken of the incident again, for fear that the widow would somehow find out where he lived and come calling in the middle of the night to finish him off.

Charlie figured that if his brother was lying about seeing the widow, then everyone else was, too. The cemetery didn't scare him, and he convinced Ellie that there was nothing to be afraid of.

Upon reaching the fence surrounding the graveyard, the pair slipped between the black wrought iron bars. Charlie was surprised at how easy it was to get past the fence, but then surmised that it wasn't there to keep anyone from getting out. Besides, he doubted many people had much of a desire to break *into* the cemetery.

They walked about 100 feet before Ellie suddenly stopped. "Shh! I heard something," she whispered nervously.

Charlie stood as still as he could and listened. Seconds later he heard it as well- a slow, rhythmic scraping. Looking to his left, in the direction of the noise, Charlie made out a black Dodge pick-up in the distance. The paint was chipped in several spots and, with its narrow bullet-shaped hood, flared sides, and headlights perched atop the front wheel wells, it appeared to be several years old.

"The caretaker, I suppose. Although, I've never seen anyone here on a Saturday unless there was a funeral," Charlie whispered back. "Let's go see."

Ellie was apprehensive. "I don't know. What if he's burying someone?"

Charlie shook his head. "No one has died this week, so it can't be that. Maybe it's a ghost after all!" he quipped, holding up his hands and wiggling his fingers.

"Not funny! Can we just go? I don't care what they're doing."

Charlie almost conceded, but then his curiosity got the better of him. "You stay here if you like and I'll go look. It'll only take a second."

"Don't leave me by myself!" Ellie gasped.

"Then come with me. There's nothing to be afraid of. It's the middle of the day. Besides, I'm sure it's just someone paying their respects."

"You're probably right," she frowned. "I just don't like it here."

"I know," he said, taking her by the hand. "But we won't get too close. They'll never even know we were here."

"Promise?"

"Cross my heart."

They moved through the grass, treading as quietly as possible, until they reached a stone mausoleum situated about thirty feet from the truck. From here, Charlie could see the front end of the vehicle, though a large oak tree, about ten paces out, obstructed the rest of his view. He dropped into a low squat and gestured toward the tree. Ellie ducked down, following his lead, and they moved forward, crouching behind the wide trunk of the oak. Brassy big band music belted from the truck radio, hiding any noise they made. Charlie recognized the song as one his father had played many times before – *In the Mood* by Glenn Miller.

Peering out from behind the tree, he saw a mound of freshly dug earth, still dark and moist from the recent rains, piled a few feet from the truck. A musty, putrid odor hung thick in the air, though he couldn't identify what it was. What he saw next chilled his blood. A muddied casket was sticking up from a dark cavernous opening in the ground. And it was moving.

He watched in horror as the casket moved back and forth, and finally realized that someone, standing unseen within the grave, was pushing the casket, heaving it up and out of its resting spot. Moments later, a hand emerged, then another, and with a grunt, a man hoisted himself out of the deep hole. It was Walter Conley.

Walter was a man of powerful stature. At over 6 feet tall, with broad shoulders, a stone-chiseled jaw, and thick calloused hands, he was well suited for his job working the oil rigs just outside of town. He was in his mid-forties, but looked much older; a combination of years of working in the hot sun and a deep affection for the bottle.

Even before the car accident that took the lives of his wife and son the previous December, Walter had been an eccentric man. He wasn't all that friendly, and had no desire to make conversation. In fact, Charlie had barely heard him speak more than a handful of words in his entire life. Walter's house was on his paper route, and when he collected each month, it was usually Alice Conley who'd paid. Since her death, Walter had taken over that duty, though he usually only muttered *Here* as he handed over the payment. Sometimes he said nothing at all.

Even more unnerving to Charlie was the man's mother-in-law, who lived in one of the upstairs bedrooms of the house. She had moved in a year earlier when disease claimed both of her legs. Catheter and colostomy bags were her permanent fixtures, attached to her body at all times, as even the simple act of climbing onto a toilet required the assistance of someone else. Charlie didn't know the woman's name, but he'd seen her sitting in a wheelchair, staring down at him from the window, when he delivered the paper. It always gave him the creeps. He thought she could give the widow Willoughby a run for her money any day.

The children watched now as Walter walked around the casket and started dragging it toward the back of his truck. He rested the top end on the tailgate and, picking up the back end, shoved it up into the bed. He then leaned over and pulled out a tarp, draping it over the casket and working to tie it down.

A hand came down on Charlie's shoulder. "I want to go. I'm scared," Ellie whispered.

"Okay," he replied without budging. He was transfixed on the scene before him. So much so, in fact, that he had failed to notice the red ants crawling onto his right hand until they started to bite.

He cried out, yanking his arm back and brushing the insects quickly away. Then, realizing he had just made his presence known, he panicked. Beads of perspiration popped out on his forehead, and his heart reverberated like thunder in his chest. He peeked around the tree, wondering if he'd been heard. Walter was nowhere to be seen.

Charlie looked back at Ellie. The girl's face was red and her eyes were wide with terror. "We've got to go before he finds us!" he said, rising up and darting back to the mausoleum. He flattened his back against the stone wall and waited. But Ellie didn't come.

Inching back to the edge of the tomb, he looked around and saw her still clinging to the tree, frozen with fear. She was crying now, her shoulders and chest heaving with uncontrolled sobs. He motioned for her, but she only shook her head. "I can't move. Help me!" she pleaded.

Charlie started to go back for her, but stopped when he heard a loud snap on the ground nearby. Ellie stiffened, the color draining from her face.

A moment later, Walter came around the tree, holding a shovel. Ellie whimpered and scurried backwards, but the man moved fast, raising the metal spade and bringing it down hard across her legs. The girl let out a pained scream, though it was silenced almost immediately when Walter grabbed her by the throat, lifting her off the ground as if she weighed no more than a stack of books. He walked toward the truck with the girl held out to his side, while she kicked and thrashed to no avail. Opening the driver side door, he flung her across the front seat, her limbs flopping like a rag doll. She came to rest on the torn vinyl seat, unconscious.

Walter jumped into the truck and pulled the door shut with a slam. The truck roared to life and tore away. Charlie watched in a state of numb shock, his eyes welling up with tears. Ellie had just been stolen in front of his eyes, and he had no idea why. Moments later, with clarity of thought returning, he stood up and ran as fast as his legs would take him, out of the cemetery and toward town.

CHAPTER 2

September 2, 2010

The dark green SUV cruised down the two-lane highway, water hissing and spitting from the treads of the tires as they cut through the rainwater on the wet road and churned it into a fine mist. Fat drops of precipitation beat down on the windshield between each pass of the wiper, the rhythmic thumping and swishing lulling Leslie into an almost hypnotic trance. Fully aware of the road, yet without conscious thought, she steered the vehicle forward. A rustling in the backseat brought her back into focus.

"How much further?" Cody whined.

"We're almost there. Maybe another thirty minutes or so. You gonna make it?"

"I kind of need to pee, but I think I can hold it."

"I can pull over."

"Nah, I'm good. If I have to, I'll just roll down the window and take care of it."

Leslie glanced up at the rearview mirror, meeting Cody's eyes; mischievous blue orbs under a spiky mass of sandy blond hair. His mouth was turned up in a playful grin between his dimpled cheeks.

"I don't think so, mister!" she said, trying not to smile.

Cody put his hand over his mouth and giggled, proud of his clever answer and the reaction it garnered.

Despite the emotional toll the divorce had taken on her, Leslie noticed that Cody seemed largely unaffected. She attributed that to a lack of attachment, which was likely due to his father's constant absence from the home. A prominent attorney, John had displayed a great affection for his job, but very little for his family, having spent his days with clients, and the better part of his evenings with other women.

Several years earlier, after the first affair had come to light, he claimed he had made a mistake and had asked for a second chance. More recently, however, Leslie had learned of several more of John's 'mistakes', some of which he couldn't even remember the names of, and had decided that she could no longer stay with a man who had such obvious disregard for his marriage and son. She and Cody were, for all practical purposes, living a life apart from him already.

Turning her attention back to the road, she saw a sign post up ahead on her right, the white letters shimmering in the bright beam of the headlights: *Millford Springs - 25 miles.*

She flicked on the radio and pressed the button that would scan for available stations. It stopped on a talk show and then a hardcore metal station, both of which she promptly skipped. She finally settled on a channel playing an old Garth Brooks tune. Cody seemed to approve of her selection, bobbing his head and singing that he was *Much Too Young To Feel This Damn Old*, though he was careful to change damn to darn. Leslie smiled, clearly amused by her son, and began singing along as well.

Twenty minutes later, they passed the city limit sign, *Population 3,326*, and approached an arched tunnel carved out of the hillside. A black iron railway bridge crossed over the top, and a large banner hung on the under truss, congratulating the Millford Strikers football team on their 2009 Division Championship win.

Crossing beneath the bridge and through the arch, they turned onto Main Street. The rain clouds had thinned now, lifting like a curtain and allowing patches of sunlight to burst forth and illuminate the town that lay sprawled out ahead of them. Two- and three-story brick buildings in alternating shades of red, tan, and white lined the street. The storefronts, with their colorful awnings and picture windows, appeared cozy and inviting. Tall arched windows trimmed in limestone, some with small balconies, dotted the upper levels, and Leslie imagined that behind them sat offices or quaint loft-style apartments.

"Look at that," Cody said, moving up from the back and pressing himself between the driver and passenger seats. He pointed toward a large marquee, framed in red and yellow and studded with lights, which jutted out from the building to their right. Standing atop the great sign, reaching high above the elaborate terra cotta cornice of the roof, was a red tower with white block letters descending in a vertical line, reading CENTENNIAL.

"That's the movie theater," said Leslie. "It's really something, isn't it?"

The metal-framed box office was flanked by bright red doors and tucked neatly beneath the wide shelter of the marquee's undercarriage which, like its outer frame, was filled with rows of flashing lights. The whole thing glowed like a carnival ride, promising sensational thrills and rousing delights just inside.

"Whoa," Cody said, his eyes still affixed on the spectacle behind them. "I've never seen one like that."

The cinema, like the rest of the town, evoked a warm feeling of nostalgia in Leslie, and she was struck by the postcard setting of this place. If not for the modern vehicles parked along the curb, it would have been easy to imagine walking out of a time warp into a bygone era with a simpler, less hurried way of life. When she'd passed through here two months earlier in search of a house, she'd immediately been taken with its quiet beauty.

"Can we go?" Cody asked, tugging at her.

"We don't have time for a movie right now."

"Please, Mom," he pleaded. "I'll clean my room, promise!"

"Nice try," she laughed. "But you don't have anything *in* your room yet. We need to get to the new house and settle in first. Perhaps, if you get your things unpacked and organized, we can come explore the town tomorrow."

"And see a movie, too?"

"Sure, if they're showing anything good."

Satisfied with that answer, Cody plopped himself back down in his seat. "I need to go soon. I've been holding it for a while," he noted casually.

"Okay, it won't be much longer," she replied, slowing the car for a red light. As she sat, waiting for the signal to change, she noticed a diner on the corner of the next block.

"On second thought, are you hungry?"

....

The bell above the door clanged as they stepped into the Springs Diner and the smell of onions frying on the grill greeted them at once. Leslie's stomach rumbled, reminding her that she hadn't eaten since leaving Dallas that morning. A waitress rushed by, pot of coffee in hand, and told them they could sit wherever they liked. Cody hurried across the polished checkerboard floor to a long row of shiny steel barstools at the counter.

"Right here, Mom!" he said, patting the red vinyl cushion.

She walked over and took a seat next to him. There were only a couple of other patrons inside, eating silently in booths near the windows. It was 4:30 in the afternoon according to the neon rimmed clock on the wall, and a little early for the dinner crowd. Leslie figured that would make for quicker service, allowing her to move on to the task of settling in that much faster.

The waitress, a buxom woman in her mid-fifties, walked back around the counter, returned the pot of coffee to a warming plate, and collected two menus, which she placed before them.

"A couple new faces," she said cheerfully. "You stayin awhile or just passing through?"

"Staying," Leslie replied. "We just got into town and thought we'd grab some dinner before heading to the house."

"Well, I'll be. We don't get too many new folks around here, just generations of the same ol' families. Good to have you. Name's Dorothy, Dorothy Myers."

Leslie nodded and stuck her hand out. "Leslie Bradford. Pleased to meet you. And this is my son, Cody.'"

"Well, aren't you a doll," the waitress said, turning toward him. "You can call me Aunt Dorothy if you like. All the kids do. And since it's your first time here, I'm gonna have to fix you up with my special double fudge milkshake, on the house. If that's okay with your momma of course."

"Can I, Mom?" he asked.

"I think that would be alright," she smiled back.

"Okay. Yes, please," Cody said, nodding joyfully in the waitress' direction.

Dorothy grabbed an order pad from her apron pouch and retrieved the pencil wedged between her red bouffant locks and her right ear, jotting down the milkshake order as she spoke. "One double fudge. And what else will you be having this evening?"

"What's good?" Leslie asked.

"The fried chicken is our most popular. All the burgers are good, too, but I'd stay away from the meatloaf if I were you."

"I think I'll try the chicken and a salad, ranch on the side, with an iced tea. And a cheeseburger for him."

"Alright, I'll get that in for you," Dorothy said, ripping the ticket from the pad and walking it back to the kitchen, where a wiry young man went to work straightaway, tossing a pink patty of meat on the grill and dropping a basket of fries into the hot sputtering oil.

Cody excused himself to go to the bathroom, making sure to tell his mother that she was not to drink any of his shake should it arrive before he returned.

"Don't you worry," Dorothy said, returning to the counter with glasses of water, an iced tea, and a bowl of cut lemons. "Aunt Dorothy has got your back. I'll keep a good eye on it for you. And if you remember to wash your hands, there may even be a slice of pie for you as well."

"Yes, ma'am," Cody grinned, and took off toward the restroom.

"What a good kid," Dorothy said, watching him. "Not many are so well mannered these days."

"Yes, he is. He forgets his manners sometimes, but he's always stayed out of trouble."

"That's a lot to be proud of."

"You're right. I don't know what I'd do without him. You have children?"

"No, I was married once, but I used a frying pan on that man more than I ever did a Sunday dinner. Ed was worse than a four year old sometimes. Honey, he was all I could handle," she chuckled.

"I know what you mean. I had one too. Only he had other hens in his frying pan, if you catch my drift."

"Oh my, I'm sorry child. What is it with some men? If Ed had ever done anything like that, I'd have had his balls in that fryer back there. Pardon the expression."

"Not at all," Leslie smiled. "I think that makes for a fine deterrent."

"Well, you and that boy of yours doing alright on your own?"

"Yes, thank you. I think we'll be much better now. I received a settlement – enough to buy the house – and I'll get child support, which will help with the finances. I did notice your sign, however." She motioned to a sheet of paper taped inside the front window with the words *Help Wanted* scrawled across it.

Dorothy lifted her eyebrows. "You lookin for work? Ever wait tables before?"

"A little. Back in college."

"Well, ain't much hard about it here. The townsfolk know what they like and the people passing through … well, if you like em', you recommend the chicken. And if you don't, just recommend the meatloaf."

Leslie laughed. "So does that mean I'm hired?" she asked.

"Come by tomorrow and we'll talk about your schedule," Dorothy replied with a wink.

"Thank you. I can't tell you how much I appreciate this."

The waitress laughed. "Oh, not a'tall. It's the least I can do, and it'll be nice having you around." She gave Leslie a little pat on the arm and excused herself to check on their order.

Cody reappeared moments later, hopping up on the barstool and giving it a quick spin. She detected the faint medicinal smell of industrial soap, and could see that his hands had been freshly scrubbed. He was usually good about washing them before he ate anyway, but the promise of free dessert essentially guaranteed it. She poked him in the ribs, anxious to share her good fortune.

"Good news. Your mother just got a job," she said, taking a sip of tea.

"Here?"

"Yes *here*, silly."

"Yay!" he exclaimed. "Free ice cream for life!"

"Umm, I hardly think so. You'll have to earn your ice cream, just like I have to earn a paycheck, which means chores, young man. You didn't think it'd be that easy did you?"

Cody rolled his eyes and groaned, then picked up a fry from the plate Dorothy had set in front of him and gave it a good dip in the cupful of ketchup on the side. As he was about to take his first bite, he stopped and furrowed his brow, deeply concerned.

"Is something the matter?" Leslie asked

"Please tell me I don't have to scrub the toilets," he replied.

"Cody Allen Bradford! Sometimes you are too much. I'm sure we can work something out. Now eat up and let's get to the house so you can pick out your new room."

....

The house was a magnificent structure. It was a pale butter yellow Victorian adorned with turned spindles and posts in contrasting white, gables accented with gingerbread trim over the second-story windows, and elaborate hand-carved brackets under the eaves of the dark patterned slate on the roof. The peak of the roof flattened in the middle, where a red brick chimney sat, surrounded by white wrought iron cresting. The whole thing topped off the house like a porcelain figure on a wedding cake.

Walking up the front steps leading to the deep wraparound porch, Leslie imagined herself spending many lazy summer evenings out here with a glass of wine and a good book. It was always the simple pleasures in life that made her the happiest. Whether this was simply a part of her nature or a result of countless hours spent alone growing up an only child, she couldn't say, but she was glad of it. Many people she knew required steady streams of entertainment, the lack of which resulted in boredom or depression. That, in her opinion, was a miserable existence. She was happiest when it was quiet, and did quite well on her own. She hoped she would find that here – the quiet peace that had been missing for so long.

"So what do you think so far?" she asked, turning to Cody.

"It looks old."

"It is. The houses in this area are some of the oldest in town. Some of them go back to 1885."

"That's cool, I guess," Cody replied, disinterested.

Leslie could see that he wasn't all that impressed, and wasn't surprised. At his age, a house was a house, and things like architectural detail or historical significance mattered little.

Stepping up to the front door, with its ornate wood scrolling and stained glass in delicate shades of lilac and rose, Leslie pushed a key into the lock. It turned with a solid click.

"Welcome to your new old home," she said, pushing the door open wide and stepping to the side.

Cody bounded inside, and ran-straight up the L shaped staircase that stood directly in front of the entry. By the time Leslie had shut the door, he was already on the landing and turning to go up the second flight.

"Don't you want to see down here first?" she hollered after him.

"Nope. I want to find a room. C'mon, Mom!" he shouted back.

"Alright, I'm right behind you."

Before following him up, Leslie stood in the entry and took a deep breath. She could still smell the fresh paint. Toffees and creams colored the walls and moldings, and the restored hardwood floors sported a dark walnut stain. With the modern fixtures and appliances installed by the previous owner, the house seemed almost new, yet still maintained all of the original details that gave it its charm; a perfect marriage of past and present.

The sudden realization that all of this belonged to her brought a surge of emotion that was almost overwhelming. It had taken a lot of courage to walk away from the securities she had once known in an effort to provide a better environment for her son, but now here they were in a home of their own, the future looking brighter than it had in a very long time. The road to this moment had been long and arduous, but for the first time in a long while, Leslie felt she could finally rest. Smiling, she turned and started up the steps.

There were four bedrooms on the second level. Coming off the stairs was a wall with a window seat inset under a large pane of glass. Turning either left or right and then back in the same direction led to the rooms, two on either side of the staircase. Cody had gone left, into the nearest room, and was looking out the window when Leslie walked in.

"You like this one?" she asked.

"I think so. I can put my computer in this corner by the window, and there's plenty of room for my bed and all my other things."

"You've got a great view from up here," Leslie said, walking to Cody's side and looking out at the tall oaks guarding the front of the house. "And, you'll have your own bathroom. The two rooms on the other side share a hall bath."

"This one for sure, then!" he muttered.

"Then I think I'll take the one next door, so I'll have my own bathroom as well. You ready to see the rest of the place?"

"Sure," he replied, racing out the door toward the rooms on the other side. "What are you going to use these for?" he asked when Leslie caught up to him.

"Probably make one into a guest room. And, then, I thought I might surprise you with the other one."

"What kind of surprise?" he asked fervently.

"You'll just have to wait and see now, won't you? It'll be your birthday next month, so you'll know then."

"It's just now September, and my birthday isn't until the end of next month! That's a long time, Mom."

"It's not that long, and trust me, it'll be worth the wait."

....

A little while later, Cody went to work finding all of the boxes with his name on them. The movers had been there a day earlier, dropping off the majority of their belongings, and leaving the heavier furniture in the areas which made the most sense. The beds and dressers were already in rooms upstairs, and a hand truck had been left on loan to make it easier to move the large items the short distances they needed to travel. All of their boxes had been stacked in the parlor, which made it look more like a warehouse than a place for socializing.

Within a few hours, Cody had unpacked most of his things. His clothes were where they belonged, the computer was up and running, and he even had a few items on the walls. His bed still needed sheets and pillows, and he hadn't found places for his books and action figures, but that could wait. He needed a break, and was ready to do some exploring. When he'd asked his mom if he could look around a bit, she'd told him to be careful and not get muddy if he went outside, but he already knew better. He felt he was more responsible than she gave him credit for sometimes. After all, he was almost ten years old. But moms will be moms, he figured.

Going outside wasn't his intended destination, anyway. He'd been more intrigued by the basement. When he toured the first floor earlier, he hadn't gone through the door off the side of the kitchen. His mom had mentioned where it led, noting that it would be great to have such a large area for storage, but hadn't taken him down there.

Opening the basement door now, Cody felt a cold draft ripple across his body. Goose pimples sprung up on his bare arms, and a damp, stale odor filled his nostrils. Staring at the wooden steps fading into darkness, he heard the faint echo of water dripping from somewhere within the bowels of the black abyss. He suddenly wondered if this was a good idea, but then dismissed the thought as a by-product of watching too many scary movies. *What could be down there after all?*

Fumbling around on the wall, he found the light switch and flicked it on. A single bulb lit the staircase, while another glowed from somewhere below, casting deep shadows along the walls. If there were any grotesque, slithering mutations or sharp-toothed, hairy creatures waiting to feast upon him, they had been relegated to the dark corners of the cave-like room, waiting with delicious anticipation until he was close enough for them to strike.

He descended with caution, allowing his eyes to adjust to the dim surroundings. At the bottom of the stairs, he stepped into the circle of light. A lamp cord and socket holding a lone bulb hung from the bare rafters above him. Glancing around, he was startled by his own reflection in an old swivel mirror, which stood in a corner. He laughed at how jumpy he'd become, and pressed onward, intent on his adventure.

Wooden shelves lined the walls and were all but empty now, with the exception of one. He walked over and found cans of leftover paint, some tubes of something unrecognizable, a glass jar holding screws and nails, some rope, a few rusty tools, and an assortment of old fixtures that had once been a part of the house. He sorted through knobs and handles, lighting sconces, and part of an old sink, then sighed. Nothing of any use to him.

In a container on the bottom shelf, he discovered a mailbox similar to the one that hung near the front door. This one had a few small dents and the paint was flaking, revealing part of a letter etched in the brassy metal underneath. He scratched at it with his fingernail, and the paint chipped away with ease. Holding the box up to the light to get a better look, he saw something move out of the corner of his eye. The hairs on the back of his neck stood straight up.

The lamp cord was swaying now; light swinging to and fro, bringing the shadows on the wall to life – a sea of black arms clawing and grabbing in a mad frenzy. Cody dropped the mailbox and ran back up the stairs, slamming the door behind him.

It was nothing he thought. *Just the light playing tricks on my eyes.*

But it had been more than that. He wasn't sure what had caused the bulb to swing in the first place, but maybe it was best to avoid the basement, after all. Now that he had seen what was down there, he had no reason to go back. At least he had managed to make out the word on the mailbox before being spooked. It was nothing though, just a name. *Conley* it had read.

The mailbox must have belonged to someone that lived here before, Cody reasoned, giving it no further thought. Feeling a renewed energy from the surge of adrenalin pumping through his veins, he hurried back upstairs to finish up in his room.

CHAPTER 3

September 7, 2010

The alarm went off at 6:30. Leslie swatted at it a few times before finding the correct button and silencing the high-pitched tones that had jarred her out of a peaceful slumber. It was still dark outside, and the ceiling fan above her whirred softly, surges of cool air swishing across the bare skin of her leg, which poked out from under the sheets. She had to fight the urge to go back to sleep, thinking it a cruel affair that work and school should start so early in the day. Mustering every ounce of energy she had within her, she slid out of the comfort of her bed and shuffled to the bathroom, feeling the chill of the hardwood on the soles of her feet. *Winter is going to be murder* she thought.

After showering and tossing on a robe, she went to wake Cody. She found him already up and dressed, wearing a new pair of plaid cargo shorts and a navy polo, which he'd picked out when they'd gone shopping over the weekend. For a boy his age, Cody was very particular about the way he looked, sometimes taking longer to get ready than she did. This seemed to be more because he took pride in a neat appearance rather than an act of vanity. That was a relief to Leslie. The last thing she wanted was a pretentious child who bemoaned anything less than designer clothing, and steered clear of those with lesser fashion as if they had been afflicted with leprosy.

Sitting upon his bed now, devouring a Pop Tart and watching cartoons, Cody glanced her direction as she entered the room.

"Well, someone's up early," she said.

"Yeah, I heard your alarm and couldn't go back to sleep. I started thinking about school."

"Are you nervous?"

"A little. What if I'm different than the kids here? They might not like me."

Leslie sat down on the bed and put her arm around him. "Of course they're going to like you. What's not to love?"

"You're my mom, you *have* to say that," Cody said, rolling his eyes.

"Yes, well, that doesn't mean it's not the truth. I see the way you are with other children and how they always warm right up to you. You're very approachable and lots of fun. Before you know it, you'll have more friends than you can count."

"I hope so," he replied.

"You will. But it's normal to feel anxious. Starting something new is always nerve wracking."

"You get nervous, too?"

"All the time. I'm nervous about starting a new job today. I want to do well and am hoping that I don't make too many mistakes before the day is over."

"You might spill coffee on someone and get fired," Cody said, crinkling his nose.

"Thanks for the vote of confidence," Leslie laughed. ""I pray that doesn't happen. But, if it did, I certainly hope my boss would be a little more forgiving."

"You'll do great, Mom."

"Thanks. And so will you. I have no doubt about it," she said, ruffling the back of his hair. "Now, I'd better get your lunch packed. What will it be today? Peanut butter? Or turkey and cheese?"

"Turkey," Cody replied. "With chocolate milk, please."

"You got it. Be downstairs in half an hour. I want to make sure you have everything together before the bus comes. Do you have all of your school stuff in your backpack?"

"Uh-huh," he said, his attention focused once more on the cartoon he'd been watching.

Leslie left him on the bed and went downstairs to prepare his sandwich. Coming around the corner to the kitchen, she found the door to the basement standing wide open. "Seriously, Cody. You know better than this," she muttered under her breath.

Shutting the door, she went to the refrigerator and retrieved the lunch meat and cheese. Once the sandwich was together, she wrapped it carefully and placed it in a bag with a container of carrots, a banana, and an individual carton of chocolate milk. With that out of the way, she poured herself a glass of orange juice and sat down to watch the morning news. She must have dozed off at some point, as the sound of Cody's footsteps pounding down the stairs woke her with a start.

"The bus is coming!" he yelled.

She looked around her, confused, then jumped into action. "Okay, you have your backpack? Class schedule? Oh, and the number to the diner?"

"Yes, Mom, I'm ready. I just need my lunch."

She handed him the bag, which he opened to inspect the contents. "You forgot the chips," he said.

She ran over and grabbed a bag of potato chips, tossed them into his sack, and knelt down to kiss him on the cheek. "Okay, better get going."

She followed him out the front door and watched as he climbed the impossibly tall steps into the bus and took a seat next to a boy about his age. He had barely sat down before the two of them were talking with one another. *You're going to be just fine kiddo* she thought, and went inside to finish getting ready for work. Clicking off the TV and hurrying upstairs to dress, she failed to notice the basement door, which was easing its way open once more.

....

Walking into the diner, surrounded by the smell of bacon sizzling and coffee brewing, Leslie recalled the days spent at her grandparent's house when she was a little girl. Breakfast had been her grandfather's favorite meal, and each morning she would wake to a wonderful aroma, knowing that there would be a stack of pancakes and warm maple syrup waiting for her at the table. There was always a fresh pot of coffee made as well and, even back then, she had liked the taste of it. Though her grandmother didn't think it was an appropriate drink for children, her grandfather would always let her sneak a few sips from his mug when no one was looking, giving her a knowing wink when grandma came back in the room. The memory made her smile.

"Hey, sugar, good to see you!" Dorothy hollered from behind the counter.

Leslie gave a wave and walked over to meet her. "How are you this morning?"

"Oh, couldn't be any better unless I won the lottery. How about you?"

"I'm well, thank you. Ready to go to work."

"Well, alright, let's get you started."

She took Leslie to the back office and showed her a place to put her purse and any other personal items she needed to store, got her clocked in and, then, took her back to the kitchen to meet a man she called Arthur. They stepped up to the grill, where an older man in a white apron stood tending to an assortment of eggs in various states of being scrambled or fried.

Dorothy made the introduction and Arthur simply nodded. He was a short, rotund man with a receding hairline, a sizeable nose, and colossal brows. To Leslie, it looked like a couple of fuzzy caterpillars had taken up residence over the man's eyes and might, at any moment, spring to life and crawl away.

"Arthur here is the owner, and works mostly day shifts. Every now and then he fills in on a few nights as well," Dorothy said.

"Oh, I thought you ran the place," Leslie replied.

"Eh, she pretty much does," Arthur said in a graveled voice. "I just cook and pay the bills. So if you need anything other than food, go to her."

"Alright," Leslie nodded, turning to follow Dorothy back out to the front.

"Arthur doesn't say much, so don't feel bad if he's not talkin to you," Dorothy said. "It ain't that he don't like you, he's just not a people person. Likes to keep to himself, which is why I pretty much take care of everything but the cookin."

There were about eight people in the diner now. Breakfasts were slower when school was in session, which gave Dorothy ample time to teach Leslie the ins and outs of the equipment, and the finer points of waiting on tables. Leslie picked up on things quickly, and after about an hour, began taking tables of her own.

Lunch was considerably busier and, for close to two hours, every table was filled. Despite the quick pace, Leslie was having more fun than she'd had in quite some time. It was nice to have something to do while Cody was in school, and she thoroughly enjoyed meeting the people of the town. Everyone seemed so affable, and the anxiety she'd initially felt had melted away. Not once did she drop a plate or spill a drink and, even if she had, she felt like the people here wouldn't mind one bit. They'd probably offer consolation, instead, and lend a hand in cleaning it up.

There were a couple of notable exceptions, the first being a man in an expensive suit. "One of them wealthy out-of-towners. Those are always the trouble makers," Dorothy had said when she saw him.

And she was right. Surly and disagreeable, he refused to drink the water, insisting on having something in a bottle instead.

"The only thing we have in bottles is beer," Leslie told him.

"That'll be fine. Bring me whatever you have in a light."

"Sure, and do you know what you'd like to eat?"

"Do you have anything in this place that isn't cooked on a grill or in a deep fryer? This all looks atrocious."

"Well, sir, we have a few sandwiches," Leslie replied, pointing to the correct place on the menu.

"A bunch of meat. And it comes with fries. I just said I didn't want anything fried."

Leslie did her best to stay cheerful and polite, but this man was really getting under her skin. This was a diner after all, not The Tavern on the Green. What did he expect he was going to find on the menu?

"You could substitute a salad for the fries, if you like," she said.

"Tell you what, just bring me the salad since that's obviously the only semblance of something decent in this shit box. Haven't you ever heard the saying, 'you are what you eat'?"

"I'll get that right out to you," Leslie replied, ignoring the question and collecting his menu. She gave him her best forced smile. Back behind the counter, she grabbed a beer from the cooler and let the door slam behind her. Dorothy, sensing she was upset, came up and gave her a little pat on the back.

"You okay, hun?"

"I'm fine. But you were right about that one."

"He giving you trouble?

Leslie recounted the conversation she'd just had at the table. "Can you believe he actually asked me if I'd ever heard 'you are what you eat'? What a jerk!"

"Well, my goodness. If that's true, then he must eat a steady diet of assholes'"

Leslie put her hand up to her mouth, trying to conceal her laughter. "Thanks, Dorothy. I needed that," she said, wiping at her eyes.

"Well, now, if he gives you any more trouble, you come tell me and I'll give him the boot. Don't need that kind of nonsense in here, and you don't have to put up with it."

Leslie quickly found that Dorothy was true to her word. While the man in the suit ate his salad and left without incident, the second one – a rough and tumble sort – was far more lewd and offensive.

"Damn, I bet I could bounce a quarter off that thing," he had said, making a kissing sound and staring at Leslie's backside as she passed by. Dorothy, who was just two tables away, marched straight over to the man, telling him if he'd like to make good on that, she would promptly bounce a skillet off of his fat head. The man's smile disappeared quickly, and he sunk down in his seat.

"Now, I'm sure your momma raised you better than that. But, whether she did or didn't, that ain't my concern. What *is* my concern are the people who work for me. So if you think you're gonna march up in here and disrespect a lady the way you just did, you better think again, mister."

"Yes, ma'am," the man mumbled. "I'm sorry."

After that, he finished his meal and left in a hurry. While neither of the men left Leslie a tip, she was just glad to be rid of them. The restaurant she'd worked for back in college required that you kiss the customer's ass no matter how unpleasant they were. Which meant you just had to deal with creeps like that. But Dorothy's hard line stance against those who were rude and contentious was a refreshing change, and she thought she was going to be quite happy working beside her.

....

It was nearly 3:30 in the afternoon and Evan hadn't stopped to eat lunch yet. As sheriff, one of his duties was to analyze the budget for his department, a task he never looked forward to. With the end of the fiscal year approaching, it was imperative that he make sure they hadn't gone into the red. Telling Bob Patterson that you were over budget was a lot like telling your girlfriend or wife that she looked fat. You just didn't do it. And if you did, you'd never hear the end of it. It had taken him all day to crunch the numbers, but it appeared he was in good shape and would come in well under the goal.

There was a knock on the door and a muffled voice from outside. "Reece, you in there?"

"Yeah. Come on in, Dan," Evan shouted.

Daniel Decker opened the door and stepped inside. At 6'4" and 340 pounds, he more closely resembled a bear with acute hair loss than an average man. His nicknames, Double Decker and Big Dan, suited him well. As deputy sheriff, he rarely had to issue threats, and had never brandished a weapon. He could have asked even the roughest looking suspect to put on a dress and sing *I'm a Little Teapot*, and Evan figured they would not only comply, but probably offer up an encore as well.

"You eaten anything today?" the deputy asked. "I haven't seen you come out of your office since you got here this morning."

"No, I've been trying to get this budget knocked out. I was just thinking about food, though."

"I thought I might head over to the diner, if you'd like to go."

"That sounds like a great idea. I just finished up here."

"How did we fare?"

"We did well. Ol' Bob will be able to keep his panties on for at least another year."

"That's always cause to celebrate."

"Indeed it is. We may just let him pick up the tab on lunch today. Business expense, wouldn't you say, Dan?"

"No argument there, boss."

....

Arriving at the diner, the two officers took their normal spot in a booth next to a window overlooking Main Street. They had barely sat down when Dorothy appeared, placing a steaming cup of coffee in front of each of them.

"Ah. You beautiful woman, you. This is exactly what I needed," Dan said.

"I always take care of my boys, especially when they talk to me like that," she said with a wink. "You havin your usual today?"

"Yes, I think that —" Evan stopped before he finished the sentence, his eyes on the other side of the room.

Dan and Dorothy followed his gaze across the restaurant, where Leslie had just come out of the kitchen with a tray of clean silverware. Evan watched her for several moments, oblivious to everything else around him, until Dorothy finally broke the silence.

"How long you gonna stir that coffee?"

Evan looked down and realized that he was still swirling the spoon around the mug, and had been for an interminable amount of time now. He felt his face flush, but tried not to show his embarrassment.

"So who is she?" he asked.

"Her name's Leslie. Been in town less than a week. And, she – is – single," Dorothy said, stretching out every syllable of her last sentence for dramatic effect.

"Oh, well, thank you for that piece of information," Evan replied in mock gratitude.

"I'm just sayin, I don't think I've ever seen anyone render you speechless like that. I was afraid if you stared any harder, your gun might go off."

Dorothy flashed a playful smile, and she and Dan burst out laughing.

"For crying out loud, what are you? Twelve years old? Don't you have something else you could be doing?" Evan asked, shooting Dorothy a look that was intended to be serious, but made her laugh all the more.

"Well, I could be getting your food, but I think watching you is much more fun at the moment. But, fine. I'll go get you some hot rolls."

"Unbelievable," Evan muttered, watching Dorothy walk away. "And don't you start in, either," he added, turning his attention back to his partner.

Dan threw his hands up in surrender. "Wasn't me, boss. I didn't say a thing."

"No, but the look on your face tells me everything. Which is to say you're eating this up as much as she is," Evan replied, taking his first sip of coffee. He had no sooner sat the cup back down when Leslie appeared at the table carrying a basket of rolls.

"Hi, guys. Dorothy sent me over with these and said you wanted to see me."

"Oh, she did, did she?" Evan asked. He rocked back in his seat and looked across the diner. Dorothy was nowhere in sight. He glanced across the table at Dan who, as much as he was trying not to laugh, was doing a poor job of it. Why Dorothy delighted in tormenting him like this was anyone's guess, but Evan thought there must surely be a special place in hell for someone like her.

"So, which one of you is the sheriff?" Leslie asked.

"That – that'd be me," Evan stammered. "Hi, I'm Evan Reece."

Evan's brain was suddenly a jumbled mess, and he was having a hard time putting even the simplest thoughts into words. *What's wrong with me? Now I feel like I'm the one who's twelve. You're a grown man. Get it together!*

"Nice to meet you, Evan," Leslie said before turning to the hulking man in the opposite seat. "And you must be Dan?"

"Yes, ma'am. People call me Big Dan, though I'm not sure why," he said.

"I don't know either, but I'll ask around and see what I can find out," Leslie laughed.

"So, I hear you're new here. How long have you been in town?" Evan asked.

"Almost a week."

"And how are you liking it so far?"

"Oh, I love it. It's such a beautiful place. And the people are all amazing. I feel right at home."

"That's great to hear. There's never much in the way of trouble around here, but if you should ever need anything, you feel free to give us a call," Evan said, handing her his card.

"Thank you. My shift is over and I was just about to leave, but I look forward to seeing you around."

"Likewise," Evan replied.

He and Dan watched as Leslie walked out the door and crossed the street to her vehicle.

"You like her, don't you?" the deputy asked.

"She's attractive. But, you know."

"No, I don't know. What?"

"Relationships. They're complicated," Evan said, averting his gaze away from the deputy.

"Life is complicated," Dan replied. "Is it about the accident? How long has that been? Ten years now?"

"Yes. Ten years."

"And we've been friends for what? Eight?"

"That sounds about right."

"Well, you're a good man, Evan. As good as any I've ever known. And you deserve to find happiness. Now I can't say that she's the one, but you sure won't ever know unless you get out there and try. So ask her out. What's the harm in that?"

Evan stared out the window, watching as Leslie's car faded into the distance. He couldn't remember the last time he'd allowed himself to get close to anyone. Honestly, he hadn't met anyone in the last ten years that had made such an immediate impression on him the way Leslie had done just now. He did like her, even if he'd just met her. Maybe it was worth a shot after all.

"Perhaps you're right, Dan. Maybe I will ask her out."

CHAPTER 4

September 10, 2010

Evan woke at just past 2:00 in the morning. His mind was hazy, and his thoughts were blanketed by a listless fog. He knew he was in his bed, but couldn't remember how long he'd been asleep, or even what day it was. The wind blew in furious gusts outside, the house moaning under the onslaught. Branches of the tree outside scratched against the window like long, bony fingers, scraping and searching as they sought a way inside.

But the room itself was still. Too still. The air felt thick and palpable, and Evan grew restless. Something felt wrong. That was when he heard the cry. At first, he thought he'd imagined it, but then the sound came again; a long slow agonizing cry.

Evan lay motionless in the dark, seconds turning into minutes as he held his breath, listening intently to every sound around him. All was quiet. He was about to chalk it up to being the wind but then he heard it again; still distant, but loud enough to determine that it was coming from somewhere within the house.

Climbing out of bed, he rubbed his eyes, as if the simple act might somehow push away the grogginess that lingered. His legs felt heavy as he plodded across the room and into the hallway.

When he got there, he stopped. Up ahead, a glimmer of light shone from underneath the bathroom door.

Had he left that on? He didn't think so.

As he approached, he watched for any flicker of movement, and listened for odd sounds. There were none. Placing his hand on the knob and exhaling slowly, he eased the door open.

The vinyl shower curtain above the tub was pulled taught, and he could hear a steady drip from the faucet. A small stream of water spilled over onto the floor from the lip of the tub, and there was a twinge of saltiness in the moist air.

Drip ... Drip

He inched forward, a deep feeling of dread building inside of him. He wanted to turn and run, but couldn't. It was as if a force greater than his own will propelled him forward, forcing him to look.

Drip ... Drip

The sound was maddening. He had to make it stop. Gripping the shower curtain, he yanked it back, unprepared for the sight that awaited him.

"No. No. Oh, God! No!"

Evan shot upright in bed, yelling. His body was sticky with perspiration, and his head throbbed. He felt as if he were going to be sick. It was just the dream again. Always the same dream. It had haunted him for years, and he feared it would never leave him.

He went to the kitchen and turned on the faucet, splashing handfuls of water on his face. After drying off with a dish towel, he opened the refrigerator and grabbed a bottle of beer, twisting the cap off and taking deep gulps, the cold liquid quickly expelling the heat in his parched throat.

Finishing the beer, he sat the bottle on the counter and went to lie down on the couch. He knew sleep wouldn't find him again for a while - maybe even hours - so he grabbed the remote and turned on the TV. There was never anything worth watching at this hour, but it was no matter. It was a distraction, and that's what he needed to banish the unsettling visions of the dream. His mind began to wander, seeking out more pleasant pursuits. It came as no surprise to him when his thoughts turned to Leslie.

JIM MARTIN

CHAPTER 5

September 11, 2010

"Hi, Dorothy!" came the familiar little voice.

Turning from the table she had been wiping down, Dorothy saw Cody strolling into the diner, along with Tyler Roberts, a slightly chubby kid with wavy brown hair, a freckled face, and rumpled clothing that looked as if he'd just dug it out of a hamper.

"Well, my heavens," Dorothy said. "It's so good to see you boys. Tyler, how's your daddy feelin?"

"He's doing better. I don't think he likes being stuck at home so much, though. Mom yells at him a lot."

Chris Roberts had fallen off a ladder while working on a roof the week before, fracturing his left ankle. Not being the type who liked going to the doctor, he'd hobbled around for two days, insisting it was only a sprain, until the pain finally got the better of him. Dorothy knew his wife, Lisa, could be quite temperamental, and was amused by Tyler's remark.

"Well, you tell him I hope he gets better real soon, and that we miss seeing him around."

Tyler nodded and Dorothy turned to Cody. "And how are you, handsome?" she asked.

"I'm fine, thank you."

"Where's your momma? Did you bring her with you?"

"Yeah, she's outside talking to someone. She said we could get ice cream today."

"You've come to the right place. What can I get started for you?"

Cody shifted his gaze upwards and tapped his finger against his lips as he pondered the possibilities. "I think I want another one of those double fudge shakes," he finally said. "I liked that one a lot."

"I thought you might," Dorothy said with a wink. "And how about you, Tyler?"

"I want a caramel sundae," he replied.

"Alright, you boys have yourselves a seat and I'll get you fixed up."

Cody and Tyler selected a booth in the corner and sat down, chatting away like two old friends who hadn't seen each other in years. They burst into fits of laughter with such frequency that one might have thought they were at a comedy club rather than in a small town diner. It was just that sort of thing that made Dorothy love her job. At one point she'd wanted to be a nurse, but a brief stint working in a hospital had quickly changed her mind. She felt it was far too depressing, and found the mood here to be much more to her liking. Certainly the pay was less, but she was happy, and in her opinion, that was worth far more than a few extra dollars in her pocket each month.

Leslie walked in several minutes later and took a seat at one of the barstools at the counter. A few feet away, the motor on the drink mixer was making a high-pitched strum as the stainless steel agitator churned a mixture of milk, ice cream, and chocolate.

"I'm so sorry to have left you with the boys, Dorothy. Mrs. Nelson stopped me as I was walking in and started talking. You know how hard it is to get away from her."

"Oh, do I ever. It's no wonder Mr. Nelson refuses to get hearing aids. He finally got him some peace and quiet after all these years. And no worries with the boys. They're certainly no bother."

"Try spending four hours with the two of them."

"Well, it's gotta be a far cry better than four hours with Mrs. Nelson."

"Touché," Leslie said with a smile.

"Can I get you anything, hun?"

"I could go for a cup of coffee."

"Just brewed some up," Dorothy said, pouring the hot liquid into a white mug and placing it on a saucer in front of Leslie. "I see Cody has himself a new friend."

"Yes. He says he's made several friends, but Tyler is the one I hear about the most. And not all of it is encouraging."

"Oh? How's that?" Dorothy asked.

"In the past week alone, he's run through the girls' restroom, hidden someone's lunch in a trash can, and put a cricket on the teacher's desk. Not exactly the kind of role model I was hoping for in my son's new best friend."

Dorothy chuckled. She had one of those laughs that was contagious, and would have you smiling whether you wanted to or not. Coupled with her wit and incessant sunny disposition, Leslie found it inconceivable that anyone could stay in a bad mood after spending even five minutes in the presence of such a jubilant soul. She smiled grudgingly at the other woman's amusement.

"Tyler's a bit rambunctious, but still a good kid. Gets into some mischief more than anything else. Besides, who's to say Cody won't rub off and be the bigger influence?"

Leslie shrugged. "I just can't help but worry a little, you know?"

"Sure, hun. What kinda momma would you be if you didn't? But at some point you have to trust that you raised 'em right and give 'em room to do the right thing. You've got a good kid there, and I know he'll do fine. You just watch."

"Thanks, Dorothy. It's just hard when you love them so much. You don't want to see them get into trouble."

"I bet that's not much of a problem for him. Now when I was younger, that was a different story."

Leslie took a sip of coffee and looked at Dorothy with disbelief. "I can't imagine you being in trouble at all."

"In my day, when my brother or I acted up, Daddy would make us cut a branch off the old willow in the back and he'd use it as a switch. Don't you know half that tree was missin by the time I was ten? Of course that was before I cut it down."

"You cut it down?" Leslie asked with surprise

"Sure did. Daddy was out of town one weekend and I told my brother we should get rid of it. So we did. Daddy about lost his britches over that one. And we still got a whippin."

"I never would've guessed you caused your dad so much grief."

"Oh, I was something alright. You ever seen that bumper sticker that says, *I'm so bad, I'm good?* Well, sugar, don't you know they were talkin about me?"

They both laughed.

"Now, I'd better get this shake out there before somebody goes puttin a cricket on my desk," Dorothy said. She placed the ice cream on a tray and scrambled around the counter with the swiftness of a woman half her age. Returning just as quickly, she poured herself a cup of coffee and joined Leslie at the counter, watching for a moment as the boys began devouring their ice cream. "Cody sure seems to have adjusted well."

"Yes, he certainly has," Leslie replied.

"How've you been farin since you got here, sugar? I mean with the divorce and the move and all. You holdin up okay?"

"I'm feeling better than I have in a very long while. John was gone so much when I *was* there that it's not much different now. I missed him for years, and just kept holding out hope that one day things would change and he would start spending time with me again. I felt alone for so long that, after a while, I just quit feeling anything. By the time we split, I'd already gone through the hurting part. Now it's just ... official."

"Well, I'm glad you're both alright. You're a fine woman that any man would be lucky to have."

"Thank you. That's very sweet of you to say."

"And already turnin heads around here, too."

"Now, I don't know about that," Leslie scoffed.

"Oh, yes indeed. Especially one in particular. Been comin and sittin in your section every day."

"Sheriff Reece?" Leslie asked with uncertainty.

"Yes, honey. He's been eyeing you like a new squad car. Don't tell me you haven't noticed?"

"I don't know. Maybe I just haven't wanted to notice."

"He not your type?"

"It's not that. He certainly seems like a good guy. I'm just not sure I'm ready to be in a relationship again so soon."

"That's understandable. But, when the time does come, you could certainly do far worse than Evan, if I do say so."

"Playing matchmaker now, are we? Did he put you up to this?" Leslie asked, raising an eyebrow.

"No. In fact, he'd probably shoot me if he knew I said anything. He's just been through a lot himself. I don't think I've seen him take an interest in anyone the whole time he's been in this town, until now. I just think he'd do you right. And I think you'd be good for him, too."

"It's not that I'm opposed to getting to know him. I just feel like I've got some pretty high walls up at the moment. Those will have to come down before I can be close to anyone again, and I'm not sure I know how to get around them yet."

Dorothy shook her head. "Oh, it's not that we don't know how to do it, dear, it's that we're afraid. Those walls are good for a time, but I think when you come out from behind them and love again, that's when you truly heal."

Leslie sat in silence for a moment, considering what had just been said. She wrapped her hands around her mug and felt its warmth on her palms, seeking some comfort. She did want to love again, and knew that someday she would, but right now though those walls were protecting more than just her heart. They were protecting Cody as well. He was her life, and she had to think about him. In some ways, it was fortunate that John had been as lousy a father as he had been a husband, for Cody was spared the pain she'd gone through. After all, how can you miss what you never really had?

Even when a new man did come into the picture, there would be uncertainties. What if Cody became attached and for some reason things didn't work out? She never wanted him to feel the sense of loss that would be inevitable if the relationship ended. For that reason, it seemed best to stay single. But then again, if it *did* work out, Cody would have the stability and love of a father figure. There were no easy answers, no matter how much she thought about it.

"Who's to say what could happen down the road?" she finally said.

"You just listen to your heart. You'll know what to do when the time is right," Dorothy replied.

She grabbed the pot of coffee from the warmer and refilled Leslie's cup, then looked up as the bell on the front door clanged. "Speak of the devil," she whispered.

Leslie turned to see Evan standing in the doorway. He waved when he noticed her, and walked over. "Hi, Leslie, I almost didn't recognize you out of uniform. You look really nice."

"Thank you."

"Not to say you don't look nice in your uniform," he said, fidgeting with his hat. "I just meant, um, you know..."

"It's okay. I know what you meant," she smiled.

Evan wiped his brow and a look of relief spread across his face. Leslie knew he was trying to make a good impression, and found his occasional awkwardness endearing.

"Mind if I join you?" he asked.

"Not at all."

"The usual today?" Dorothy asked Evan as he sat on a barstool next to Leslie.

"You know, I think I'll go with the grilled cheese and tomato soup instead."

"My, my. You're just finding all sorts of new things to like around here, aren't you Sheriff?"

He knew what she was inferring, and shot her an exasperated look. Had she been taunting anyone else, he would have derived a certain pleasure from her game, but now that he was in the hot seat, her clever remarks weren't nearly as regaling. Dorothy, unperturbed by his look, grinned with self-satisfaction as she went to the kitchen to place his order.

"I think this is the first time I've seen you in here without your sidekick," Leslie said.

"Oh, Dan? He's holding down the station right now. Not that there's much to hold down, but he stands by diligently in case someone does something unscrupulous."

"Now there's a big word for a small town sheriff. I'd almost think you weren't originally from around here."

"And you would be correct. I grew up in Tulsa and came here about eight years ago. So, like you, I was once the town newbie. I hadn't necessarily intended to be here indefinitely, but the place kind of grew on me. It's hard not to love it here."

"I know what you mean. And I've only been here a couple weeks."

The door to the diner opened again, interrupting their conversation, and in walked a middle-aged man with disheveled hair and an unkempt beard. His clothes hung loosely on his thin frail frame, appearing to be two sizes too big, and his tanned leathery skin suggested that he spent a fair amount of time outdoors. Despite his ragged appearance, he had an almost scholarly look to him, like someone who may have, at one time or another, entertained discussions on the works of Hemingway or Hawking but now, mumbling to himself and reeking with the biting scent of whiskey, would have been hard pressed to discuss even the simple merits of Dr. Seuss.

"Who is that?" Leslie asked, watching as the man staggered over to a booth at the far end of the diner.

"Larry Wilkins. You haven't seen him before now?" Evan asked.

"I've heard Dorothy mention the name, but I guess he usually wanders in here in the evenings after I've already gone home for the day. What's his story?"

"No one really knows too much about him, but he must have hailed from a wealthy family. He showed up here a couple years ago, rented an apartment above the hardware store, and started pulling money from a trust fund. No job. No real friends. He just walks around in an inebriated state most of the time, rambling about things that don't make any sense."

"That's sad. And scary."

"Everyone was pretty cautious of him initially, but he's harmless. If he gets too intoxicated or becomes a nuisance, we lock him up for the night and let him sleep it off. His antics can actually be quite amusing at times."

"Do tell," Leslie said, raising her eyebrows and leaning in closer.

"Well, let's see," Evan smiled. "He once decided to skinny dip in the public pool, which was not a pretty sight, let me tell you. And another time he showed up at the hospital with a gash in his forehead, which he claimed to have sustained while roller skating with Marilyn Monroe."

"No way. You're making this up," Leslie laughed.

"Honest to God truth. Of course my personal favorite is the time he tried to give CPR to Ms. Tremont's dog."

"Oh, well what's wrong with that? He was trying to help, I'm sure."

"Yes, except that there was nothing wrong with the dog. She was just out taking him for a walk."

"Oh, was he okay afterwards?" Leslie asked.

"There were a few minor injuries - bruises and a couple of stitches."

"Stitches? That poor dog."

"No, the dog was fine. The injuries belonged to Larry."

"I have to say, that's quite a story. I bet Cody would get a kick out of that one."

"Your son, yes. How's he doing, by the way?"

"That's right, you haven't met him yet. He's right over there with his friend," she said, pointing in the direction of the boys. She waited until Cody looked her direction and motioned him over.

"Cody, I want you to meet someone. This is Evan Reece. He's the sheriff."

"Hi, Mr. Reece," Cody said, extending his hand to shake.

"Hey, sport. I've heard a lot about you. Your mother talks about you all the time."

Cody gave a bashful smile. "Do you arrest a lot of people, Mr. Reece?"

"Not really. Most people in this town stay out of trouble, which is good. Well, all except for this guy next to you," he said in a playful manner. "I may have to arrest him if he keeps acting up."

"No, Sheriff! I'll be good. I don't want to be in jail," Tyler pleaded.

"Alright, I'm holding you to that, then. Cody here is a pretty good kid, from what I've been told, so I'm sure he'll help you stay out of trouble. Won't you, Cody?"

"Yes, sir," he said, standing tall and looking pleased that the sheriff regarded him in such a favorable light. He looked over at Leslie, who gave him a wink and a proud smile.

"Hey, Mom, can we have some quarters for the jukebox?" he asked, transitioning smoothly into the real reason he'd looked at her.

Before she could answer, Evan stood up and reached into his pocket, pulling out a handful of change and handing each of them several coins. "This one's on me."

They both thanked him and took off toward the jukebox. The 1946 Wurlitzer, with its gold foil accents and neon tubes glowing red, yellow and green, was one of the few original pieces that had been a part of the diner since it opened over sixty years earlier. Though the 45's inside were all songs that were decades older than either boy, the real satisfaction for them was punching one of the chunky selection buttons and watching the metal arm pick up a record and flip it onto the turntable, where the tone arm would lower and make its way across the grooved black vinyl.

"Do you hear them?" a gruff voice said.

Cody turned to see Larry Wilkins glaring at them. "Hear who?" he asked.

"The voices. The little ones."

"I don't hear anything," Tyler said.

"Do you want to hear a certain song? We can play something for you," Cody added.

"No. There's already music playing. Don't you hear it?"

Cody shook his head.

"He's weird," Tyler whispered. "Let's just pick out a record."

Tyler turned back to the jukebox, but Cody's gaze remained fixed on the old man, who sat there seemingly spellbound, staring at something unseen in the distance.

"I hear the band playing, and the little ones, they're afraid."

"What are they afraid of?" Cody asked apprehensively.

Larry began to rock back and forth. His eyes glazed over with fear and his mouth drew open in a silent scream, strands of saliva stretching between his dry cracked lips. His voice trembled when he finally spoke. "Walter. Walter is coming."

JIM MARTIN

CHAPTER 6

September 25, 2010

The tires on the silver Porsche screeched and smoked as the car barreled around the corner, painting the road with thick black tread marks and leaving behind an acrid stench of burned rubber. The low rumbling of the engine increased to a guttural roar as the driver jammed the pedal to the floor, opening the throttle and launching the car onto the highway with furious speed.

The tachometer jumped as the speed rose, quick and steady – 80 … 90 … 100 mph. The lights of a police cruiser flashed in the rearview mirror, still a decent stretch behind, but keeping up nonetheless. Passing into a tunnel, the roar of the engine amplified and the great silvery beast pressed on, picking up more speed and rocketing out the other side like a bullet from a gun.

The road block came into sight now, a long line of police cars stretched across each lane. The Porsche steered left and vaulted across the grassy median onto the opposite side of the highway, clipping another vehicle and going into a spin before colliding with an oncoming truck. There was an explosion of shattering glass and twisted metal, and the words *You Lose* popped up on the screen.

"Want to go again?" Cody asked.

Tyler sighed and tossed his game controller on the couch. "That's like the tenth time in a row you've won. Even when I play as the cops, you still win."

"Don't worry. You'll get better with practice."

"Yeah, I think it might be easier if you had one of those steering wheel controls. Those are pretty sweet."

"I know. I'm hoping my mom will get me one for my birthday," Cody replied.

"Me, too. I'd come over even more."

"You're already over here all the time. My mom says she feels like she has two kids now."

"Yeah well, it's more fun hanging with you. My brother is lame. He's either hogging the TV or having his girlfriend over and telling me to get lost. Probably because they're doing it."

"Doing what?" Cody asked.

"You know, like that gross stuff you see in the movies. All sticking their tongues on each other, and kissing and taking off their clothes."

"Oh, I think girls make their boyfriends do that stuff even if they don't want to. Otherwise the girl gets really mad."

"Well, I don't ever want a girlfriend then."

"I don't know. They always smell good, and some of them are pretty to look at."

"Don't!" Tyler exclaimed. "It's a trap. Just don't talk to them."

Cody rolled his eyes. He didn't understand girls, or what all the fuss was about, but whatever it was, he certainly didn't think it was a trap. Abby Parker sat next to him in Mr. Jenkins' class and there was no denying that she was cute. He liked talking to her, and there were moments – when she would look at him a certain way – that he'd feel all tingly inside. He wasn't sure why that happened, but the last thing he was going to do was tell Tyler about it. There would be no end to the ridicule. Besides, it wasn't like he was in love or anything.

"So what do you want to play next?" he asked, holding up a game case in each hand. "*Zombie Battle Zone* or *Mad Mercenary 3*?"

"Let's do zombies. You get it loaded up while I go to the bathroom," Tyler replied.

He hopped off of the couch and made his way out of the parlor and down the hall to the restroom. Stepping inside and shutting the door, he was taken aback by the strong aroma of floral air freshener.

Another crazy thing about girls...why do they always want the house to smell like that kind of crap?

Lifting the seat on the toilet and undoing his pants, he took aim and began relieving his bladder. A sudden chill passed over him, and he shivered. The temperature in the room seemed to drop 15 degrees in a matter of seconds. Then his peripheral vision caught a flash of movement. Looking to his right, he saw a bright yellow balloon attached to a strand of ribbon ascending from above the shower curtain. It hit the ceiling with a dull thud.

What the...?

Buttoning up his pants and keeping his eye on the balloon, Tyler reached over towards the tank, fumbling around a second or two before feeling the handle, and flushed the toilet. He took a step toward the tub and pulled back the shower curtain, searching for the source of the balloon. A stab of fright cut through him when he saw the girl.

She was sitting at the far end of the tub with her legs pulled close to her chest, rocking back and forth. Her clothes were dirty and tattered, with rips in the pink skirt that covered most of her legs, and she was missing her right shoe.

"Who are you? Are you okay?" Tyler asked, his voice shaking with fear.

The girl stopped rocking and her head began to rise up, strands of greasy, matted hair falling across her deathly pale face. Where her eyes should have been, Tyler saw only dark pits; deep voids that now stared back and unnerved him. She lifted a grimy, blood-smeared finger and pursed it against her cold purple lips. "Shh," she said, her voice wispy and ethereal, "he'll hear you."

Tyler backed slowly away from the tub. He wanted to run, but was afraid to turn his back on the girl for fear that she would spring up and grab him. The lights began to flicker, and the balloon moved as if caught by a torrent of wind, becoming larger as it bounced and scraped across the rough ceiling. Something was inside of it; something dark and growing. The once bright yellow balloon turned brown in color, bulging and swelling until, with a great pop, it burst, slinging torn bits of latex and a warm crimson liquid across the walls. Blood.

Tyler looked in the mirror and saw bright red streams running down his face. Two more apparitions appeared from behind the glass and began to scream; cries of anguish and despair that made his flesh crawl.

Panicked, he ran to the door, twisting and pulling on the handle. It was locked. He pounded hard, frantically yelling for Cody, for anyone. "Help me! Oh God, please! Somebody, help me!"

The lights flickered again, and went out. He heard the shower curtain rings slide across the metal rod, clinking, as one by one they pushed against each other. It was opening. He screamed and pounded harder, tears starting to roll down his hot flushed cheeks. With a sudden click that startled him even more, the door opened.

"Hey, what's wrong?" Cody asked.

Tyler tumbled out into the hallway. Without stopping to answer, he ran out the front door and took off across the front lawn, tripping over his own feet. Rolling over to get back up, he glanced back at the house. High up in one of the second floor windows, the curtains parted and a dark, menacing face looked down on him.

"Cody, get out of there!" Tyler screamed. Not knowing if he had even been heard, and not daring to go back, he picked himself off the ground and sprinted away.

CHAPTER 7

October 3, 2010

Dusk approached and the temperatures began to drop on what had already been an unseasonably cool day. Cody pulled the strings on his jacket, cinching the hood tight against him as a cold damp drizzle started to fall.

It was Friday night, which meant a new movie would be showing at the Centennial. Because it still only had one screen, the movies were cycled more frequently here than at the huge multiplexes of the big cities, which housed anywhere from twenty to thirty auditoriums under one roof. But what it lacked in number of screens, it made up for in its grandeur. Adorned with balcony seating, ornate plaster columns and corbels, gold enameled wall sconces, crystal chandeliers, and plush red velvet curtains, the place was a palace as much as it was a cinema.

Stepping into the lobby with his mom close behind, Cody could feel the chill in his pink windblown cheeks start to subside. The large metal kettle behind the concession counter announced a fresh batch of popcorn as it drummed loudly, golden yellow kernels spilling out into the bin below and filling the warm air with a buttery aroma. He loved going to the movies more than just about anything, and the sights and sounds of the theater always filled him with a sense of wonder and delight.

"Now, this is a surprise," said a voice nearby.

"Well, hello, Evan. I didn't expect to see you here," Leslie said.

"They do give me a night off from time to time," he said with a laugh. "This is my favorite place to escape, other than the diner of course."

"This is my favorite place, too!" Cody exclaimed.

"I knew there was something I liked about you. It's good to see you, little man," Evan said, extending his hand out for a high five.

Cody laughed. "Yeah, you too," he replied, giving the sheriff's palm a good smack.

"If you haven't already found seats, I've got dibs on the front row of the balcony if you'd like to join me. I'd be happy to have the company."

"I've never been in the balcony before. Can we, Mom?" Cody asked, jumping with excitement.

Leslie was hesitant at first, but then reasoned that she was being silly. It wasn't like this was a date, after all. He hadn't asked her to be here tonight. So what could it hurt? And, since they were just two friends running into each other, it almost seemed rude to say no. Accepting his invitation, she and Cody followed Evan up a long flight of stairs and down a steep aisle to the bottom of the balcony.

"After you," Evan said, gesturing toward the long row of unpopulated seats.

Leslie went in first and selected a seat mid-row, placing her directly in line with the center of the screen. "So, are you a big movie fan?" she asked, turning back to him.

"Huge," Evan replied. "Have been since I was a kid. You could find me at the drive-in just about every weekend."

"A drive-in?" Cody asked. "Those are for food places aren't they?"

"You've never been to a drive-in theater?"

Cody shook his head.

"Oh, they're great. You watch the movie from your car on a big screen outside. Some of my best memories as a child were of my father taking my brother and me there on Fridays nights for the double feature. We would load up on snacks from the concession stand and pile into the bed of his old pickup truck with blankets and pillows. There's nothing quite like watching a movie under the stars on a cool summer night."

"That sounds like fun," Cody said. "My dad never took me to anything like that."

Evan's heart sank, and he regretted what he'd just said. He didn't know all the details of Cody's relationship with his father, only that he hadn't been around much. What little he did know had been picked up in bits and pieces through his conversations with Leslie at the diner. When it came to personal matters, he was never one to pry, unless laws were being broken and his job necessitated it.

"There just happens to be a great drive-in thirty minutes outside of town, over in Bakers Grove. Perhaps when they open up next season, you'll get a chance to see what it's all about.'

"That would be cool. You should go with us," Cody said.

"Oh, well, I wouldn't mind, but your mother might want to spend that time with you without someone else tagging along."

"She wouldn't care. Right, Mom?" Cody asked, turning to Leslie.

"Summer is almost a year away. We'll have to see what's happening when that time comes."

"So, where's your buddy Tyler tonight?" Evan asked, changing the subject. He could tell that Leslie didn't want to talk about going to the movies right now, and didn't want to press her.

"He's at home, I guess," Cody frowned. "He hasn't been to my house all week."

"Why's that? Did he get in trouble with your mom?"

"No, he said there were ghosts in the bathroom."

"Aw, I see. It sounds to me like maybe he got himself grounded and doesn't want to fess up. Maybe he's trying to save face."

"I don't know. He was kind of freaked out. And sometimes I hear things down in the basement."

"Basements can be notorious for that. Old pipes and drafty windows can make all sorts of spooky sounds. It's nothing to be afraid of, though. Maybe Tyler just let his imagination get the better of him. He'll come around, I'm sure."

"Yeah, I hope so. He's going to have to if he wants his games back."

Evan laughed. "Now you're talking. A little incentive never hurts."

"Besides, my birthday is coming up, and he has to be there for that."

"Of course he does. A best friend has to show up for his buddy's birthday party. Perhaps we should have Dan work security detail and make sure those bathrooms are clear. I'm pretty sure even a ghost would be intimidated by him."

"Okay," Cody laughed. "And maybe you could come, too?"

"Well, I'll check my schedule and see what I can do."

He already knew that regardless of what day the party happened, he'd be able to carve out the time to go. It was his uncertainty of how Leslie felt about Cody's impromptu invitation that prevented him from accepting outright.

Almost as if she sensed the reason for his hesitancy, Leslie reached into her purse and pulled out a twenty, handing it to Cody and asking him if he would run down to the concession stand and buy them a popcorn and soda.

"You can spend half of this," she said. "The other half is part of your allowance, so if you go crazy down there with the treats, just know that anything over $10 is your money."

"Okay, sure," he said, tucking the bill into his jeans pocket. "You want anything, Mr. Reece?"

"I'm good. But, thank you."

"Alright, I'll be back," Cody said, turning and darting down the aisle.

"He really seems to like you," Leslie said, turning to Evan.

"I guess so. An invitation to two outings in the span of two minutes is quite an honor. I'm not sure what I did to make him like me so much."

"I think he looks up to you. You actually pay attention to what he has to say rather than treating him like he's a bother."

Evan took a deep breath, thinking that now was as good a time as any. "Leslie, I have to be honest. I wasn't sure how to respond to him just now. I know he kind of put you on the spot, inviting me to his party on a whim."

She waved a hand casually. "Oh, it's fine. You're more than welcome to come. "

"As long as you don't mind."

"Not at all. I don't know what it will be like hanging out with a bunch of nine year olds on a sugar high," Leslie laughed. "But if you think you can handle it, the party is on Friday, the 29th. I can give you the details later."

"Hey, it has to be more exciting than most of my Friday nights."

"That bad, huh?"

"It's usually bowling with Dan and his family. That wouldn't be so terrible, except that I get partnered up with his father-in-law, who can't bowl to save his life. The ball usually ends up somewhere behind him, or in another lane. Once, he even managed to lose his teeth in the ball return, and jammed the thing up for a good half hour."

"And I thought I was a bad bowler. I guess that means you'll come then?" Leslie asked with a smile.

"Yes," Evan said, smiling back. "I think it will be a nice change of pace."

....

"Is it okay if I look inside your car?" Cody asked Evan as they sifted through the crowd and exited the theater.

"Sure. Just don't try to drive off or anything."

"I won't," he laughed.

"Be careful," Leslie whispered. "You might not be able to get him out of it."

"In that case, I'd just have to deputize him," Evan joked.

He unlocked the door and Cody crawled up into the driver's seat, looking as awestruck as if he'd just discovered an alien ship in his backyard.

"Would you like to turn the flashers on?"

"Seriously? Of course I would!"

"Right there," Evan said, pointing to a black box with a toggle switch.

With a quick flick, the light bars flashed on, pulsing in rapid succession and painting everything in their path with bright hues of red and blue. A colossal grin spread across Cody's face. "Is this your police radio?" he asked picking up a handheld microphone.

"That's actually for the speaker mounted under the hood. It's there so we can talk to people from inside the car."

Without hesitation, Cody pressed the button and held the mic up to his mouth. "You're under arrest," he bellowed. "Get your hands up or I'll pump you full of lead."

Sixty-five-year-old Raymond Fisher was leaving the cinema, and had just stepped in front of the car. He jumped at the sound of Cody's voice, dropping the soda cup he was carrying, and turning around with a petrified look on his face.

"Oh boy," Evan said, flushed with embarrassment. "I was just showing the kid the car, Mr. Fisher, and he got ahold of the radio. I'm so sorry. Hope we didn't startle you too bad. Can I buy you another soda?"

Raymond lifted his hand and waved dismissively. "Ah, don't bother. Just be careful before you give someone a heart attack," he grumbled.

"Certainly. You have yourself a good evening."

"Cody Allen!" Leslie exclaimed. "I can't believe you just did that."

"Sorry. I didn't know it was going to be so loud," he replied, dropping his head and slumping down in the seat.

"No harm done," Evan said, reaching in and placing the mic back in its holder. "But we should probably play with that when there's no one else around. Or, maybe at your birthday party."

Cody's face lit up once more. "You're coming?" he asked.

"Wouldn't miss it," Evan grinned.

....

Larry Wilkins stumbled through the cemetery. The faint glimmer of the moon cast a tinseled glow on the leaves of the trees, but only vaguely illuminated the path before him. It was of no consequence, though. He had been here enough that he could find his way through the maze of headstones in even the dimmest light.

The darkness, like the bottle of whiskey he carried, was his friend, and in it, he found solace. These days, they were the only friends he had. There had been others – real people – once, but they'd taken from him what they could over the years and gone on their way. Leeches they were, feeding off of easy money and possessions rather than blood. *To hell with them all.*

Now, he thrived on solitude; desired it as much as the next person desired social interaction. Out here amongst the dead, there was no one to bother him. He was aware of the stories of the old widow who supposedly walked the cemetery at night, but he'd never seen her. If she did exist, she was either painfully shy, or found him to be the more frightening soul. Regardless, she remained out of sight.

If memory served right, the widow's ghost was searching for her lost husband, or something to that effect. He was fairly certain he, too, had been in love once, but his mind was so fragmented these days that he couldn't recall much about it. Sometimes, he would remember a face, beautiful and hauntingly familiar. Had they been married? He wished he knew. Even her name escaped him now.

He cursed at not being able to think straight. The last few weeks had been especially difficult for him. Then there were the voices. How did they find their way into his head? And why wouldn't they leave him be? He shuddered at the memory of the echoing voices, and took a long drink from the bottle of whiskey, feeling the burn of the liquid as it slid down his throat. Wiping the sleeve of his shirt across his mouth, he nearly collided with the black truck camouflaged in the thick night around him.

It was old, like those he had seen at vintage auto shows, only this one was nowhere near as pristine as the ones on display there. Even in the low light, he could make out the chipped paint and rusty metal underneath. Thinking it to be another trick of his mind, he reached out and pressed his palm flat against the tailgate. To his surprise, it was real.

The truck's radio clicked on at that moment, breaking the reticent stillness with a myriad of brass instruments, which wailed through the cab's speakers.

I hear the band playing, and the little ones, they're afraid.

At those words, memory came crashing back. He remembered now – that day in the diner - he'd heard the same big band music playing, while the voices of the children ran through his head and cried out in terror. It had been the same song. He was sure of it.

"Hello? Who's out here?" he stuttered, moving cautiously toward the driver's side door.

The only answer came in the form of music, as it escaped through the small opening in the window and retreated into the night air.

A haze of condensation on the glass shrouded the interior of the truck's cabin, but Larry detected a small amount of light pulsing inside. Its glowing mass ebbed and distended in intensity, as if it were a living breathing thing that sat waiting, and watching. A single bead of moisture rolled down the glass pane, and for one brief instant, he thought he saw something move inside the truck.

Larry stopped. "Is someone in there?" he asked, his heart beating faster, moving steadily up into his throat.

There was no answer, and he realized he hadn't really been expecting one.

He reached up and wiped his hand across the window, clearing away the fog that covered the outer surface so he could see into the cabin. Without warning, two children appeared inside the truck, their faces blurred and contorted; disturbing abstract masks, with mouths that screamed. They pounded desperately on the window, until the skin of their palms cracked from the beating and painted the glass with blood streaked smears.

Larry's bladder released and a hot rush of liquid ran down his leg. The bottle slipped from his hand and smashed against the pavement, mingling whiskey and urine among shards of broken glass. His head was spinning, the voices all yelling at once.

Then, he heard a new voice, deeper and more sinister. *"Murderer,"* it whispered.

The image of the beautiful woman returned, only now, she was sprawled out on the floor, rivers of blood coursing from the wide gash in her throat. Her mouth hung open in silent protest.

"No!" Larry yelled, pressing his fists against his temples in an attempt to drive the image out of his head.

"You killed her," the voice said.

He saw the image of her lifeless face, corkscrews driven through her once vibrant emerald eyes. "No!" he screamed again. He had loved her. He knew it. He wouldn't have done this. "Stop it. Please, stop."

But the voice kept chanting. *"Murderer ... Murderer ...."*

He had to get away, had to run, but how could he escape the voices? They were everywhere. A sickening sweet urge was mounting within him in response – the urge to kill. He was going mad. Someone, or something, was taking control of his mind, releasing a steady swarm of venomous thoughts that slowly poisoned his reasoning. He turned and staggered forward a few steps before falling to his knees and retching violently, his stomach heaving and twisting in painful knots. The grim voice relented, and for a moment, his thoughts were his own.

"Larry ..."

It was a woman's voice. Memories long since buried under years of emotional pain and substance abuse came rushing back. The woman that lived in the deep recesses of his subconscious spoke to him now.

"Larry, it's alright. I'm here, darling."

"Anna? Is it really you?" he asked, gasping for breath.

"Yes. I'm right here."

Looking up, Larry could see her standing no more than 15 feet in front of him. She wore the green sweater he had gotten her for her birthday six years before. It was her favorite thing to wear, and he loved the way it brought out the color of her eyes; eyes that now looked upon him with adoration.

"Come here, darling. I won't let them hurt you anymore."

A deep peace fell over him as he rose to his feet, barely able to comprehend the reality of what he was seeing. He took a step toward her, his heart swelling.

"Anna, I've missed you so much. Can this really be?"

"Yes, and I've missed you. I can't tell you how long I have yearned to feel your touch again. Come to me, my love, and let me rest in your arms."

Wiping away tears, Larry reached out his hand and closed the gap between them. *Why had they been apart for so long?*

Then, the answer came, stopping him cold. He hadn't killed her. Someone else had. She had been robbed while using an ATM late one evening. The gunman had driven her to a remote location, where she was bound and brutally beaten, her throat slashed at the end.

"It can't be you. You're…you're…d-d-dead," he stuttered.

Her cold hand reached out and seized his wrist, pulling him forward. "Join me!" she growled, her expression turning savage.

Losing his footing, Larry screamed and plummeted into an open hole in the earth. His cry was silenced a moment later, as the sound of ripping flesh and the dull snap of shattering bone rose from out of the deep void.

CHAPTER 8

October 4, 2010

Entering the diner without so much as a word, or the usual wave, Dan walked toward the window and squeezed his massive frame into the booth that he and the sheriff normally occupied. Noticing his arrival, Leslie poured him a cup of coffee and walked it over to the table.

"Good morning, Dan. You're in here early today. Lunch isn't for another hour and a half yet."

The mug clattered as she sat the saucer down, creating small waves that rippled across the surface of the warm liquid. But Dan sat motionless, staring out the window, at nothing in particular, and without even the slightest acknowledgment he had been spoken to.

"Dan," Leslie said again, snapping him out of his trance.

He appeared disoriented, as if he were unsure as to where he was, or how he had come to be there. "Oh, Leslie, I'm sorry. I guess I just zoned out for a moment."

"Is everything alright?"

"Not really. It's been a bit of a rough morning."

"What's wrong?"

"We found Larry Wilkin's body this morning, out in the cemetery."

"What?" Leslie asked, taking a seat on the opposite side of the table. "That's awful. Why was he out in the cemetery?"

"Who knows? One thing I do know, is that he'd been drinking again. We found a broken whiskey bottle near the grave he was in."

Leslie's imagination began to run wild. Had Larry been murdered? In this small corner of the world, such a violent act seemed as foreign a concept as 5 o'clock traffic jams. "A grave? Did someone kill him?"

"Too soon to tell until we get the autopsy results back. The grave he was found in was for a funeral tomorrow. The light isn't good out there at night anyway, and in his state, he could have just taken a fatal misstep. I hope that's all it was. There hasn't been a murder in this town as long as I've been on the force, and I'd like to see it stay that way."

Dan took a sip of coffee and let out a long sigh. "Either way," he continued, staring off into the distance. "Tragedies like this, when someone loses their life, you never really get used to working those. But maybe that's just me, a big softie instead of a hardened cop."

"I couldn't do what you do at all," Leslie replied. "I cry watching the evening news. So, it's hard to fathom actually being on the scene for something like that."

"It doesn't happen too often around here, nothing like in the cities. But there, the people involved are strangers. Here, you know everyone. You say hello on the streets, you go to their kids' little league games, and eat with them at backyard barbecues or church socials. They're all neighbors and friends. Hell, some are like family. And that makes it a lot tougher."

"That has to be heartbreaking. Are you alright?"

"Just a bit stunned still. Larry may have been an odd one, but he was still a part of this town, you know?"

"What's going to happen to him? He doesn't have any family, right?"

"We'll initiate a thorough search, see if he has any living relatives elsewhere, and then hand them the responsibility. I'm hoping that pans out, because otherwise the state will claim him, and he'll be cremated. I mean, where's the dignity in that? Everyone should be remembered in some way."

"So, he may not even get a funeral? That's sad."

"I suppose it gives you a deeper appreciation for the ones you care about, doesn't it?"

"Yes, it does," Leslie replied.

It came as no surprise that her thoughts turned to her son who was, without a doubt, the most important person in her life. Nor was it unexpected when Dorothy came to mind, for she was the closest thing to family that she and Cody had here. What was a surprise, was the image of Evan that popped into her head. While she hadn't expected this revelation from her subconscious, she had to admit that he had indeed become a good friend. His laid back manner and easy going charms were growing on her, and she found herself looking forward to their conversations more with each passing day.

"Dan darlin," Dorothy's voice interjected from behind the counter. "I got a couple biscuits left over here if you want 'em."

"Why, yes ma'am. If nobody else wants them that is."

"If someone doesn't eat 'em, Arthur will. And he's done had enough."

"I heard that," Arthur said, stepping out from behind the swinging door that led to the kitchen. "I've only had a couple. And since when do you worry about what I eat?"

"Since Dr. Miller told me about your cholesterol. Someone's gotta watch out for you, and it may as well be me. Too many biscuits aren't good for anyone, let alone someone your age."

"My age? I'm only a year older than you. That's only middle age, I'll have you know. I bumped into Edna Harris at the market the other day, and she said I don't look a day over forty."

"Ha!" Dorothy laughed. "Everyone looks like a child to her. That woman is as old as the town itself. She might think she's makin herself look younger with all that make-up she cakes on, but she ain't foolin no one. Why, it's like puttin Avon on an alligator."

Arthur waved his arms in exasperation and mumbled something under his breath. He knew he had about as much chance at winning this argument as he did of being crowned the next Miss Texas, but he wasn't about to make it easy for her. "I'm going to go prep for lunch. And maybe I'll have a biscuit while I'm at it," he grumbled, marching back into the kitchen with Dorothy at his heels.

"And another thing," she yelled after him. "Where's that banana cream pie I fixed up yesterday? I don't see that it ever made it to the case out here. Did you eat all that, too?"

As the metal door swung shut behind the squabbling pair, Dan looked across the table at Leslie and they both started to laugh.

"On second thought, maybe I'll just take another cup of coffee."

....

74

The lunchroom at Millford Elementary filled quickly after the ringing of the 11 o'clock bell, the crescendo of voices echoing through the rafters and forming a cacophony of laughter, yells, and unintelligible conversation.

Cody walked past several of the wood-veneered folding tables before finding one that was unoccupied. As he took a seat on the bench and started unwrapping his sandwich, a tray of food slid across the table and halted about a foot away from him.

"Almost made it," Tyler said, pushing the tray the remainder of the distance and taking a seat directly across from his friend.

Examining the contents of Tyler's platter, Cody identified the green beans, mashed potatoes, hot roll, and even the wedge of cake, but the entree remained a mystery. "What *is* that?" he asked, wrinkling his nose suspiciously.

"I think it's supposed to be meatloaf."

"Oh. I guess it kind of resembles meat."

"It's gross. I've tried it before. It's worse than the meatloaf over where your mom works."

"That's why I bring my own lunch. At least I know I'll have something I like."

"What do you mean? I've got something I like, too," Tyler said, picking up the piece of cake and gobbling up half of it in a single bite.

Cody laughed, then grew serious. "Hey, are you ever going to come over to my house and play games again?"

"I don't know. Whatever was in your bathroom scared the piss out of me."

"But I didn't see anything."

"That's weird. You probably think I'm a big baby, huh?"

"No. I used to be scared of noises down in the basement, but now I think it was just drafts and stuff. I still don't like going down there, though. Are you at least coming to my party?"

"Yeah, sure. Maybe I just won't go in the bathroom."

"Well, you could go in the backyard if you have to. Or you could wear some of those diapers for big people."

"You dork," Tyler replied, picking up his roll and hurling it across the table.

It smacked Cody in the forehead, bouncing off and rolling across the floor, before coming to a stop at the foot of Vice Principal Sanders. Unlike the principal, who was generally an amicable guy, Mr. Sanders was the discipline enforcer of the school, and a visit to his office was one that was best avoided at all costs. Glancing down at the wayward roll, his expression turned sour and he shot a piercing gaze in Tyler's direction.

"You are so busted," Cody said.

"Time to go," Tyler replied, nonchalantly grabbing his tray and making a hasty retreat, as Cody laughed hysterically.

....

Abby Parker made her way toward the desk next to Cody as the bell rang, signaling two minutes before the start of class. The quiet room contained only a handful of children, though it would soon be abuzz with a flurry of activity as the other students made their way back from the lunchroom in droves.

"Hi, Cody," Abby said.

"Hey," he replied, looking up from the notebook he'd been doodling in. "Mr. Jenkins says he has a surprise for us today."

"I guess that's what this is for," she replied, pointing to sheets of newspaper splayed across the top of her desk. "Maybe we're going to paint or something."

"Maybe," Cody replied. "Whatever it is, it's gotta be more fun than math."

Over the next few minutes the noise level in the room escalated, as the children murmured and speculated over what sort of activity awaited them. There were a few dares between the boys to open the box on the teacher's desk to get a peek at what was inside, but while one or two pondered the idea, none were brave enough to risk getting caught.

A hush fell over the room as the door swung open and Mr. Jenkins entered, pulling a cart filled with pumpkins. The class erupted in a deluge of delighted whispers as the students realized what was happening.

"Alright, boys and girls," Mr. Jenkins said, holding up his hand and motioning for silence. "As I'm sure you can see by now, our class won the attendance award last month, and we've been chosen to carve the pumpkins that will be displayed in the front of the school for Friday's talent show."

Several hands shot up, and other students simply started shouting out questions.

"Can I make a monster?"

"Will we get to take them home for Halloween?"

"Do we get to use knives?"

"Okay, okay, quiet please," Mr. Jenkins said, laughing. "I know you're all excited, but let me finish. You're free to carve whatever you like as long as it's in good taste. Happy, scary, funny – it's all up to you. I have several pre-made templates if you don't feel like being creative. You will each be given a set of tools for carving – a crafting knife, a chisel, a scoop, and a small hammer. These are not toys, and can be very dangerous. If I see anyone using them in a careless manner, or jabbing at their friends, I will confiscate them, and you will be given a book assignment instead. Does everyone understand?"

There was a flood of nods and vocal acknowledgements around the room, and he called for the students to come up, one row at a time, to select a pumpkin and pick up their tools. Cody was closest to the window, and would, therefore, be in the last row to go up front. While he waited, he began thinking about the type of face he would carve. He had seen a Grim Reaper jack-o'-lantern, once, and wondered if he could pull that off. He dashed off a quick sketch in his notebook and thought it looked good. Grim Reaper it would be.

When he looked up, he saw that there were still two rows before his turn. He looked outside, waiting, and watched a group of kids on the playground. Two boys traversed the steel frame of the jungle gym, making their way to the top before hooking their legs on the high bar and hanging upside down. Had it been any normal day, he would have wanted to be out there with them, but the lure of making jack-o'-lanterns was more appealing at the moment.

A gust of wind kicked up, and his gaze followed a patch of crimson leaves as they danced and twirled across the grounds and past a girl standing at the edge of the play area. He hadn't noticed her until now, but as the leaves rushed by, he saw that she was only wearing one shoe. Taking in her appearance as a whole, he realized he'd never seen her at school before. In fact, everything about her seemed strange. Her pink skirt was tattered, and the white shirt she wore was covered with dark stains, as if she'd been drug through mud and muck. Her skin was pale and bruised, and her eyes looked as if they'd been blackened. She was staring at him, and probably had been for some time. When his eyes met hers, a sudden chill, reminiscent of the first day he'd been down in the basement, shot through him.

A second later, a ball sailed through the air, missing the girl by only an inch. She didn't flinch; didn't so much as blink. The boys playing with the ball laughed and scurried past her as if she weren't there at all.

That's so weird. Where did she come from?

He gave a small wave but she only stared back, her face void of all emotion.

"Cody, go! It's your turn," Abby's voice broke in.

Breaking his gaze from the girl outside, he realized he was still sitting at his desk, while everyone else in his row had gone to the front of the room. He jumped up and joined the group, selected a suitable pumpkin, and returned to his chair. As he sat back down, he looked out the window. The mysterious girl was gone.

Turning back to the task at hand, he sketched the image of a bony reaper with methodical precision, paying close attention to every menacing detail. When it was perfected, he taped the lucent sheet of paper containing his drawing to the front of the pumpkin and transferred his design. Ten minutes later, he was ready to begin carving what he felt would, surely, be the single best piece of work in the class.

Picking up the scalpel-shaped crafting knife, he carefully pressed the blade into the orange flesh, and pulled downward along his traced line. Instead of cutting smoothly, though, a thick gush of blood oozed from the incision and trickled down the face of the pumpkin. Cody gasped and dropped his blade. "Mr. Jenkins!" he cried.

Before the teacher could arrive, something slammed hard against the window. Cody turned, shocked. It was the girl. Her hands were pressed against the glass, and blood poured from her eyes, nose, and ears.

A surge of fear welled up inside him, only this time it seemed to suck the very air from his lungs. The room started to spin, and everything went silent - all but one sound. Breathing. At first he thought it was his own, but as it quickened and intensified, it was clear that it was coming from Abby's desk. She was hunched over, clutching the knife in her fist and furiously etching the surface of the pumpkin.

"Abby?"

The heavy rapid breathing ceased, and for a moment the girl was still. She turned and looked at him, her eyes filled with torment. Then, she picked up the pumpkin and turned it around for him to see. There was no face or image, only frenzied erratic scratches and lacerations spelling a single word: RUN.

"What are you doing?" asked an angry voice.

Mr. Jenkins stood over Abby now, his face red with anger. Without waiting for a reply, he grabbed the hammer off the desk and bludgeoned the girl in the back of the head. There was a dull crunching sound as bone splintered and cracked. Abby slumped forward, the pumpkin rolling out of her hands and falling to the ground. It split open with a hollow thud, spilling long threads of wet, sinewy pulp across the tiled floor.

"You're ruining it. You're ruining everything!" Mr. Jenkins snarled as he brought the hammer down again, sending a spray of blood and tissue into the air. Abby tried to speak, as one last bit of breath passed across her trembling lips.

"Help me," she pleaded.

"Stop!" Cody screamed, jumping from his desk and shrinking back against the wall.

All the kids in the class turned and stared. Glancing around the room, Cody's vision cleared, and he saw Mr. Jenkins standing by the blackboard, and Abby at her desk, as alive and well as ever.

It hadn't been real. Was it some kind of dream? But how could it have been? He hadn't been asleep.

"Did you hurt yourself, son?" Mr. Jenkins asked.

"No. No, I'm okay." Cody replied, making his way back to his seat. His heart was pounding, and he was shaking, but he breathed a sigh of relief.

"What happened?" Abby asked.

"I ... I thought I saw something is all."

He turned and looked out the window. The girl was gone. He scanned the playground, but saw no trace of her amongst the other children. Thinking he had somehow imagined the whole thing, he went back to work on his carving, and tried to push the image from his head.

Had he watched a few seconds longer, he would have seen the clouds part on an otherwise overcast day, brightening the sky just long enough to reveal a single line of blood running down the glass of the window.

JIM MARTIN

CHAPTER 9

October 29, 2010

Evan steered the police cruiser into the driveway of the old yellow Victorian and shut off the engine. He couldn't make out the house number from where he sat, but he recognized the green SUV that was parked in front of him as Leslie's. If that hadn't been enough of an indicator that he was in the right place, the colorful array of balloons and streamers affixed along the banister of the front porch provided all the assurance he needed.

Gripping the steering wheel with cold clammy hands, Evan closed his eyes and tried to gather his thoughts. He was nervous. It wasn't the thought of making conversation with Leslie that had his stomach in knots, after all, he spoke with her nearly every day at the diner. There was more at stake on this particular day, though, for he'd decided the time had come to ask her out. He had played the scenario out in his mind a thousand times over, thinking about what he might say. Of course, he knew that rarely, if ever, did situations like this go exactly as one imagined.

It had been so long since he'd asked a woman on a date that it felt like he was figuring it all out for the very first time. Dan had tried to offer encouragement by telling him it was just like riding a bike. The problem was, he wasn't sure he could manage that anymore without falling over, so the analogy hadn't worked the way Dan meant for it to. Then there was the old adage that said *the worst thing she could say was, no.* He'd always hated that. Certainly, whoever came up with it, had never faced much rejection. He could see how it might be fine if you were asking a woman out at the bar, having just met her, but when it was someone you'd already developed feelings for, being turned down was akin to your doctor giving you two months to live. A slight exaggeration, perhaps, but crushing nonetheless.

"Get it together, Evan," he said aloud. "You can do this."

He took a deep breath and climbed out of the car, making sure to grab the gift he'd brought for Cody. It was crudely wrapped in bright blue foiled paper, and he was less than thrilled with the results of his handy work. He figured a ten year old wouldn't be all that critical, wanting to unwrap the thing as fast as possible to see what was inside. Should he ever buy something for Leslie, however, a gift bag might be in order.

Walking up the front porch steps, he could hear the playful shrieks and laughter of the children well before he reached the door. It took several knocks before his presence was even noticed. He heard a voice, which he was sure was Tyler's, telling everyone that they must be making too much noise, because the cops were at the door. He laughed, not just at the remark itself, but because he knew that if any of the children had been guilty of making too much noise, Tyler would likely be the culprit.

A moment later, Leslie opened the front door, looking frazzled, yet still wearing the warm smile that was her trademark, seeming as natural to her as the act of breathing was to every other living creature. Just one of the many things that he found so endearing.

"You made it," she said. "I'm glad the thought of wrangling a houseful of kids didn't deter you."

"I'm quite adept at entering dangerous and uncertain situations. Besides, I can always call for backup," he replied, patting the radio clipped to his belt.

"Oh, I'm going to have to get me one of those," she laughed.

"I'll see what I can do. How are you holding up?"

"Pretty well. It hasn't been too bad, really. Mostly trying to guard the cake and keep little fingers away."

"I think I might be able to help you out with that. Sorry I'm a little late. Hope I didn't miss anything."

"You're just in time, actually. I was about to gather them all at the table. Come on in," she said, stepping back and gesturing him inside.

"You've got a beautiful home," Evan said as he crossed the threshold and looked about.

"Thank you. I'm happy with how it all came together."

"It's great. You have a flair for decorating. I'm afraid my place pales in comparison."

"Nothing a woman's touch couldn't fix, I'm sure."

Before Evan could say another word, Cody came running into the room with the speed of a comet. "Mr. Reece!" he exclaimed, following the greeting with a string of questions for which he gave neither pause, nor time to answer. "Did you see all the balloons out front? Did you bring your police car? Do you want to see my cake?"

"Yes, yes, and yes," Evan said. "But before I see the cake, I've got something for you."

He pulled the package out of his jacket pocket and handed it to Cody.

"Can I open it now?"

"If your mom says it's okay, then it's fine by me."

They both looked at Leslie, who nodded. "Go ahead," she said.

In the brief time it took for Evan to shift his gaze back to Cody, the wrapping paper had already been ripped away and dropped to the floor.

"Cool! This is the video game I was wanting! Thanks, Mr. Reece."

"You're welcome. And, you can call me Evan. I like to be on a first-name basis with those whose birthdays I celebrate."

"Okay. Thanks, Evan. I've gotta go show this to Tyler!" he said, turning to go.

"Not so fast, mister," Leslie said. "Pick up your trash before you leave."

"Oh, sorry," he replied, scooping up the remnants of the wrapping paper before dashing out of the room.

Leslie smiled after him, then turned back to Evan. "You didn't have to spend so much on him, but thank you. He'll certainly put it to good use. How did you know he wanted that? Or that I hadn't already got it for him?"

"Small town, you know. People are supposed to know everything about each other, right? Little birds always talking and whatnot."

"Hmm. I'm thinking more like one big bird named Dorothy."

"A man of integrity never compromises his sources."

"You don't have to. She's the only person I told. Nice try, though. Now, how about some cake?"

....

Several minutes later, after all of the children had been gathered up and escorted to the dining room, Cody took his seat at the head of the table and admired the triple layer chocolate fudge cake that sat before him. Dorothy had insisted she make him a proper birthday cake, one that would outdo any of those cheap store-bought cakes that were, in her words, nothing more than tasteless piles of sugar and shortening.

Though he hadn't yet taken a bite, it was already apparent that she had succeeded. He marveled at the perfect swirls running through the thick chocolate buttercream as one might admire a work of art. He thought it was every bit as stunning as anything found in a stuffy old museum, and no doubt vastly superior in taste. It was all he could do not to reach out and dig in while his mom lit the ten candles perched atop the decadent mound of heaven.

"Happy birthday to you ..." she began singing as the last candle began to glow. Everyone else followed suit, singing in his honor; a mish-mash of out-of-sync, and out-of-tune, voices, but all of it music to his ears. Though he tried hard not to blush, a warm rush flooded his cheeks and a sheepish grin spread across his face.

"Happy birthday to –"

There was a quick flash of light, and the happy scene turned to one of horror. The children looked cold and pale, and Cody knew they were dead. Tyler was slumped over the table, a chunk of skin and hair missing from his scalp. Blood pooled beneath his face, as red as the punch in the crystal bowl next to his lifeless body. Other children sat upright, heads tipped to the side, their eyes rolled back in the sockets. Nothing but ghostly white tissue behind their open lids, incapable of sight, yet, somehow seeming to stare back with ominous intent. The cake that had tempted him only moments before now looked as if it had been ripped apart; hunks of stale festering rot, now fodder for the thousands of maggots that writhed across its surface.

Cody gasped, and closed his eyes. When he opened them again, all was normal. The song was ending and everyone clapped and cheered. What was happening? Why was he seeing these things? Maybe Tyler really had seen something that day in the bathroom. Cody hadn't told his friend about the girl he saw on the playground, and didn't want to tell him about this, either, for fear that it would alarm him further. Then, he might never come over and play. But whatever was going on, Cody didn't like it one bit.

"Blow out your candles," one of the children said.

"Yeah, let's eat!" exclaimed another.

"You have to make a wish first," Tyler interjected.

A wish, Cody thought. *I wish all this scary stuff would go away.*

With that he took a breath to blow out the candles. It was then that he heard the noise – a loud menacing groan - coming from the vicinity of the basement. This time, everyone heard it. The room went quiet, and Cody knew it hadn't been a figment of his imagination.

"What was that?" Tyler asked breathlessly.

There was a slow creak of wood on the basement stairs. Cody noticed a change in the flames of the candles, which now flickered and sputtered, whipping at the air as if seeking refuge from whatever was coming.

Another creak.

With a suddenness that startled everyone, the basement door flung open with great force, rocking back on its hinges and slamming into the wall hard enough to knock out a chunk of sheetrock.

Evan hurried over to investigate, with Leslie close behind. "Oh, that stupid door!" she cried. "I'm always finding this thing open. I don't think it latches right."

Evan opened and closed the door a few times, pulling on it to see if it would come open without turning the knob. "It seems to be in good order. I'm guessing it doesn't always open with such intensity?"

"No. That's the first time I've seen it do that."

"That was one heck of a noise before this blew open. Sounds like you've got some major drafts going on down there. I can get Doug Mason to come have a look, see if there's some insulating or resealing that might need done."

"Please do. I don't want to fix the wall, only to have another hole knocked in it."

"I'll call him today, then. Maybe he can get out here as soon as Monday."

Watching as his mom and Evan talked, Cody could see that there was no one in the basement. Maybe it was only a draft, but the recent visions had made him wary, and his imagination ran wild with dark images of ghosts and monsters.

Perhaps it would help if I finish that wish, he thought. But, turning back to the cake, there were only little pillars of smoke where the flames had once been. Someone, or something, had already extinguished them.

....

When the last child had gone home, Leslie basked in the tranquil silence of the empty house. She loved children, but trying to keep up with a dozen of them all at once was enough to strain even the most patient of souls. Though she wanted nothing more than to settle down on the couch and relax, there was cleaning to be done. While disposable plates and cups would be easy enough to take care of, the bits of confetti and smudges of frosting that had infiltrated nearly every room of the house, would prove to be more daunting. Before she could begin the task at hand, however, there was still one very important thing left to do.

When she reached the dining room, Evan and Cody were hard at work piecing together a new space station Lego set. Now, instead of paper plates containing remnants of cake and ice cream, multitudes of plastic blocks in various colors, shapes, and sizes littered the table instead.

"I don't know which was a bigger mess, the dishes, or this," Leslie said.

"Right," Evan chuckled. "The box says this is for ages ten and up, but you'd need an engineering degree to figure out how to get this thing together. Whatever happened to Lincoln Logs?"

"What are those?" asked Cody.

"Careful, Evan. I think you're showing your age," Leslie grinned.

"Yeah, I guess I am. Lincoln Logs are wooden sticks that are notched out at each end. You'd stack them together using those notches to build cabins and fences."

"What else could you make with them?" Cody asked.

"That was about it. If you had more than one set, you could build even bigger cabins and fences. Spaceships were out of the question, I'm afraid. Unless, of course, you wanted one that looked like a wooden box."

Cody eyed Evan quizzically, trying to determine if his leg was being pulled, or if this were indeed a true story. "Well," he finally said, "That's kind of ridiculous."

Evan laughed. "Yes, I suppose so. Toys just weren't as cool when I was little."

"Since we're on the subject of boys and their toys, I think there's still one more big surprise left," Leslie said.

Cody's eyes widened with excitement. "Is it the thing you were doing with the room upstairs?"

"It just might be. Why don't you go take a look?"

She pulled a small key out of the pocket of her jeans and handed it to Cody, who looked as if he might burst from the mounting anticipation. A second later, he was already halfway up the stairs, while Leslie and Evan followed at a more leisurely pace.

"This must be big," Evan remarked.

"It might be a little more than any kid should have all at once, but he's been so good with the move and starting a new school. I remember moving when I was about his age, and having to leave everything I'd ever known behind. I think I cried myself to sleep for two months, and constantly begged my father to take us back. It's a hard thing for any child, but Cody has never complained, not once. When I picked this house and had the extra room, I knew immediately that I wanted to do something special for him."

"I think that's nice."

"You don't think I'll be spoiling him?"

"I'm not sure what the gift is yet, but no. Cody always seems very appreciative of what's done for him. In my opinion, those are the kinds of kids who actually deserve a little spoiling from time to time."

They reached the top of the stairs just as Cody was inserting the key into the lock. With a quick turn of the knob, he pushed the door open and disappeared inside the room. A profusion of enthusiastic whoops and hollers commenced, as the long-awaited surprise was met with unequivocal approval.

Evan stepped out of the hall and into a game room that would be the envy of any boy, and many grown men for that matter. A large flat screen monitor hung on the wall, flanked by speakers that made up a portion of the surround sound system. A low-profile black cabinet beneath the monitor housed a console, controllers, and audio components. Two game rockers were placed strategically in the middle of the room, facing the television, and, between those, was a racing seat mounted to a metal chassis with steering wheel and pedal attachments.

"This is the best present, ever! Thanks, Mom!" Cody exclaimed.

"You're welcome. I thought you might like it."

"I love it! Wait until I tell Tyler. He's gonna freak out. Can he spend the night?"

Leslie had been looking forward to some quiet time and wasn't keen on the idea, especially after having spent the last few hours with a houseful of children. But the lure of the game room likely meant that she would see neither hide, nor hair, of either of the boys for most of the night. In fact, it was possible that she would have to drag them out of the room when it was time for bed. With some reluctance, she agreed to the sleep over, and Cody raced back downstairs to find the phone.

"This is really something," Evan said. "How did you pull it off without being seen?"

"I ordered everything online, and arranged for it to be delivered and installed while he was in school yesterday. I locked the room afterwards, but I don't think it even occurred to him to look until I said something a few minutes ago."

"I must say, I'm quite impressed."

"Are you one of those men who still likes to play games?"

"Oh, I played my fair share growing up. Games now are so much more complex than they were then. I've attempted one or two, but the controller alone intimidates me. There are more buttons on those things than in most cars."

"Stick around awhile and Cody will be giving you lessons, I'm sure."

"All I need is to end up getting hooked. Then I'd have to come up with the money for my own setup. That, or live here part-time like I imagine Tyler will be doing."

"At least you're better behaved," Leslie joked. "When I envisioned all of this, Tyler was not a part of the plan, although, I should have known that Cody would want friends over on a regular basis. I guess I'm just going to have to put some limits on it for the sake of my own sanity. If the boys had their way, they would probably hole up in here all weekend."

"Fun for them I suppose, but for you it sounds like a good way to get cabin fever."

"Exactly. While I wanted to do this for him, I don't want him incessantly playing video games, either. He needs to have other outlets to occupy his free time."

"Fall Festival is this weekend. I think you'd both enjoy that," Evan said.

"Yes, I've seen the banner downtown. Is it like a fair?"

"Not quite the same scope as a big city fair, but along those lines, yes. It's a pretty big deal around here. There's the usual gamut of arts and crafts, games, a chili cook-off, hay rides, a corn maze, live music, and, my personal favorite, loads of great food. Oh, and there's a livestock barn, too, in case you're in the market for a cow."

"I think I'd have to pass on the cow," Leslie laughed. "But the rest of it sounds like fun."

Evan had initially thought about asking Leslie to a movie, but where was the originality in that? It dawned on him that the festival could work out for the better. If she accepted of course. It was a little less formal, and would give them more time to talk with one another. He opened his mouth and spoke before he could think any further. "I'm thinking I might go out there tomorrow night. Would you and Cody care to join me?"

There. He'd done it. The asking hadn't been as hard as he'd made it out to be. No, the hard part would be what to do if she turned him down. It wasn't that he couldn't handle rejection – he'd been turned down almost as much as not. But, he was never graceful with words after a letdown, and always ended up feeling like a bumbling idiot. Standing here now, he felt the prickling heat of nervous perspiration on the back of his neck.

"Are you asking me out, Evan?"

"I, uh. Well, yes, I am … asking you. Not Cody. I mean, of course I wouldn't ask Cody. What I meant to say is, Cody is welcome to come along and, oh, shut up! I'm really blowing this, aren't I?"

Leslie bit her lip in a playful sort of way and smiled, shaking her head. "No, not at all."

Evan let out a sigh of relief.

"I like you, Evan. I really do," Leslie continued. "And you're great with Cody. He's really taken to you since we've been here, and that's a major sticking point for anyone that comes into my life. It's just I wonder if maybe …"

"It's too soon?" Evan asked.

"Well, yes."

"That's alright. I understand. I shouldn't have been so hasty."

"No, I'm glad you asked. I just want to be sure I'm ready. It wouldn't be fair to either of us if I rushed into things too fast. But, maybe somewhere down the road …"

"Sure. I can appreciate that. I'd never want to rush you, believe me."

"Thank you for understanding. That means more than you know."

"You're quite welcome. And thank you for not laughing at my dreadful tongue-tied rant a moment ago," Evan replied. While he had initially felt some disappointment that she had declined his invitation, it was overshadowed by a greater sense of hope. He certainly understood her point of view, and was delighted that she had left the door open for something in the future.

"I know you were nervous, but I think that's sweet," Leslie said. "It's far nicer than an arrogant man acting like

I should feel privileged because he's asking me out. Please!"

Evan laughed. "Well, good. I feel much better now."

"So, what time should we be ready for the festival tomorrow night?"

"Wait," Evan said, looking perplexed. "I thought you didn't want to go."

"Of course I want to go. I'd just like to go as the friends we are, if that's alright by you."

Evan grinned. "I'd like that, yes."

"So, what time?"

"How's 7 o'clock sound?

"Seven it is. Cody and I will be ready."

"Perfect. I'll see you then."

············

Cody woke with a start in the dead of the night. He blinked several times as he met up with his senses, and came to the realization that he was lying in his bed. The green glow of the clock on the nightstand announced the time as 2:08 am. He wondered why he was awake at this hour, for he was usually one to sleep straight through the night, never finding it necessary to heed the call of nature or have want of water, snacks, or any other such things in the middle of his slumber. Nor did he suffer from nightmares; rarely dreamed at all, actually, at least not that he ever remembered upon waking. Whatever had disturbed his sleep was a mystery, one he was more than happy to let remain unsolved. Rolling over on his side and pulling the blanket up under his chin, he closed his eyes and prepared to doze off.

Then he heard the footsteps. Three of them, and, then, silence. They were somewhat distant, and seemed to have come from downstairs.

Sitting up in bed, Cody's first thought was that Tyler had woke up and gone downstairs for a glass of water or, perhaps, to sneak some leftover cake. Glancing down at the foot of his bed, he found the sleeping bag lying on the floor. Tyler was still in it. Even in the dim light of the room, he could see the slight movement of the heavy cotton sack as it rose and fell with his friend's breathing.

Perhaps it was his mom, but he knew she was a heavier sleeper than he was. Without the aid of an alarm, she was rarely ever out of bed before 10:30 in the morning. Besides, his bedroom door was open and, as best he could tell, there were no lights on in the house. If she'd been up, she wouldn't have worried that a light would disturb him.

He heard the footsteps again - one, two, three more. They stopped.

Crawling out from under the warmth of his blankets, Cody eased himself out of bed and tip-toed across the floor. There was a creak of wood, and he stopped and held his breath. It hadn't been him. The creak had come from the staircase. The footsteps were getting closer, sounding hollowed as they trudged up the stairs - one, two, three.

Cody traversed the remainder of the distance to the doorway of his bedroom, and very carefully peered around the corner. Someone stood at the top of the stairs, silhouetted by the moonlight streaming through the panes of glass above the window seat. The dark, faceless shape was motionless.

It was too tall, and too large, to be his mom, and certainly too big to be the girl Tyler had seen in the bathroom. This was a man, wide and broad shouldered. Though there was no light to illuminate the man's eyes, Cody could feel their gaze burning into him.

"Hello," the boy said, voice cracking.

The shape didn't move, and made no attempt to say anything in return. The uneasy feeling Cody had felt at the party returned, and he was sure that this was the being who'd been making the noises in the basement. He felt a deep sense of terror, for whatever this was before him, it wasn't friendly. He started to cry.

"Please," Cody sobbed. "Please, stop scaring me."

He grabbed the sleeve of his pajamas and wiped away the tears. When he looked up, the figure was gone. Without hesitation, Cody ran to his mother's room and climbed up into the bed, burrowing beneath the blankets and clutching her tight. She didn't wake up, but that was of no consequence. He felt safe again once he was next to her. For what seemed like an hour, he listened for more footsteps, hearing none. After a while, he became listless under the weight of drowsiness and, closing his eyes, found sleep once again.

JIM MARTIN

CHAPTER 10

October 30, 2010

"Cody, sweetie, you just had a bad dream," Leslie said again.

Her repeated attempts at reassuring her frightened son had thus far been met with stubborn denial, a trait he had no doubt inherited from his father.

He shook his head again. "Someone was in here, Mom. Why won't you believe me?"

"Now don't get upset. If someone had been here, don't you think we would have found some indication of how they got in?"

It was a valid point and Cody knew it. He had accompanied her downstairs earlier, as each and every door and window received a thorough inspection. All were locked and secured, with no trace of tampering.

"Yeah, I guess so," he admitted. "But if it was a dream, why didn't I wake up? If I have a nightmare, I always wake up during the scary stuff."

"Dreams are crazy things, sometimes. I've come out of one, and thought I was awake, only to wake up a second time to find that I was still dreaming. I know it felt very real, but a dream is the only thing that makes sense, and there's no sign of it being anything to the contrary. Even if someone had managed to get in here, and then leave again without disturbing the locks, surely they would have taken something, don't you think? What self-respecting thief with that kind of talent would leave empty handed?"

"I dunno," Cody mumbled. He knew there was no point in arguing. If he chose to believe that what he'd seen had been real, he would be alone in that belief unless he could come up with some sort of proof, or convincing theory otherwise, both of which seemed impossible at the moment.

"What do you say we go to the diner for breakfast? Arthur is making your favorite this morning – blueberry pancakes."

At this, a small grin appeared across Cody's face, and for a brief moment he forgot about the man on the stairs. After all, pancakes are always good medicine. "Can Tyler come, too?"

"Sure. I nearly forgot he was here. I haven't heard a peep out of him yet this morning. Where is he? And what is he getting into?"

"Don't worry, Mom. He's playing in the game room."

Leslie looked relieved. "Alright, let me get my makeup done and we'll leave. Make sure Tyler is ready to go, will you?" she asked as she walked out of the room.

Cody got up from the chair at his computer desk and went to the bathroom, where he picked up a tube of hair gel and squeezed a dollop into his palm. He rubbed his hands together and worked the clear blue-tinted goo through his hair, transforming the short straight locks into a series of random soft spikes. Once he was satisfied with his look, he brushed his teeth, and went to go check on Tyler.

As he walked past the stairs, a cold chill swept through his body. For a brief second he went still, frozen with fear. He wondered if the cold was a part of the dark presence he had encountered the night before. Though he saw nothing now, he had the distinct feeling he was being watched, and another shiver ran through him. Regaining sensation in his limbs, he ran the rest of the way to the game room, away from the invisible eyes that stalked him, and towards the sense of safety he felt in the company of one of his own.

When Tyler had first told him about the dead girl in the bathroom, he'd wondered if his friend was pulling some sort of prank. But the events of last night had convinced him otherwise, and he couldn't help but think he and his mom weren't alone in their new home. It seemed Tyler had good reason to be scared. Maybe they all did.

....

Breakfast at the diner had been a good idea. Leslie had several tasks to accomplish before going out for the evening, and did not want to add cooking to the list. Sure, she could have just let the boys eat cereal, but Cody always loved going to the diner, and she thought it would be a good way to take his mind off of the unsettling nightmare and end the standoff they'd been in. She was right on both counts. However frightened he may have been earlier, it certainly hadn't affected his appetite. He easily consumed half a dozen pancakes, a side of bacon, and a plate of hash browns before conceding to Tyler, who outdid him by eating two more cakes.

Leslie chose the lighter option of a Florentine egg white omelet, wheat toast with jelly, and coffee. Normally, she would have enjoyed one of Arthur's famous blueberry pancakes, but she figured there would be plenty of other calorie-laden temptations at the festival to test her willpower. It was a test she already knew she would fail, but it was no matter. Fairs and festivals were special occasions, when she felt it was acceptable to give in to her sweet tooth.

"Now, where did those boys run off to?" asked Dorothy, appearing beside the table with another plate of pancakes.

"I let them walk down to the Centennial to see a movie. I think I'll be able to get my errands done much quicker without their assistance. And, would you believe that after all this food, they asked for money to buy popcorn?"

"Well, they're growin' boys, and they need lots of food to keep up those energy levels."

"Is that what it is? For my sake then, would it be wrong to make them have an occasional day of fasting?"

"Oh, now, you be good," Dorothy chuckled.

"I'm always good. You need to give that speech to them."

"I think your son might listen, but tellin that to Tyler would be like tellin a cat to fetch. It ain't gonna do a darn bit o' good, honey."

"Hmm, I dare say that applies to most of the male population."

"Ain't that the truth? I used to tell Ed to stay out of the kitchen when I would bake, but every time I turned my back, he'd be sneakin in there. He'd try to deny it, but I knew better. Sometimes there would still be frostin on his lip, or cake in his teeth. I'd chase him outta the house, but he'd always show up awhile later with a jar of Millie Ellis's homemade apple butter. Ed knew how much I loved that stuff. God love him, I could never stay mad for long."

"That's sweet. I wish I'd had the chance to meet him. I never did ask how the two of you met."

"I was workin for a laundry just out of high school. He showed up there one day to get a pair of pants done. And, after that, he started showin up every single day with the same pair of pants. Most of the time they didn't even need washin. The ol' coot wouldn't leave me alone. I figured I either had to give him a date, or get a restrainin order."

"Sounds like his persistence paid off in the end," Leslie laughed.

"I was a tough nut to crack, but, yes, it did."

"How did you know that he was the one you wanted to marry?"

"He always did whatever he could to make sure I was happy, and there wasn't a sacrifice he wouldn't have made. I wasn't about to let a good man like that slip away, no matter how many cakes he snuck into."

"I sometimes wonder about that. If I had dated John longer than I did, would I still have married him? I was just so caught up with his charm and good looks, and I'm not sure I really saw him, if you know what I mean."

"Sure I do. No offense, hun, but it takes longer to buy a house these days than it does for people to meet and get married. There just ain't no way you can know a person and their character that fast. Maybe I'm old fashioned, but you gotta let em' court you awhile."

"No offense taken. I learned the hard way. Ed sounds like a wonderful man and I'm sure you miss him."

Dorothy's eyes misted over, and she smiled a bittersweet smile. She paused for a moment and, then, in a tone that was almost a whisper, replied, "Everyday, honey, every day."

....

Leslie had finished all her errands by mid-afternoon. Though it was almost November, the weather was still quite pleasant, and some of the people in town speculated that a mild winter lay ahead. Though every year was temperate compared to say, Maine or Minnesota, northern Texas was still no stranger to cold weather. Just eight months prior, the Dallas area saw a record snowfall of 9 inches, and that was more than enough for Leslie. She wasn't a big fan of the cold.

Autumn, on the other hand, was a different story. It was, without a doubt, her favorite time of year. The cool air tempered the stifling heat of summer, and the trees radiated with brilliant shades of amber, orange, and red, giving her a reason to make her way outdoors as much as possible. Today was one such day. Instead of driving to each of her stops, she left her car parked outside the diner and went through town on foot, enjoying the affable climate, and feeling good about getting a bit of exercise in the process.

With her tasks completed, she picked the boys up from the theater and retrieved the car. They talked nonstop all the way back to Tyler's house, making plans for Halloween the following evening. Tyler said he knew which houses gave out the best candy and, with pen and paper in hand, cobbled together a map diagraming their intended route for trick-or-treating. He didn't put his own house on the map because, as he put it, his mom handed out crap. Leslie laughed as she recalled the dreaded peanut butter candies in the orange and black wrappers that she sometimes received as a child. They were hard to the point of being nearly inedible, and her grandfather had always said they must surely be made by the devil himself.

A few minutes later, while the boys said their goodbyes in front of Tyler's house, Leslie spied a blazing maple across the way, and watched as colorful leaves cascaded towards the ground, dipping and diving as they danced in the wind. Caught up in the simplistic beauty of the scene, she reflected on her afternoon thus far, and how ideal it had been. But, the day would soon give way to night, a night in which a dark and malevolent evil lurked, watching and waiting in silence like a coiled serpent poised to devour its prey. Before the first rays of dawns light, it would strike.

CHAPTER 11

Henry Tucker was a fifth-generation farmer, inheriting not only the land he worked and lived on, but his name as well, which he shared with both his father, and grandfather before him. While wheat was his staple crop, covering over 90 percent of his expansive property, a few acres were dedicated to corn. Henry had no real interest in the corn itself, though he did sell what he harvested at the local farmer's market. It was the tall stalks left behind that served his purpose.

The Tucker farm had been host to the Millford Springs Fall Festival since its inception, and Henry had come up with the idea of implementing a corn maze after seeing one during a trip to Ohio. While it required a good deal of extra work and planning, it had been an instant success. And, at $3.00 a head to enter, a fairly profitable venture as well. For Henry, though, it wasn't really about the money. He was a man who took great pride in his work, and the real reward was seeing the delight on the faces of the people who were out enjoying the festival.

With the start of the big event only hours away, he walked the manicured grounds, checking to make sure that everything was ready to go. Strolling through the main thoroughfare, he carefully examined the strands of lights that crossed the walkway for any non-working bulbs. There was a flurry of activity on both sides of him, as food vendors in flashy stands busied themselves prepping for the hungry crowds that would soon arrive. The unmistakable aroma of ripe apples and cinnamon lingered in the crisp autumn air, and Henry craved a warm mug of cider and a funnel cake. Until he was finished with the tasks at hand, though, it would have to wait. The tractor and trailer for the hayrides still needed to be hitched up, and the band had requested another generator at the stage area to accommodate the extra equipment they'd brought in.

Moving past the food stands, gaming booths, and merchandise tents, Henry reached the shed at the edge of the cornfield, where the generators were stored. He fumbled with a large ring of keys, searching for the one which would open the padlock securing the clasp on the door. "Too many of these damn things," he muttered to himself.

It didn't help that he was a portly man; his chunky sausage-like fingers got in the way more than they helped. To make matters worse, the sun was already slipping behind the tall rows of corn, casting deep shadows on the shed and making it hard to see. After several tries, he found the right key, popping the padlock free and slipping it into the pocket of his overalls. It took a couple of firm tugs before the door finally loosened on its rusted hinges and swung open with a loud creak.

Stepping into the dark musty interior of the shed, Henry took a few cautious steps, grasping for the pull string that would turn on the light. Not finding it, he took another step, and slammed his foot into something hard.

He gritted his teeth against the pain and cursed. Then, not wanting to take another step for risk of injuring himself further, he leaned forward and moved his arm through the darkness, finding the string, but then batting it away with his swinging arms. Cursing again, he held his hand steady and caught the string on its backswing. With it firmly in his grasp, he clicked on the light.

The sudden brightness caused him to squint. He used the palm of his hand to create a visor, shielding his eyes until they could adjust. Once he could see clearly, he saw a generator sitting at his feet. "What the hell?" he grumbled aloud.

Why anything would be in the middle of the floor was beyond him. He was a very organized person and, just as every item in his house had its place, so it was in his shed also. He would never leave something out that could cause him to trip. But, if he hadn't moved the generator, who had? No one else possessed a key, and the lock outside had been intact.

He glanced around the room, taking a quick inventory of his belongings, and looking for a point of entry where someone could have forced their way in. It was then that he noticed the black faceless figure standing in the corner. Before he could react, a numbing throb began to pulsate through his body, and he fell to his knees. The shape took a step towards him and tilted its head to the side, observing him like some sort of curious animal.

The light in the room flickered, and Henry's mind buzzed with a myriad of images; graphic and twisted pictures of madness, that dug into his skull like the razor-sharp claws of a predator piercing the skin of its prey. The black figure moved forward, and the light bulb shattered, plunging Henry into physical darkness. He heard himself scream, yet the cry seemed disembodied, distant, and as foreign as that of a stranger. Something was taking him over. "Who are you?" he wailed.

As the final piece of his old self slipped away and descended into an empty void, a voice answered and said, "I'm Walter."

....

The pale ghoulish face peered at Leslie, its eyes pleading from beneath deep furrowed brows. With a black hoodie pulled up over his hair, and a zombie makeover courtesy of the face painting booth, Cody was all but unrecognizable. When he wasn't speaking in clear sentences, he could easily be mistaken for any other number of pre-teen zombies, roaming the festival grounds in search of food. Fortunately, brains were not on the menu this night, and most of the walking dead were content to feast on caramel apples, cotton candy, and other assorted confections.

"The band is getting ready to start. Don't you want to hear them play?" Leslie asked.

"No," Cody replied, letting out an exasperated sigh. "I want to do the corn maze. Can I? Please?"

"This shouldn't last too long, and then Evan and I can go with you."

"But I want to go by myself."

Leslie frowned. "I'm not too sure about that. What if you get lost in there and can't find your way out?"

"Tyler said he got lost last year, but still found the way out by himself. Besides, I'm ten now. I think I can handle it."

"Oh, you think so, do you?" She was always amused when he played the age card. It didn't always work, but if he thought he was old enough to tackle something on his own, he would say so, and, in most instances, prove himself more than capable. Like it or not, her little boy was growing up. While she was always proud of his accomplishments, she still missed the days when he depended on her for nearly everything. Days when she could find stick figure variations of herself depicted in crayon, and hung with pride on the refrigerator, the endless shrieks of laughter as she pushed the swing at the park ever higher, while he hung on with white-knuckled enthusiasm, and goodnight kisses that were as plentiful as the peanut butter and jelly smudges left throughout the house by his little fingers. Cody growing up was inevitable, of course, she just wished it didn't have to happen so fast.

"I bet he could do it," Evan chimed in.

"Just whose side are you on here, anyway?" Leslie asked, feigning a sense of displeasure.

Evan laughed and held up his hands in submission. "I'm just saying, Cody is a smart kid, and I think he would do just fine. Even if he did get turned around, all he would have to do is stay put and wait for the worker who sweeps the maze every half hour. In the five years of that attraction being here, we haven't lost anyone yet."

"So, does that mean I can go?" Cody asked.

"Alright," Leslie sighed. "But when you're done, I want you to come straight back here."

"I will," Cody replied, dancing with excitement as Leslie retrieved a handful of bills from her purse. He grabbed the cash without hesitation, thanking his mother and tossing in a quick *I love you* for good measure, before darting off in the direction of the corn field.

"You sure made his day," Evan said.

"Oh, you had a hand in that as well," Leslie replied.

"How so?"

"You made a case for him. I try to tell myself that I need to give him more freedom as he gets older, but it's just in my nature to be overprotective. Sometimes, I need someone to remind me he's not five anymore, and doesn't always need me there to hold his hand."

"That's a relief. You could have just as easily been upset with me. I wasn't intending to step on your toes in any way. I guess I just remember when I was his age, how exhilarating it was to get to go places and do things on my own."

"I know what you mean. My mother was somewhat strict, but my father, well, he would say yes to just about anything within reason. If it weren't for him, I wouldn't have even been able to ride my bike around the block until I was fifteen. I loved those little moments of independence, when he was the one taking care of me."

"So, essentially you were spoiled rotten," Evan said with a smile.

"Hey, now, I happen to think I turned out pretty well, thank you."

"I guess I can't argue with that."

"I didn't figure you would," Leslie laughed. "You know, of course, that if you keep going to bat for Cody like you just did, you're going to end up being his best friend."

"That could be a bad thing for Tyler."

"Oh, but such a good, good thing for me."

Evan choked on a mouthful of cider, sending him scrambling for a napkin, as the beverage expelled through his nose and mouth. His face went red with embarrassment, and Leslie burst out laughing.

"Not the classiest display there," he said, regaining both his voice and composure. "But, in my defense, you should never make a man laugh while he's in mid-drink."

"I'm so sorry. I'll try not to do that again. Are you alright?"

"Yes. Although I think I'm going to need another cup of cider, and maybe a bandage for my pride. Can I get you anything while I'm up?"

"Hmm, a corn dog and lemonade sounds great."

"You got it. I'll be right back," Evan replied.

After he had taken several steps, Leslie called after him and, with a devilish grin, said, "Hey, perhaps you should grab some extra napkins for yourself, too. Just in case."

Evan turned and shook his finger at her. She laughed, and he flashed a charmed smile back. Although it had been agreed that they were here together only as friends, to Leslie, the evening still had the feel of a date, even an unofficial one, and there was no denying that she was having more fun than she had in years.

Surely things can only get better from here, she thought, and then turned her attention to the stage as the band began to play its first song.

....

Cody raced out of the stage area and past the long corridor of concession stands, zigzagging his way around the other patrons who were either standing in line to order, or walking much too slow for his liking. He was on a mission, and the sooner he reached his destination the better. His momentum was slowed for a short time when he passed through the big red barn that housed the multitude of handcrafted items for sale. It wasn't the array of pies, cakes, jams, and pastries that mired his expeditious pace, though on most occasions it would have been. Rather, it was the sheer number of people funneling through the narrow walkway, and creating a bottleneck as they stopped to admire and purchase the edible souvenirs on display.

Once he reached the other side of the building, his step quickened as he traversed the dirt path behind the barn. It took only a minute or two to reach the iron gate that opened up to the corn fields. A crude wooden sign was lashed to the beams with the word *Maze* painted in bright red blocky letters. Further ahead, in the distance, Cody could make out a small, dimly lit booth.

Somewhere behind him, faint echoes of music and applause rose through the air as the band struck up. It was then that the thought occurred to him. He hadn't seen a soul since leaving the barn. Looking around him now, he saw that the whole area appeared to be deserted. Had they closed already? They must have.

Cody shoved his hands in his pockets and kicked at the ground, as a wave of disappointment flooded over him. If only he'd have come here immediately upon arriving at the festival, he wouldn't have missed out. But, nothing could be done about it now. No, he would have to wait until next year, and right now that felt like an eternity. Lowering his head and slouching his shoulders, he shuffled back toward the gate.

"Going so soon, son?"

Cody whipped back around, looking to find the source of the voice. He hadn't noticed it before, but, as he peered hard into the night, he saw the silhouette of a man sitting inside the booth at the field's edge.

"Are you here for the maze?" asked the voice.

"Uh-huh," Cody nodded.

"Very good, then. Come this way, and get your ticket, my boy."

Cody took a few steps toward the booth. Just a few moments ago he would have wasted no time running to the counter, eager to put his money down and begin his adventure. But now he was reluctant. Not only was his heart still pounding from being startled, but the dark outline of the man brought to mind the shadowy figure outside his bedroom the night before. That, coupled with the complete absence of other people in the area, was more than enough to give him pause.

"Wh-wh-where is everyone?" Cody stammered.

"At the concert, I suppose, or maybe getting something to eat. It is about suppertime, after all. It's like this every year. But they'll be back," said the man. "They always come back."

Cody had drawn close enough now that he could make out the features of the booth's sole occupant. Heavyset, with a round face, and a midsection that was even rounder, the man wore a plaid shirt and denim overalls, the clasps pulled taught as they strained to contain the massive bulk that lie within. He leaned forward as Cody approached, tipping back the straw hat on his head and eyeing the boy.

"Are you...all alone?" the man asked, looking towards the gate and shifting his gaze back and forth.

Cody stopped just shy of the counter and nodded his head, wondering if the man would tell him he couldn't venture into the maze alone, and would need a parent to accompany him after all. A part of him would have felt a sense of relief if that were the case, but he knew deep down that if he didn't do this on his own, he would regret it later. Besides, he was intent on breaking Tyler's completion time of an hour and ten minutes, and would never be able to do that with his mom tagging along.

The man pointed a chunky finger towards the maze. "You won't be afraid of going in there all by yourself?"

"No," Cody replied, with an assertiveness that belied any residual apprehension he was feeling.

"Well, aren't you the brave one?" the man replied with a crooked smile. He reached beneath the counter and pulled out a small flashlight, clicked it on to ensure it was working, and then handed it to Cody. "Best keep this with you while you're in there. It can get awful dark, especially on a night such as this, where the moon can duck behind the clouds for a spell."

He paused for a moment, and when he spoke again, his tone was lower and more foreboding. "The darkness hides many things; dreadful, terrible things that take refuge from the light and lurk in the shadows, feeding on the souls of men. Darkness is a friend to no one, and those who think it can be trusted do so at their own peril."

Cody gripped the flashlight tightly. He wasn't sure if this was a speech that everyone received - a scare tactic of sorts - to heighten the intensity of the maze experience, but he didn't like the man. It wasn't so much what he said, as it was the way he said it. And, the way he looked at him with those dark, empty eyes. Dead eyes.

"Here you are," Cody said, fishing the crumpled bills out of his pocket and setting them on the counter. He was anxious to pay and move along, to be far from the grim company of the man and his unnerving stare. "Can I go in now?"

"Of course, my dear boy. It's all yours to explore. Do be safe now, you hear?" the man replied with a sinister grin.

Cody wasted no time retreating from the booth, making his way to the edge of the field in a matter of seconds. He raised his flashlight and shined the beam of light into the mouth of the maze, illuminating the murky pathway in front of him. A quick glance at his watch revealed the time to be 8:34. One hour. That was the goal he had set to find the exit and beat Tyler's time. He had until 8:49 to find the first quarter marker.

A cold gust of wind swept through the rows of corn, rattling the thousands of thin papery stalks together in unison. The resulting sound was akin to thunderous applause from a great crowd, and, for a moment, Cody imagined it to be for him alone. Smiling at the thought, he took a deep breath and stepped into the maze.

His pace was slow and steady for the first few minutes, but then, remembering that he had a time limit to adhere to, he picked up his stride. Having already taken a few wrong turns, Cody took to cutting a line in the soft ground with the heel of his foot at each junction, making it easy to see where he had been should he hit a dead end and need to backtrack. It appeared to be working. Only twelve minutes had elapsed before he came upon a red flag marking the first quarter.

"Yes!" Cody exclaimed, throwing his arms up in a show of victory. At this rate, he would easily finish in under an hour. He wondered what the all-time record was, and thought about how great it would feel to break it. That would sure burn ol' Tyler.

With that, he jogged on. He reached another junction, cut a line, and made a left. Then another thought sprung to mind. Even if he were to finish in record-breaking time, who would know? There wasn't anyone else around. With no witnesses, it would be his word alone, and that wouldn't cut it. There was the man at the booth, of course, but it was doubtful he was monitoring time. Besides, Cody hoped to avoid having to talk to him again, anyway.

So lost was he in his musings, that he didn't notice the object in his path until it was just inches in front of him. Veering right in order to avoid a collision, he lost his footing and fell to the ground. The flashlight rolled out of his hand, flickering several times before finally going out. Perhaps it was only his imagination, but he thought he had seen something; something terrifying. Looking around now, there was only blackness.

"The darkness hides many things. Dreadful terrible things..."

Lying motionless, Cody listened. There was a rustling in the corn. He hoped it was just the wind, but, then, there was something else; the sound of breathing. And it was close. Suddenly he knew. She was here. The girl from the playground. The dead girl.

....

The man rummaged through the items under the counter until he found what he needed. He discovered the sign first: *Closed - Ya'll come back soon!* it read. He had to search a bit longer to find the padlock for the gate, which was buried under a stack of newspaper and an assortment of half-consumed beverages in paper cups. That should do it. Closing the field would ensure no one would interrupt him.

"Hey, there, Henry," said a husky voice. "What's up?"

Henry rose and found Michael, one of the local high school kids who worked the festival, leaning on the counter. He held a soft pretzel wrapped in wax paper, and was busy working a bite of the doughy bread between his jaws. Next to him, holding a large stuffed giraffe, was a girl that Henry presumed was Michael's girlfriend, based on the couple's close proximity to one another.

"What are you doing here?" Henry scowled.

"My job," Michael replied, with a hint of sarcasm.

"No need. I'm closing it up for the night."

"But, it's early. There'll be another crowd after the concert."

"I'm not feeling well," Henry said.

"Do you want me to cover? Katie could watch the booth when it's time for me to sweep the maze."

"No!" Henry snapped. "If they want to go in, they can come back tomorrow."

"Wow, you really must be feeling bad. That's not like you. Whatever you say though, boss. I'll go ahead and do my final sweep and then we'll close it up."

"No need, I said. There's nobody in there."

"What about the boy?" Michael asked.

"Boy? You're mistaken. There's no boy."

"Katie and I saw a boy walking down this way a bit ago. He had to have come through here. Surely you must have seen him."

"No," Henry replied, glaring at Michael.

"Well, maybe he got by you and snuck in. I'll do a quick run through and double check."

Henry sighed and began to chuckle, a low babble that was almost a grunt. He stepped out of the booth, and walked around the counter to face Michael. "I'm sorry," he cackled.

"What?" Michael asked with a snicker, wondering what he had missed that was so funny. He looked at Katie, who simply shrugged her shoulders with equal confusion. Turning his gaze back to Henry, he barely had time to register the knife, seeing only a brief glimmer of light before the cold steel slid across his neck. Wide eyed with shock, he stumbled backwards, clutching his throat as thick spurts of red jetted from the open gash.

Katie froze. She fought to catch her breath as her mind tried to make sense of what she was seeing.

This isn't happening. Oh god, this isn't happening.

A knot was rising in the back of her throat. She was going to be sick.

No, you have to run. You have to get away.

She tried to take a step but her legs were heavy and numb.

I don't want to die.

A new wave of adrenaline surged through her veins, and she started to run. Dropping the blood spattered giraffe in her arms, she ran towards the gate. The ground felt spongy beneath her, and she feared the man would catch up at any moment, but she pressed on harder. Her side was aching now, and her legs felt rubbery and unsteady. She stumbled.

"Help me!" she shouted. "He's killing him! Please, somebody help me!" she screamed, finally finding her voice.

She saw a man run down the path towards her, and shrunk back, kneeling and burying her head in her arms, crying hysterically.

"Katie," said the man, "Its Dan, honey. What is it? What's the matter?"

The girl looked up, her face smeared with tears and mascara. "He killed him. He's dead," she wailed.

"Who's dead?"

"Michael. Back there, at the maze," she replied, pointing a trembling finger in the direction she had come from.

"Who killed him?"

"Henry."

Dan was dumbfounded. "Katie, can you make it up to the barn? I want you to call an ambulance and get some help. Can you do that?"

She nodded, and Dan helped her to her feet, giving her a pat on the back before taking off down the path. "Dear God," he whispered when he reached the cornfields.

Henry knelt on the ground, howling with laughter as he stuck a knife into Michael's chest over and over, his crazed maniacal shrieks intensifying with each swing of the blade.

"Drop the knife, Henry!" Dan shouted, drawing his gun and taking aim at the man.

Henry stopped laughing and looked up with a blank stare, as if the officer had him confused with someone else. He smiled a second later, and with a cool, calm tone replied, "You can't stop me this time. He belongs to me."

"I don't know what you're talking about, Henry. Just put the knife down. Let me help you."

Michael gasped, rolling his head to the side and staring at Dan with desperate eyes; eyes that were teeming with fear and pain. His chest rose, emitting a wet gurgling sound, as he struggled to hold on to life. "Please," he wheezed with a frail voice and an outstretched hand.

"Jesus, he's still alive," Dan muttered to himself.

Henry drew back his lips in a twisted grin and raised the knife. There was a violent crack in the air, and a split second later, the bullet found its mark. Henry's head snapped back, the side of his skull exploding in a cloud of blood, bone and brain tissue. His body convulsed several times, the knife falling from his hands, and his lifeless form slumped to the ground.

Holstering his sidearm, Dan ran over to Michael, who lay motionless, shrouded in black inky pools of blood. A quick check for a pulse confirmed what the bewildered officer already feared. The boy was dead.

Dan fell to his knees, cupping his face in his hands. Two lives had been lost tonight, and he had taken one of them. He had pulled the trigger for the first time in his career, something he'd hoped he would never have to do. What made the situation even more dire was who he'd killed.

"Why?" Dan wondered aloud, glancing toward the man who had wielded the knife; a man who had been his friend for many years.

Henry had been a good person, kind-hearted and generous beyond reproach. It was inconceivable that he could ever commit such an atrocious act. The man he had come upon moments ago, however, was a stranger. The insane look in his eyes, the deranged laugh, and the cryptic way he spoke were all indicative of an unhinged mind, and that was not Henry. He'd just spoken with his friend that morning at the diner, and Henry had been the jovial soul he always was.

So why? Dan knew the question would forever echo in his mind, and that the answer would remain as elusive as it was this very night; a night that would surely haunt him the for the rest of his life.

JIM MARTIN

CHAPTER 12

Cody lay still. He reasoned that if he couldn't see the girl, then, maybe, she wouldn't see him either. If that held true, and he could stay quiet long enough, then surely she would go away. The thunderous hammering in his chest was deafening, yet he could still make out the faint graveled rasping of the ghostly girl a few feet away. Each discordant breath was unwavering, but also stationary. She wasn't moving.

A dull ache began to creep into his forearms where he was supporting the weight of his body. He was desperate to change positions, but doing so could be detrimental if he were to make any noise.

He suddenly wished he'd waited for his mom and Evan to come out here with him. Why did he have to be so insistent? Beating Tyler's time seemed of little importance now. He just wanted to be back at the festival where it was safe.

The breathing stopped, replaced by a new noise, a clacking sound, followed by a long groan, then silence. "Cody," a voice whispered.

Terror-stricken, he scrambled to his knees, turning and patting the ground in a frenzied search. He only had to move a few feet before his fingertips felt the cold metal casing of the flashlight. *Oh, please work! Please!*

With a click, he depressed the power button. A welcome beam of light lanced the frigid black night around him, pushing back the darkness and restoring visibility.

The girl was directly in front of him now. The hollows that were her eyes seemed impervious to the light, nebulous pits that swallowed up the luminous rays like a black hole. She lifted a cadaverous arm and stretched out her hand, her purpled lips parting as if she were about to speak.

Cody didn't wait around to hear what she had to say. He spun around on his heels and fled, taking a right at the next junction. There was no time to stop and cut a line in the ground. No time to think about which direction to go. He just needed to get away. Having gone only a few steps, he couldn't believe his eyes when another girl, as ashen and dead as the first, stepped out from behind the rows of corn.

Grinding to a halt, Cody nearly twisted his ankle turning and running back in the opposite direction. There was still one unobstructed pathway, and he sprinted toward it. Shadows sprung from every direction, crouching and leaping as the beam from the flashlight bounced about in an erratic dance. There was one, however, which moved in a different manner than the rest; straight ahead. A vague inky pillar that loomed ever larger as he neared.

Cody slowed just enough to hold the light steady, focusing it on the indeterminate object before him. It was another child, a boy this time. Thin and skeleton-like, his left arm dangled at his side, swinging like a pendulum as he ambled forward.

He was in the last pathway, which meant there was nowhere to run. Cody backed up as far as he could until he brushed the tall stalks behind him. For a brief moment, he considered darting into the thick growth, but feared even worse terrors may be lurking amidst the narrow rows of corn. A dense fog began to blanket the ground, rolling and swirling with a malevolent life of its own. The ghostly children drifted atop the pillowed mist, gliding closer like spectral surfers riding an ocean of death.

Cody's mind reeled, and his body trembled uncontrollably. A sweet, acrid odor filled the air, twisting his stomach with nausea – the smell of rotting flesh.

The girl in the tattered pink skirt was just inches away now. Cody squeezed his eyes shut as she put her face to his. He waited for the dreaded moment when he would become as dead as she, the vapid fog consuming his lifeless body and leaving no trace of the boy he'd once been.

"Don't be afraid," whispered the phantom voice.

Cody opened his eyes. What he saw was not hostile, but instead a being full of desperation and despair. As he looked around, he felt a pressing anguish invade his mind, the same heavy weight of sadness that encumbered the lost souls standing before him. In one brief moment, an unspoken connection was forged, and the gravity of their emotions, their torment, struck him hard. His anxiety subsided, replaced by the misery of a burden that was not his own, and an oppression he did not understand.

"I'm sorry," Cody lamented. "I don't know how to help."

"There is no help for us," the girl replied in a low, mournful tone.

"Because you're ... dead?"

She lowered her head and nodded.

"What happened? How can you still be here?"

"There's no time. You have to go. Run far away."

"What do you mean?"

"He's coming for you."

Cody's throat constricted and he started to shake. "Who?"

"The shadow man. The one who lives outside your –"

The abrupt manner in which the girl stopped speaking was as unsettling as the cryptic message she conveyed, maybe even more so. Something was wrong. Like a deer sensing an unseen hunter, the girl lifted her gaze and scanned the night around them.

Cody could feel a collective anxiety amongst the children. It seemed ironic that the dead would still experience fear, for what harm could possibly befall them? But, perhaps there were things more terrifying than death.

He heard something now, faint and rhythmic, rising through the air. As he strained to listen, it became more clear – music. At first he thought it was just the concert, the haven of safety which may as well have been a million miles away, but then he realized the sound was getting closer. More distinct now, he could make out trumpets and saxophones blaring. While the song was likely an anthem of cheer at one time, there was something off about the rendition playing now. Dragging like an old vinyl record being played at the wrong speed, the refrain was disconcerting. It was the music of nightmares.

The phantasmal melody emanated from within the corn, creeping up through the dark rows and drawing ever closer, until it seemed only a single veil of stalks stood between Cody and the source of the hellish tune. Then, just as quickly as it had materialized, the music stopped.

"He's here," said the girl.

The other two children wailed in a high pitched cry that sent chills down Cody's spine. He watched as they dissipated before his eyes, their essence mingling and disappearing into the fog, its thick rolling currents whisking them out of harm's way.

Two streams of bright light spilled out from behind the stalks, casting a harsh, eerie glow on the milky skin of the remaining corpse-like girl before she, too, began to vanish. "Come with me!" she cried, reaching out to Cody.

He recoiled, fearing that taking her hand would end his life and curse his soul to share in her torment. He turned and ran before the last of her faded away.

Behind him, there was a low grumble of an engine starting, followed by the spitting of tires kicking up dirt, as an old black truck lurched out from behind the stalks of corn.

Cody gasped. The air was even heavier and more rancid than before, as if it, too, had bloated and spoiled from death's touch. He raced back in the direction of the entrance. It was the shortest route out of the maze, and he thought he stood a better chance of avoiding the blocked paths. He would have to remember the steps he'd taken before, however, as the fog made it impossible to see the lines he'd drawn in the soft ground.

He looked behind him as the truck fishtailed around the corner, mowing down a large swath of corn. The wheels spun, and the crops beneath ripped and crunched as the tires found traction, shooting the vehicle forward in a swirl of dust and fog. The rumble of the engine rattled Cody's bones as it growled with a fierce intensity, pushing the metal monster onward even faster.

Then there was that music again, the same terrible music, rising up and ringing in his ears. His teeth clacked with each stride, and his entire body throbbed from the intense pounding in his chest. He twisted and turned through the narrow maze, propelled by a sort of instinct, as if he had been down these paths a hundred times before. He gained ground with each corner as the truck slowed to maneuver the turns, but now it took to crashing straight through the flimsy stalks, seemingly desperate to reach him.

He could feel the heat bristling from the radiator as the truck closed in on him. The noxious odor of burning oil and exhaust filled his lungs, and his head started to ache. He rounded another corner, struggling to stay afoot. Sharp, crushing pains tore through his chest and he stopped, leaning forward and grasping his knees as he sucked in deep gulps of air. He couldn't go any farther. He wasn't going to make it.

The truck tore through the stalks to his right as if they were tissue paper, spinning and grinding to a halt. Cody lifted his hand in the air, shielding his eyes from the brightness of the headlights, and tried to look inside the cab to see who it was that had come for him. He was met with only darkness. The door creaked open and the ground crunched as someone stepped out of the vehicle.

Cody let out a wet sob and stepped back. The moment he reached the path's edge, a pair of arms shot out from the corn and seized him by the wrist. He screamed, spinning around and seeing the face of the dead girl. Ice surged through his veins and his vision blurred. There was a great rushing sound, and he was overcome by a sudden sense of weightlessness. *This must be what dying feels like*, he thought. And with that, everything went black.

In the next instant, he heard screams. There were voices, too, but they were low and unintelligible. Though his eyelids were heavy, he was able to open them long enough to realize he was lying at the entrance to the maze. He could make out a group of people huddled around something several feet away, the grass around them painted red with blood. He'd never seen so much. It was everywhere.

Beyond the mass of people, in the middle of the crimson pool, was someone else; someone lying on the ground watching him. It was the big man who had sold him the ticket, staring back with the same cold, dead eyes as before. Only this time, it wasn't just his eyes that were expired.

Cody heard another voice now – his mother's. She sounded frantic as she cried out to him. He tried to answer, tried to move, but couldn't. Too weak to do anything, he closed his eyes and slipped into the darkness once more.

....

Waking with a start, Cody sat up in bed and glanced around his room. The green numbers on the digital clock indicated that it was 3:15 in the morning. He searched his memory for what had happened. The carnival, the maze, and the dead children – had they all been nothing but a lurid dream? It must have been, had to have been. It was too crazy to be real. Even so, he didn't want to sleep alone tonight. Though he knew he was too old to be sleeping in his mom's bed, right now he didn't care. The vivid memory of the dream still frightened him.

Brushing the perspiration from his forehead, he felt a sharp sting near his wrist. He leaned forward and moved his arm into the dim light of the window. His eyes widened with alarm when he saw the deep red marks etched into his skin; finger-shaped welts from where the dead girl had grabbed him. It hadn't been a dream at all.

Crawling out of bed, he turned on the light to examine the marks closer. The prickling sting intensified when he poked at the wound with his finger. It didn't look too bad, though. No worse than the time he had burned himself on the hot stove when he'd tried to make macaroni and cheese. At least he was still alive after his encounter. Touching the girl hadn't killed him. In fact, it seemed she had saved him.

Cody flicked off the light and made his way to the door. As he reached for the knob, he heard a thump downstairs. He listened, hearing nothing but the stillness of the room and his own hushed breathing. Then it came again; another thud, then another - footsteps. Someone was coming up the stairs.

The shadow man. The one who lives outside your —

"Room," Cody whispered, finishing her sentence.

Thump ... thump ... thump.

There was a shuffling outside the door, and the knob began to turn. Cody ran to a corner and cowered down, closing his eyes and hoping that when he opened them again, everything would go back to normal.

Please. Please, stop.

The abrupt pop of the latch scraping across the strike plate startled him, and his eyes flew open. It hadn't worked. The shadow man was coming for him just like the girl had said. He held his breath as the door swung open and the black shape stepped into the room. It stood motionless for several long seconds, and then, without sound or warning, charged forward.

Cody tried to scream, but his vocal chords produced only a hoarse rasp. He called out again, harder, expelling all the air in his lungs, but the fleeting cry was no more than a whisper; a whisper which was silenced forthwith as the darkness fell upon him.

CHAPTER 13

October 31, 2010

Evan watched as the black liquid churned and swirled inside the mug, staring beyond its inky vortex into the even darker recesses of his own subconscious. It had been two months since the nightmare had invaded his sleep, but last night it had returned with a vengeance.

While he had, for the most part, moved on since the incident ten years ago, the dream forced him to relive the horror of that night time and again. Not just the ache of the emotional wounds, mind you, but every gut wrenching detail. Sights, sounds, and smells that elicited profound guilt and fear, so much so that at times he thought it capable of driving him mad. Perhaps it was his penance though, an endless attrition for the blood on his hands and a personal hell of his own making.

A voice from behind broke his train of thought, and he turned to see Dan standing in the doorway.

"Hey, boss," the deputy mumbled. With a haggard countenance, bloodshot eyes, and tousled hair, he looked like someone who had just stumbled out of bed after a night of hard drinking.

"You're looking well this morning," Evan jested.

"Liar," Dan quipped, doing his best to smile and play along. "I still look better than you though."

"Yes, well, who doesn't? In all seriousness though, are you doing alright?"

"I suppose so. Can't feel much of anything right now. Still in shock I guess."

"I think we all are. You want to talk about it?"

Dan shrugged his shoulders. "I don't know what to say, really. I mean, you saw what happened."

"I did, but trying to shoulder something like this on your own doesn't work, even if you are the size of King Kong. It's heavier than you think. Trust me on that."

"You saying I should talk to a shrink?"

"Heavens, no. I want you to get better, not worse. I mean talk to Linda. She's your wife, after all. Talk to me, or Dorothy, or whoever you want. Just talk to someone."

"If anyone can possibly understand what I'm going through, it would be you. Right now, I just want to understand why."

"I know Henry was your friend, and it may not feel like it, but you did the right thing."

"I wish I could be certain of that, but I'm not," Dan replied, walking into the room and pacing back and forth. "I hoped I would never have to fire that weapon, and in a town like this, I shouldn't have had to, especially on one of our own."

"He was stabbing that boy, Dan. It doesn't make a damn bit of sense, and I can't fathom what sort of motive he could possibly have had for doing so, but you did what any officer would have done to save a life."

"But I didn't save anyone. Michael was dead, anyway. I should have taken Henry alive."

"You didn't know that. There was a chance he could have lived. But if you had stood there and let Henry put that knife in him again, he certainly would have been dead. I don't think that's something you'd want to live with, either. This wasn't a win-win situation. Somebody was going to lose, and it shouldn't have been that kid. You tried to save him, Dan, and that's what matters."

"But why didn't Henry stop? Why did he just look at me and raise that knife again? He had to know I would pull the trigger. Why did he force my hand like that? I just want to understand why!" Dan shouted, slamming his fist into the side of the vending machine. The sheet metal buckled under the impact, rocking the entire cabinet back on its legs and dislodging a bag of chips from the wire spiral inside.

He stood there for a moment, face red and eyes damp. After he had collected himself, he walked over to the worn mahogany table in the center of the room and slumped down into one of the fabric chairs nestled underneath.

Evan retrieved a mug from the cabinet over the sink and poured another cup of coffee. He put the drink down in front of Dan and took a seat in the chair across from him. The room was quiet as both men sat in silence, listening to the steady hum of the fluorescent lighting overhead. Somewhere in the station a phone began to ring. Neither of them moved.

"You want me to get that?" Dan asked after the third ring.

"It can wait," Evan replied. "Probably Bob calling to inquire about the incident. I'll call him back."

"Guess I'm about to be on an involuntary vacation, huh?"

"I'm sorry, Dan. It's procedure, and my hands are tied. You know I'd much rather have you here. Shouldn't take long. Seems pretty open and shut to me. Nothing to worry about."

"I'm not worried. Just don't know what I'm going to do in the meantime. Sitting at home is the last thing I need."

"Well, if the media gets wind of this, you won't want to be around here, anyway. Better to lay low until it blows over."

Dan was quiet for another long moment, staring down at the floor as if he were counting the individual tiles. "Evan, that wasn't Henry last night. If you'd seen the way he looked at me, it's like he didn't even know who I was. I've never so much as seen him raise his voice in anger the whole time I've known him. Something just feels wrong about this."

"I agree. I'm just thankful he didn't hurt Cody."

Dan's eyes widened, and he sat up with a start. "Oh God, I've been so wrapped up in my thoughts that I forgot to ask if he was alright."

"He was pretty dazed after he came to. I'm not sure he even realized Leslie and I were there. Doc Miller looked at him and said he was most likely suffering from emotional anxiety and mental shock. His vitals were good, and there were no signs of blunt trauma, so he told Leslie to take him home and keep him comfortable. He is supposed to go by and check on him again this morning."

"You think he saw the murder?" Dan asked.

"Hard to say until he can tell us himself. I just hope he's okay."

"Have you talked to Leslie yet this morning?"

"No, I didn't want to call too early. Figured I'd stop in and take care of some business, then run some breakfast by and see how things were going."

"Well, don't let me keep you. We can talk more later."

"You could come with me."

"You go ahead. I'm going to wrap up a few things around here while I still can. Maybe I'll meet you for lunch. Oh, and sorry about the vending machine."

"I'm not worried about that old thing. But you do know you're going to have to pay for those chips, right?" Evan said with a grin.

Dan let out a slight chuckle. "Does Leslie know what an asshole you are yet?"

Evan laughed as he walked out the door and headed towards his office. Reaching the end of the hall, he could hear Dan chortling back in the break room. At first, he thought his friend was still laughing, but when he listened a bit closer, he wasn't so sure. It may have been the sound of weeping instead.

....

The phone call with Bob Patterson lasted half an hour and went exactly as Evan had imagined it would. He wanted to know the details surrounding the shooting and asked if the state bureau of investigation had been called yet. He inquired about Dan's mindset, about the boy that was killed and what, if anything, the family had said. He discussed potential liabilities and legal issues that could arise, and what steps Evan should take to protect the welfare of the town.

Bob wasn't a bad man, but he was all business. A good trait for any mayor, no doubt, but having some compassion wouldn't have hurt. Two people had just been killed, and the lives of others had been irrevocably altered or shattered. But Bob spoke of it all like he was planning a public works project. Evan assured him he would handle everything to the letter, and placated the man to the best of his abilities. It was a relief when he ended the call and left the station.

On the drive to the diner, Evan planned an itinerary for his day. Talking to Michael's family was going to be the hardest part. He knew they would want to know why an upstanding and well-respected member of the town had suddenly murdered their son, and he currently had no answers. He hoped that they might be able to offer up some sort of clue, no matter how small, in regard to Michael's working relationship with Henry in the days leading up to the festival. Perhaps Henry had already shown some signs of instability that were shrugged off instead as eccentricities.

Turning the corner a block from the diner, Evan pushed the thoughts of the investigation out of his mind and started thinking about breakfast. He knew Cody would want blueberry pancakes, and Leslie was an omelet kind of gal. He himself preferred anything smothered in cream gravy. Biscuits, eggs, pork chops, it didn't matter, as long as there was plenty of gravy to be had.

He also wanted coffee. Good coffee, anyway. He tried to finish the cup at the station that Dan had brewed but, as always, was unable to take more than a few swallows. Dan used more ground beans than any rational adult ever should, creating a finished product that might be capable of fueling the human body for days at a time. There could be upsides to that, of course, but only if you could get past the fact that it tasted like shit.

Pulling up in front of the diner a moment later, Evan was surprised to see Dorothy running out the front door towards him, wringing her hands and yelling out his name.

"Where's your phone?" she cried. "Leslie has been tryin to get a hold of you all mornin!"

"I forgot to grab it when I left the house today. What's the matter? Is she okay?"

"No, you gotta get over there now. It's Cody. No one can find him. He's gone, Evan."

CHAPTER 14

Leslie hung up the phone and was once again struck by the oppressive emptiness that had settled throughout the house. It seemed a desolate place now, a lifeless vacuum transcended only by the deep chasm widening in her soul. There were no busy feet racing across the floor above her, no video games blaring, no laughter over the whimsical melody of morning cartoons, and no spirited little voice asking a hundred questions before noon; all things that had become the soundtrack of her life. The only audible noise was that of the clock on the wall, an intonation that seemed to swell in magnitude as the seconds rolled by, each methodical tick feeling like a blow.

"Nothing yet," Evan had said just moments ago. "We still have a lot of ground to cover though, so don't lose hope. I'll call you again soon."

He had tried not to sound worried, but she detected a measure of grief in his voice. Subtle, but there nonetheless. There was genuine concern on his part for Cody, something made all the more apparent by the events of last night and today. He'd insisted on driving them to meet the doctor, staying to make sure Cody was okay, and then seeing them home again. When he'd arrived at the house this morning, his sense of urgency and the sentiment in his eyes put to rest any lingering doubts she may have had in regard to his devotion to her and her son.

But, while Evan was a model of compassion, John was far from it. "Why would anyone take him, Les?" he had said when she called his cell earlier. "He'll turn up. I'd love to chat but I have a deposition to get to. Let me know when you find him, okay?"

His indifference infuriated her. She wanted to lash out, but it would have been a waste of energy. Years of experience had taught her that John was only interested in John. She should have expected nothing less from the man, who didn't have an altruistic bone in his body. How he could be so calloused towards his own flesh and blood was something she would never be able to comprehend.

Not wanting to sit and brood over it, she got up from the couch and made her way to the kitchen, opening up the refrigerator and staring at the contents. She didn't feel much like eating, but knew she needed to keep her strength up, now more than ever. Grabbing a carton of milk from the top shelf and selecting a box of granola from the pantry, she poured herself a bowl of cereal. The simple act of consuming food was a task now, something done out of necessity rather than enjoyment, and after several bites she pushed the bowl aside.

The relentless ticking of the clock receded, giving way to the chime of the hour, it's toll resonating through Leslie's mind like the cold hollow ring of a death knell. It was 4 o'clock in the afternoon, and she was growing more restless with each passing hour.

When she hadn't been able to find Cody that morning, her first thought was that he may have wandered off, still disoriented from the trauma of the night before. In searching the house, though, she discovered all the doors and windows locked tight. If he had ambled off in a befuddled state, she doubted he would have had the presence of mind to take a key and latch the door behind him.

After a call to Tyler's house, and a quick walk through the neighborhood, turned up nothing, the panic began to set in. By the time Evan showed up a little while later, she was a trembling wreck.

Though she tried to reassure herself that everything would be alright, the unthinkable kept creeping into her head. Part of the reason she had moved to this town was because it had seemed so much safer than the big city. Perhaps that was naive on her part, but had it not been for last night, her beliefs would have remained unchanged. It stunned her that a man she'd served several times in the past, a man who appeared harmless, could turn around and murder a teenage boy in such a brutal and savage manner. She couldn't help but wonder if he had somehow been involved in the death of Larry Wilkins. Or, perhaps, there were other closet psychotics in this town, depraved monsters masquerading as kind and simple country folk who said hello on the streets, but then butchered you when no one else was around.

Leslie's thoughts turned to Michael, and her heart ached for his family. She couldn't begin to imagine what his mother must be feeling. How does one deal with the loss of their own child? Had Dan not intervened when he did last night, she may have already known the answer.

A wave of nausea rippled through her, sending her running for the bathroom. Her chest heaved and she fell to her knees and gripped the rim of the toilet bowl, gagging and coughing as her insides twisted back and forth, expelling what little food she had ingested.

Once the retching had subsided and she was certain the sickness had passed, she trotted up the stairs to her bedroom. She disrobed and stepped into a cold shower, shivering as icy cascades of water lapped against her hot bare skin. Up to now, she had resisted the urge to cry, but the fear and pain were becoming more than she could bear. Sinking down against the tiled wall and burying her head between her knees, her body convulsed with heavy sobs, and the tears fell unrestrained. "My baby," she cried. "Please, let them find my boy."

....

The vibration from the phone on the nightstand jarred Leslie awake. Still feeling flushed after the shower, she had curled up on the bed unclothed, letting the cool wisps of air from the ceiling fan temper her fevered body. She hadn't intended to fall asleep, but the soft purr of the fan motor had alleviated her troubled mind long enough to lull her into a deep slumber.

Reaching over and picking up the phone, she pressed the button that lit up the screen. One missed call and a voice mail. Without haste she navigated to the message. It was from Evan. She paused for a moment, afraid of hearing anything other than good news. Taking a deep breath, she tapped the screen and put the phone next to her ear.

"Hi. We're still searching, but thought I'd call and see if by chance there was any news on your end. Are you doing alright? Stupid question, I suppose. Of course you're not. I'm sorry. Anyway, I'll stop by in a bit and let you know how things are progressing, Call if you need anything, alright?"

Leslie's heart dropped as she heard the click of Evan's phone hanging up. It was almost dark outside, and as the sun slipped away below the horizon, so too did the chances of finding Cody, at least for today.

She felt helpless at home, and wanted to be out searching along with everyone else, but Evan had suggested that somebody stay at the house in case Cody returned on his own. It made sense, but after calling everyone there was to call, the sitting and waiting had become torturous.

A loud knock at the front door stirred her from her thoughts. She threw on a robe and hurried downstairs, securing the tie as she walked. She hoped to find Cody waiting, but if he had used a key to lock the door earlier, then surely he would have used it to get back in. It was probably Evan. She had no idea how long she'd been asleep, and hadn't paid attention to what time he had called. For all she knew, the message he'd left her was hours old.

Reaching the bottom of the staircase, she saw the bowl of candy sitting atop the side table in the entryway. With everything that was going on, the fact that it was Halloween had escaped her. The neighborhood was probably crawling with trick-or-treaters right now. Though she hadn't left a light on, some of the more adventurous souls may have decided that even the dark houses were worth investigating, especially if it resulted in the addition of another piece of candy to their bucket.

Regardless, Leslie didn't have it in her to entertain droves of cheerful, costumed kids when the whereabouts of her own child were unknown. She would open the door this time, but then make a sign saying there was no more candy. She considered just setting the bowl on the front steps, but if one or two greedy ghouls came along and cleaned her out, she might continue to get knocks from other treat seeking visitors.

Leslie flipped on the porch light and cracked open the door. No one was there. "Pranksters. Not what I need tonight," she muttered.

Irritated, she hit the light switch and went to close the door, when a faint orange glimmer caught her eye. Stepping outside, she was baffled by what she saw. There on the banister, some twenty feet away, sat a lit jack-o'-lantern. She approached with caution, as if the thing intended to do her harm. It was only a pumpkin, of course, but for reasons unknown it unnerved her.

Scanning the front yard, she noticed the silhouette of a young girl standing beneath one of the oaks. "Hi there," Leslie said.

The girl stood rigid and silent.

"Did you put this here? Or did you see who did?"

Still no response.

Reaching out and turning the pumpkin around in order to extinguish the candle, Leslie gasped when she saw the grim reaper carved into its face. This was the jack-o'-lantern Cody had made in class. He had displayed it at the school talent show, but never bothered to bring it home, saying it would be rotten by Halloween. Yet, here it was, as pristine as the day he had created it. If this were some sort of twisted joke, it wasn't at all funny.

Leslie hurried down the porch steps and marched across the yard toward the little girl, thinking she must know something about how the pumpkin ended up here. As she neared the tree, the girl took a step behind it, concealing herself.

"It's alright, you're not in trouble. I just wanted to ask you a couple questions. Do you know my son, Cody?"

Rounding the tree, she stopped short. The girl was nowhere to be seen.

Rattled, Leslie ran back in the house to call Evan. As she headed up the stairs to retrieve her phone from the night stand, there was another knock. It seemed inconceivable that someone could have crossed the yard and made it to the door in the few seconds since she had come in, yet there was no mistaking the muddled shape of a person standing outside now.

Easing back across the entryway and turning on the porch light, Leslie saw a child's hand pressed against the glass. Had the girl come back? Or could it be ...

"Cody?" she whispered, and flung the door open.

The sight of the thin pale boy standing on the porch repulsed her. His bluish complexion may have been part of an elaborate costume, although she wasn't sure what he was supposed to be other than a diseased child on the verge of death. There could have been no faking the left arm, which dangled at an unnatural angle, nor the malnourished frame and protruding bones, over which skin was drawn so tight and thin that it resembled paper rather than living tissue.

As shocking as his appearance was, the three words that spilled from his bruised lips were even more terrifying.

"Help me, Mommy," he wailed.

....

"Here you go," Dorothy said, setting the mug of hot chamomile tea in front of Leslie. "This always helps me if I'm anxious. Should ease your stomach as well."

After her shift had ended at the diner, Dorothy boxed up some food and stopped by the house to check in on Leslie. Walking up the porch steps, she had discovered the front door ajar and her friend curled up in a ball on the floor of the entryway. Paranoid and incoherent at first, Leslie rambled on in a nonsensical manner.

"The children," she said, over and over. "Where are the children?"

Dorothy made a call to Evan, who arrived minutes later, his car screeching into the driveway with lights flashing and sirens blaring. Together, the two of them managed to get Leslie to the couch and lay her down, though several minutes passed before she was composed enough to articulate the details of her encounter from earlier.

"Thank you for the tea," Leslie said now, her voice weak and afflicted. Her hands shook as she raised the mug to her lips and took a small sip.

"It's inexcusable what those kids did to you tonight. You sure you didn't recognize them?" Evan asked.

"I never got a good look at the girl, but the boy," she trailed off, squinting and shaking her head as she tried to recollect every child she knew in town. "No, I've never seen him before. I wouldn't forget someone like that."

She shivered at the image of the pallid young boy that sprung to the forefront of her mind. It was a disturbing picture, which would be ingrained in her conscious for some time to come, with the distinct possibility that it might never be completely expunged.

"If you had seen him, you would know what I mean. I've never come across anyone so thin and ailing. He was sick, Evan, and if I didn't know better I'd say he looked dead."

"Seeing that it's Halloween, looking dead wouldn't be out of the ordinary. I'm sure it was just a good makeup job."

"I've seen some elaborate costumes in my time, but nothing to this degree, and certainly not on a child. For the sake of argument, though, let's say it were makeup. That still doesn't explain his weight. No one is that skinny unless there's something wrong with them."

"Maybe them Anderson kids," Dorothy said, shooting Evan a sidelong glance. "That youngest one barely has a speck of meat on his bones."

"Possible. I'll stop by and have a chat with them. See if I can find out where they've been tonight."

"Wouldn't surprise me if they had somethin to do with it. They're always stirring up some kind of trouble," Dorothy huffed.

"Who are the Andersons?" Leslie asked.

"They live in the next county, just outside of Baker's Grove. Dad is a long haul trucker and the mother bartends at the local tavern. The kids are left unsupervised quite often. The oldest is fourteen and is given charge over the two younger boys when the parents are gone, but I'd say she's every bit as unruly as they are," Evan replied.

"It's a shame," Dorothy interjected. "That so-called mother of theirs ain't much of one a'tall. Even when she is home she lets em' run amok. Those children look like they ain't got a home, but she rides around in that fancy car of hers with her skin tight pants and manicured nails like she's high society. She can try all she wants to look like some Barbie doll, but it's like wrappin a septic tank with Christmas lights. Don't matter how flashy it is on the outside, it still ain't nothin but shit underneath."

Red faced, with hands on her hips, it was clear that Dorothy bore no good will toward the ways of this woman and her undisciplined kids. Not surprising, considering her own strict upbringing. "Pardon my language, hun, but I'd sure like to give that ol' hussy a piece of my mind. And them kids, too, if they done this. Ain't right, them having so little respect for what you're going through."

"I know you are both just looking out for me," Leslie replied. "If it were those children, though, how did they know about Cody?"

"Everyone within 100 miles knows by now. Dan faxed pictures to the neighboring counties in the event Cody was to be seen outside of town. We have to assume that if someone did take him, they might be on the run. There are roadblocks set up as well, to check all cars leaving the area."

Leslie lowered her head and covered her face. "Why?" she cried. "Why would they take him?"

"We all want to know that," Dorothy said, wrapping an arm around Leslie. "There are so many of us that love that boy to pieces, and we're hurting with you, darlin'."

"I'm just afraid. I try not to think it, but a part of me wonders if we'll ever know."

"That's only natural," Evan replied, moving from the chair he'd been in and kneeling in front of Leslie. "I know what it's like to suffer to the point you can't take another step, to have so much anxiety that you can't breathe, and to feel like the biggest part of your soul has been ripped away. The emptiness it leaves behind is indescribable. But, even when you think you have nothing left in you, it's still possible to find the will to press on. You're a stronger person than I ever was, so I know you can fight."

Leslie wiped away the tears with the back of her hand and stared into Evan's eyes. She saw a pain there that she hadn't seen before, an anguish that had been locked away in the most private corner of his heart, and was now laying bare before her. He spoke not as someone who tried to sympathize and find words of comfort, but as a man who had, at one time, been crippled by a deep emotional torment of his own. "How? How can you understand what I'm feeling?"

When the sheriff replied, his voice cracked under the weight of what he was trying to say. "I know, because ten years ago, I lost my little boy."

CHAPTER 15

"Why don't you have a seat, hun," Dorothy said to Evan as she got up from the couch. "I need to run on home, and I think it's better the two of you get to talk alone."

Shifting her attention back to Leslie, she went on. "Darlin, I set some food in the fridge, along with a pitcher of tea for when you feel like eatin. And don't be worryin about work. Arthur and I will keep things goin. You take all the time you need, and call if I can help in any way, alright?"

Leslie nodded, and Dorothy turned to go, straightening the skirt on her uniform and feeling alongside her tower of red hair, making sure everything was in place. One might have thought she was leaving for a date instead of going home, but this was a common ritual that Leslie was accustomed to seeing. *A girl's always gotta look her best*, Dorothy would always say, and it was a motto she lived by without exception.

Evan walked her to the door, waiting on the porch until she was in her car and on her way. He returned to Leslie a moment later and took a seat on the cushion beside her.

"A son, Evan? I'm stunned. I mean you never even mentioned you had a child. What happened?"

"It's just difficult for me to discuss, even after all this time. Since I've moved here, I can count on one hand how many people I've told."

Leslie recollected the conversations she and Evan had shared and realized that she knew very little about his past. He had never pried or questioned hers. In fact, everything she had divulged about her relationship with John and the divorce was done voluntarily. Perhaps he never asked because he was afraid of having to answer questions about his own painful past.

"I'm sorry. I shouldn't pry into something so personal," Leslie said.

"Don't be sorry. I wanted to tell you, and would have eventually. But under the circumstances, I think it's time you know."

"Was he abducted?"

"Not exactly."

Evan lowered his head and began to fidget with a stray thread on his police jacket, letting several moments of silence pass before the words finally fell from his trembling lips. "My son died. I made a mistake and because of it, I lost Ryan."

Leslie threw a hand up over her mouth. The revelation ripped through her as if it were her own child he spoke of. That was no surprise to her since she had always been a compassionate person, but now she empathized in a way that would have been impossible only twenty-four hours ago.

"He was just three when it happened," Evan continued, wringing his hands together so tight that the ends of his fingers turned a deep shade of crimson and purple. "I was drawing his bath water when the phone rang. It was my weekend on call and I needed to answer. Ryan was in his room playing so I shut the bathroom door behind me and ran downstairs to catch the phone."

He paused, agonizing over each torturous word. Leslie told him he could stop, that he didn't have to go on, but he only shook his head and continued.

"I had child safety covers on the knob, but in my haste I must not have shut the door all the way. When I came back up ..."

He stopped again, his face burning with grief. Leslie reached over and touched his arm as he struggled to maintain his composure.

"I lost him," he choked, fighting back the tears. "Just like that, he was gone. My boy was gone."

"I'm so sorry, Evan."

"Me, too," he said, pressing his lips together in a melancholy grin and shaking his head. "I'm not even sure how I made it through that first year. People told me it was just an accident, as if that should somehow make me feel better. But it didn't. His mother never said it aloud, but I know she blamed me for what happened. Things were never the same between us afterwards, and neither of us knew how to deal with the emptiness. We tried therapy after a while, but we were too far gone. She left shortly thereafter. How could I fault her though? If it weren't for my carelessness, Ryan would still be alive."

"Evan, I wish I had the words."

"It's alright. I just wish I had things to do over, you know?"

"Hindsight can be a slap in the face. There are always the questions, the what-if's. I wonder what if I had taken Cody seriously when he told me about the man on the stairs? Or, what if I had stayed next to him last night while he slept? But I didn't. And now I have to live with that. I guess we both wish we could go back and do things differently."

"You know Leslie, I don't think you should fault yourself for thinking this man Cody saw was a bad dream. I would have thought the same thing. You said yourself that all the locks were secure, and I didn't find any indication of forced entry. If someone took Cody, I believe they did so after he wandered out of the house. You couldn't have known what was going to happen."

"Maybe not. But, then, you couldn't have known with Ryan either. I don't doubt you were a terrific father," Leslie replied.

"It's hard for me to feel that way, but thank you," Evan sighed. "And thank you for listening. I hope I haven't upset you further."

"No, it's fine. I'm just heartbroken for both of us. And I'm sorry for Ryan. I wish I'd had the chance to know him."

"Would you like to see a picture?"

Leslie nodded and inched closer to Evan as he retrieved a worn photo from one of the slots inside his wallet. In the middle of the image sat a dimple-faced boy in a numbered baseball jersey. He clutched a stuffed rabbit which, from the looks of it, had been an object of affection for quite some time. Patches of brown fur had been worn down to the underlying canvas, and one of the ears was conspicuously absent, a small cluster of loose stitching the only telltale sign of where it had been. Ryan held the rabbit close, his entire face radiating with laughter, the kind of wonderful simple joy that springs from, and exists, wholly in the soul of an innocent child.

"He's beautiful. And he's got your eyes," Leslie said.

A warm smile spread across Evan's face and he thanked her for the compliment. He beamed with pride as he stared at the picture of his son.

"From the looks of it, he sure must have loved that bunny," she added.

"That was Max," Evan replied. "They were inseparable. Even after Max lost that ear, Ryan wouldn't think of replacing him. Every night, when I would read him a story and tuck him in, he'd ask me to tuck Max in, too. No matter how many times I did, Ryan would always laugh like it was the funniest thing he'd ever seen. I think those are the moments I miss the most.

"That's sweet. And I was right about you. You were an amazing dad. I think that's one of the reasons Cody loves you the way he does, because he knows you're a good man, Evan."

"After Ryan's death, there was no real joy or purpose in my life anymore. It's like I was alive, but I wasn't living. At least not until you and Cody came along. Being around the two of you has made me remember what it is to be happy. I wasn't sure I could ever feel that way again. I love your son like he were my own, and I can't, I won't, lose another child I care about. I've got to get him back. That's all there is to it."

Leslie leaned in and kissed Evan's cheek. "Thank you," she whispered. "I'm so very glad you're here."

....

The first attack happened that night. Leslie had gone to bed at her usual time of 10 o'clock, though more from routine than anything else. While the stresses of the day had left her both physically and mentally exhausted, there were still too many worries and concerns churning through her brain to allow her to sleep. She tossed and turned indeterminately, stretching well into the midnight hour. It was then that she heard the sound.

An abrupt squeaking, like that of a wheel axle thirsting for oil, pierced the room. It was faint, and at first Leslie chalked it up to one of the many thumps and rattles common to any old home. But, as she lay there listening, the shrill chirping seemed to change in tone, as if it were drawing nearer. Even the hardwoods groaned under the weight of something moving up and down the halls.

Sliding out of bed, Leslie tip-toed across the room and pressed her ear to the door. All was quiet. Then she heard it: *Squee-cha, squee-cha, squeee.* It was definitely moving. Leslie nudged the door ajar and peered through the crack. She saw nothing, but the sound came again. It was originating from Cody's room.

A part of her wanted to believe her son had returned, but logic told her it didn't make sense that he would be gone all day only to sneak back in during the middle of the night. So then who was it? Her thoughts turned to the man on the stairs, and panic set in. Who was this stranger that was finding his way into her home? And if he had made off with Cody, what had he done with him? She needed to know. This was her son's life at stake after all, and if there were a chance she could find some answers, then she was going to do just that. With heart racing, she began easing her way down the hall.

Squee-cha, squee-cha.

The noise grew louder as she approached the doorway to Cody's room. She reached for the knob and took one last step, the floor letting out an emphatic crack as her foot came down. The squeaking stopped.

Leslie froze, expecting someone to burst out of the room at any second, but no one came. She opened the door and clicked on the light. The room was empty. No mysterious man, no emaciated children, and no ghostly squeak. Just her son's room exactly the way he had left it. She checked the closet and the bathroom, even went so far as to look under the bed, but there was nothing. Then she noticed the one small detail which had almost gone unnoticed. The window blinds were open.

She remembered closing them the night before. Cody always slept with his blinds drawn, and rarely opened them himself during the day. That was usually something she did each morning, but not today. Someone else had done that.

Leslie sat down on the bed and tried to reason with herself. The noise she had heard earlier was gone, but she knew she hadn't imagined it. And, though it might have seemed silly to some, she was certain those blinds had been closed before. So what was going on? Admittedly, she was an emotional mess right now, but she wasn't crazy. At least not yet.

She fell back on the bed and buried her face in the pillow. It smelled of the strawberry-scented shampoo that Cody loved so much. She remembered him picking it out for the first time when he was just four years old, and how he'd insisted on using it the moment they got back home. Bittersweet tears crept to the corners of her eyes, and for one brief moment, she smiled. Hugging the pillow tighter and holding on to this sweet redolent reminder of her son, scores of other happy memories began to dance through her head, gradually shifting from mind's eye to dream. Before she knew it, she had cried herself to sleep.

Waking sometime later, the pleasant remembrances she had dozed off with were replaced straightaway with absolute horror. Opening her eyes, Leslie was struck by a suffocating heaviness in the room, and an immediate sense of dread mounted inside of her. The lights, which had been on when she fell asleep, were now off.

Someone else was there. She could feel eyes on her, watching in silence from some unseen spot, their gaze burning into her like hot embers. There was a sudden rustling, and the shadow of a person drifted across the wall. Leslie's breath quickened and she felt the mattress give behind her.

Oh God, no!

Her mind was in a terrified frenzy, telling her to run, but she was paralyzed. The weight of the entity was upon her now, jarring her with a sudden blow to the back. She struggled with all her might to move, to turn her head and see who was attacking her, but it was of no use. Unseen hands crushed and pummeled, violently shaking her, and she was helpless against them.

She tried to scream, but her throat only produced a wet choking sound. Closing her eyes and mustering one final surge of willpower, her body sprung to life. Rolling onto her back with arms swinging, she thrashed at the air but connected with nothing. She stopped fighting and looked around.

This can't be. They were right here!

Dizzy and shaken, she tried to make sense of what had happened. It wasn't possible that any human could disappear in such a manner. But the alternative, that she was dealing with something else, something supernatural, seemed equally implausible. Maybe it was a dream, but it all seemed too real. Her body ached where she had been struck, and the angry growl of her attacker resonated through her mind like a clap of thunder.

Leslie tried to dismiss the experience as best she could, but the event had left her anxious and afraid. She made her way to her own bed, but found it impossible to sleep. As much as it had been a long and trying day, the night, it seemed, would be even longer.

CHAPTER 16

November 12, 2010

It was a cold, dreary morning, and the usually colorful palette of Millford Springs and the surrounding autumn foliage appeared dull and achromatic, having been muted by a solid wall of gray, which blanketed the sky and held hostage the life-giving rays of the sun.

Leslie pulled into a space along Main Street directly across from the diner and shut off the engine. She opened the car door and stepped out into the frigid morning air, suddenly wishing she'd brought a coat with her. A light mist was falling, adding to the already dismal feel of the day, and the wind had begun to blow in sharp gusts, its icy fingers chilling her exposed skin.

She hurried across the street and retreated into the warmth of the diner. The breakfast rush had ended a half hour earlier, and the place was all but empty now. Only a couple of tables remained occupied by those lucky enough to have ample time to dawdle over an extra cup of 40-weight and the daily edition of the *Millford Messenger*.

Though the crowds had dissipated, the familiar smells of crisped bacon, brewed coffee, and fresh-squeezed oranges lingered. There was something else as well, a warm spicy scent that Leslie recognized before she ever saw it – pumpkin pie. It was one of those small seasonal pleasures she normally looked forward to, the aroma alone evoking an overall cozy feeling and cherished memories of autumns past. With Cody still missing, however, and having had no promising turn of events, her insipid mood matched the dullness of the weather. Happy remembrances held no place in her mind now, having been eclipsed by unbearable sadness.

The door to the kitchen swung open and Dorothy emerged, carrying a pie in each hand. She was hollering something about how *running a diner was enough, and that she wasn't operating a daycare as well.* This was presumably directed toward Arthur, who mumbled something in response but remained unseen, choosing to either acknowledge defeat, or refocusing his energy for another round once his foe returned to the kitchen.

Upon seeing Leslie, Dorothy sat the pies down and hurried over. "You were the last person I expected to see in here today, darlin. I hope nothin's the matter. At least nothin worse, anyhow."

"No, there hasn't been any news, I'm afraid. I went to see Dr. Miller this morning and wasn't quite ready to go back home. I really needed to get out of the house for a while."

"Well, of course, hun. I imagine you would. C'mon over here and talk to me," Dorothy said, nodding toward the barstools. Leslie rubbed her arms as she walked, attempting to brush away the last remnants of the chill residing in her bones.

Dorothy shuffled back around the counter, instinctively grabbing a mug and pouring a hot cup of coffee, which she placed in front of Leslie. She then hollered for Arthur, telling him they had a visitor. There was a clanging sound, and a moment later a pair of eyes, nestled under tufted woolly brows, peered over the kitchen window. After an initial look of surprise, Arthur made his way through the swinging door, wiping his hands on a white linen towel and draping it over his shoulder, before greeting Leslie with open arms.

"It's good to see ya," he said in his graveled voice. "I only wish it were under better circumstances."

"Thank you. It's good to see you, too," Leslie replied, reaching out and shaking Arthur's outstretched hand.

"It's a terrible, terrible thing what happened. I'm very sorry. I ain't very good at this sorta thing, but I hope they find your boy soon. He's a good kid. Father O'Banion reached out to the congregation after mass last night, so you got a lotta prayers going up for ya," Arthur said, firming his grip and giving Leslie a pat with his other hand.

"Thank you again. Cody and I both appreciate your thoughtfulness."

"I hope this ends soon so things can return to normal. Besides, it'd be nice to have you back. This one's making me lose my mind," he jested, motioning towards Dorothy.

"You're one to be talkin," Dorothy replied. "The way I see it, turnabout is fair play, honey. You done made me lose mine years ago!"

"Eh, you'd have to have had one to begin with," Arthur cracked, tossing his hands up in the air.

Leslie couldn't help but grin. She missed being at the diner. The endless squabbling and fussing between Arthur and Dorothy was as much a staple in this place as the burgers and, for Leslie, was a constant source of amusement.

After another moment of banter, Arthur made his way back to the kitchen to prepare for lunch, and Dorothy moved the pies to their rightful spots in the glass display case. "So how you holdin up, hun?" she asked, returning to the counter.

Leslie shrugged. "I'm trying to stay hopeful, but that's harder to do with each passing day. Every morning I wake and there's that brief moment where I start to get up and get Cody ready for school. But then the reality of everything sinks in. I just don't know how long I can go on like this."

Dorothy reached for a napkin and dabbed the corners of her eyes, which had begun to mist over. "God knows how many tears I've cried these past few days. I just wish there was more I could do."

"You've been a great help to me. And I know everyone is doing all that they can right now. If it weren't for you and Evan, I don't think I could have kept myself together this long."

"Speaking of Evan, I'm sure he'll be in here again before long. That man is living on caffeine right now. He tells me otherwise, but I don't think he's sleepin a lick. And speakin of sleep, you look pretty worn out as well. You gettin any rest, sugar?"

"Not really. I know that's to be expected with the worrying and all, but it's more than that. It's the attacks also."

"Attacks?" Dorothy asked, her voice rising with concern. "Good heavens, what do you mean? Who's attacking you?"

"According to the doctor, nobody," Leslie replied. She recounted the attack from the first night, as well as the ones which followed each subsequent evening after. "Dr. Miller says I'm suffering from sleep paralysis."

"I don't think I've ever heard of such a thing," Dorothy said.

"Neither had I. But, apparently, it's fairly common. He said that when we're in a dream state, there's a disconnect between the brain and the muscles in the body, which prevents acting out. What happens with sleep paralysis is that the person becomes conscious and aware before the brain plugs back in, making movement impossible."

Dorothy had stopped wiping the pepper shaker she held in her hand and stood motionless, her curiosity clearly piqued. "But how does that explain the attack?" she asked.

"Panic, anxiety, and hallucinations are all symptoms. Apparently, many people report sensing a presence in the room, being shaken, or feeling a crushing weight on their body. To say it's a terrifying experience would be an understatement."

"Oh my, I reckon so. What on earth brings that on? And how do you stop it?"

"Several things. But in my case, most likely increased stress. He did say that it's rare for it to persist. For most, the experience happens once or twice and then never again. Guess I'm a special case. Lucky me."

"You poor dear. There's nothing he can do for you?"

"He said it would go away on its own, and prescribed some sedatives to help me sleep."

Leslie stared down at the mug clasped in her hands, her thumbs tracing the lip of the cup back and forth. The doctor's diagnosis made sense, even if she'd never heard of the condition, but there were other things of late that she couldn't explain. She hadn't intended to say anything to anyone, for fear of appearing crazy, but the words spilled out nonetheless. "Dorothy, do you believe in ghosts?"

Just then, the bell on the front door clanged as the last remaining customer made their way outside, creating a rush of cold air which robbed Leslie of what little warmth she had regained. A thousand tiny goose bumps sprung up on her arms and stood at attention, sending her body into an uncontrollable shiver.

Dorothy clucked like a mother hen, seeing Leslie shake. "You're gonna make yourself sick dressed like that in this weather. Give me just a moment," she said, excusing herself to the back and returning several seconds later with a knit button-up sweater, which she draped around Leslie before taking a seat on the barstool next to her. "Now what's all this talk about ghosts?" she continued.

"Just odd things happening in the house – strange noises, footsteps, lights left on, or things moved around that I'm sure I had nothing to do with."

"And you think it's a ghost in the house?"

"Sounds pretty silly to hear someone else say it," Leslie said with a small laugh. "I don't know. I've never been one to believe in that sort of thing, but what I'm experiencing is real, and I don't know how to make sense of it. Do you think I'm crazy?"

"Oh no, honey. Not a'tall. I just think you've been under a lot of stress this past week. I imagine it's all a result of that, and a lack of rest'."

"Maybe so. But something just feels off to me. I've been having these unsettling dreams also. Well, one dream anyway. It's been the same each night since Cody went missing."

"I'm all ears if you wanna talk about it,' Dorothy said.

"I see a little girl around Cody's age standing in the bath tub with her back to me. I ask her name, but she acts as if she doesn't hear. She's holding a yellow balloon on a string that suddenly turns a bright red and begins to drip blood. It's slow at first, but then it begins to gush until her clothes are as red as the balloon. I try to reach her, try to help, but I can't move. The little girl doesn't turn around but I hear her say, *Find him.*

"I ask who, and she starts to write a name in blood on the wall. She gets the letter *C* finished and then I hear someone screaming like they're angry. I don't see anyone, but it's a man's voice. *Look what you've done. You're ruining it*, he yells, and the next thing I see is the girl lying in the blood smeared tub. Her eyes are hollowed out and her complexion is blue. I know she's dead, but it's as if she is somehow still looking at me, pleading for help. And that's when I wake up."

"Lord, have mercy," Dorothy exclaimed. "I ain't no psychiatrist, but even I know that's pretty messed up."

"It's horrifying. But I feel like it's trying to tell me something. She drew the letter C. It's Cody. She must be talking about Cody. Maybe she knows where he is."

"But who is *she*? I don't wanna dash your hopes, darlin, but you don't even know her name. And even if you did, I don't think this is someone you're gonna find listed in the phone book."

"No, of course not. But what do you know about my house? Did anything bad ever happen there?"

"I don't rightly know. This town has a long history, and I've only been here for the last twenty years. Certainly nothing's happened in that time. There was an elderly couple lived in your house before you, but they never reported anything outta the ordinary."

"Maybe it's just me. Maybe I am going crazy," Leslie said, lowering her gaze and fidgeting with her mug again.

"Now don't be talkin like that. You most certainly are not. Heaven knows anyone who's gone through what you have the past few days would certainly be dreamin all sorts of terrible things. That don't mean you're crazy."

"But I'm sitting here talking about ghosts. And not just talking, but starting to believe it. Pretty extreme, wouldn't you say?

"I always thought that the only real ghosts were those we made for ourselves. Bad decisions, regrets, people we done wrong, or life choices we wished we could change. All those things can come back to haunt you in the worst ways sometimes. But who am I to say that literal ghosts don't also exist? I just never seen one is all."

"Are you only trying to make me feel better?" Leslie asked.

"You know I always say what I think. And I think anything is possible. But if they are real, and I ever see a bloodied dead girl in your house, I don't think I'll be comin around to visit much."

"Fair enough," Leslie laughed.

"Now, I better get myself back to work before ol' ape eyes gets to fussin back there. You want somethin to eat?" Dorothy asked.

"Oh, I've still got plenty at home, but thanks. And thank you for listening."

"Anytime," Dorothy replied, giving her friend a hug before making her way back around the counter to retrieve a bus tub and a wet rag.

Leslie collected her purse and car keys and was about to leave when she remembered the sweater that wasn't hers and began to peel it off.

"Keep it!" Dorothy shouted from across the way. "You need to stay warm out there and I've got another in the back."

"Okay, I'll take you up on that," Leslie smiled. "I'll get it back to you soon."

"No hurry. Just take care of yourself and try and get some rest."

Leslie pulled the small amber bottle of sedatives out of her purse and gave it a quick shake. "That shouldn't be a problem. Ghosts or no, nothing is going to be haunting me tonight."

....

Within ten minutes of arriving back at the house, Leslie heard the doorbell chime. She was in the middle of changing into warmer clothes and hurried her pace, pulling a sweatshirt over her head as she jogged down the stairs.

"Who is it?" she asked, reaching the front door.

It was Evan. She was still fumbling with her shirt when she opened the door, and her midriff was exposed. The sheriff turned and looked away, as if he had just caught her wearing nothing at all.

"I'm sorry. I guess I should have called first," he said.

"No, you're fine. I've been up awhile. Just needed to change into something more befitting the weather today. Come on in," she replied, opening the door wide and stepping to the side.

Evan crossed the threshold and waited for Leslie to close the door before following her into the living area.

"Any news?" Leslie asked.

"No, but there's something I wanted you to look at."

He pulled a thick colorful envelope out of his jacket and Leslie immediately recognized it as one of the photo pouches from the one-hour lab at the drugstore. "I was at Thompson's this morning picking up some allergy pills, and they reminded me about these. Pictures I took at Cody's party."

"Oh, Evan," Leslie replied, taking a small step back and shaking her head. "I don't think I can look at those right now. It's just too much."

"No, no, I understand. I wouldn't normally ask you to, but there's one I think you need to see."

"Why? What is it?"

"I'm not sure. Will you have a look?"

Leslie stood in silence for a long moment, biting at her lip the way she always did when she was nervous, before finally agreeing to look at the picture. Evan pulled the stack of photos out of the pouch and handed her the one on top. Just as she feared, her heart began to ache the moment she saw her son smiling back at her. Cody was sitting in the driver's seat of the police cruiser with the lights on and a 90-mile-wide grin on his face. He had played around in that car for nearly half an hour, and she'd had to practically drag him out of it when Evan was ready to leave.

"I miss him so much," she said, cupping her hand over her mouth to stifle a cry.

"I know. I'm sorry," Evan replied.

Leslie saw anguish in his eyes and knew he hated having to show her something that caused her pain. She glanced at the image again, but wasn't sure what it was she needed to see. Nothing seemed out of the ordinary. "What am I supposed to be looking at?"

"I didn't see it at first, either. It's not Cody. It's the house."

Leslie scanned the photo again and there it was – a figure in the upstairs window. The blinds were peeled back in Cody's room, and the face of an old woman stared down toward the car where her son sat. She dropped the photo and gasped. The entire floor seemed to shift beneath her feet. She stumbled backwards, knocking into an end table next to the couch. Evan ran over and put an arm around her for support.

"Someone was in the house. Oh God! Someone was in here!"

"You don't recognize the woman in the window?"

"No!" Leslie shrieked.

"This doesn't make much sense. I mean we had been upstairs minutes before this picture was taken."

"A lot of things don't make sense lately. Maybe she came in the back while we were outside, but why? Who is she?" Leslie asked, her eyes filled with horror. She met Evan's gaze, hoping beyond all hope that he could answer her question, though she already knew he was as lost as she was.

"I don't know. It's a lead, perhaps. More than we've had to go on thus far. But, given the circumstances, I think I'd feel a lot better if you weren't staying here alone."

"I need to be here. What if Cody came back and no one were here? Besides, where else am I going to go?"

"I don't want you to feel like I'm being too forward, but I have an extra room at my place and you're welcome to it. At least consider it until we figure this out."

"I just think I feel better being here. I know if he's out there and can get back, this will be the first place he comes."

"I worry about you right now," Evan sighed. "If someone is getting into this house, anything could happen to you."

"I appreciate your concern. I really do. Maybe you could stay here, if it would make you feel better."

"Well, that still leaves you here during the day, but at least you wouldn't be alone at night."

The police radio on Evan's belt began to crackle and sputter. *"Evan, you there? Come back."*

"Yeah, I'm here, Dan. What have you got?"

"I'm here at the Harvey place. I've got a bit of a situation."

"What's going on?"

"I'm not entirely sure. A lot of blood. You probably need to see this."

"I'll be there in five," Evan replied, clicking off the radio and turning his focus back to Leslie. He knew by the look in her eye what was on her mind before she even spoke.

"You don't think?" she cried.

"No, I'm sure it's fine," Evan said, unwittingly lying to himself as much as Leslie. He didn't want to believe it could have anything to do with Cody any more than she did.

Leslie marched over to the coffee table and grabbed her purse. "I'm going with you."

"That may not be a good idea. I mean I'm sure it's not Cody, but –"

"If you don't want to take me, I'll get in my car and go myself. I have to, Evan. Good or bad, I just need to know. You can understand that can't you?"

He couldn't argue. Had it been his own child, he would have been just as determined. Losing someone was devastating, but not knowing where they were, or if they were even alive, was a feeling he was only now learning. "Okay," he conceded. "Let's go."

CHAPTER 17

The house on Sycamore Road belonging to Ray and Miriam Harvey was easy to spot. An ambulance sat alongside the curb half a block away, its flashing lights bathing the small white home in shades of red. Throngs of neighbors, some adorned only in bathrobes and seemingly oblivious to the bitter temperatures, stood across the street, craning their necks in the general direction of the scene. A few others had ventured closer in an attempt to get a better look, and now stood huddled together in a small cluster at the end of the driveway. It was just past noon, but thick charcoal-colored clouds had stalled overhead, graying the world below and making the hour seem much later than it was.

Evan brought the car to a stop and threw the shift lever into park. Leslie reached for the door handle and paused, watching out the window as a visibly distressed Dan peered into the backseat of a newer model Buick. Sensing her hesitation, Evan placed a hand on her shoulder. "You sure you want to do this?" he asked.

"No, I thought I could, but if it's him...."

"I know," Evan said, giving her a reassuring glance before climbing out of the car and starting up the drive. The twenty feet to his destination could have been one hundred, as everything seemed to move in slow motion. A ringing sound flooded his ears, and a heavy throb lashed against the backs of his eyes. It was the same fear he felt during his nightmares. The sense of knowing something terrible waited just behind the shower curtain. But this was no dream. The circumstances may have changed, but he was terrified the ending would be the same – with the discovery of a lifeless body belonging to someone he loved. He prayed that whatever was in the back of the Buick would be anything but Cody.

"Hey, boss. Am I ever glad to see you. Two days back on the job and I get this? I'm starting to think this whole town has gone crazy," Dan said.

"I'm beginning to agree," Evan replied. He stopped just short of the car and mopped his brow. Despite the chill in the air, he was perspiring like he'd just run a marathon. "Is it him?" he asked, his mouth turning to sand.

"Cody? No, it's not. Thank God for that."

Evan closed his eyes and took what was probably his first breath since exiting the vehicle. Drawing in a long gulp of air and slowly exhaling, he felt the tension in his body melt away. He turned toward Leslie and shook his head. She cupped her hands over her face and slumped back in the seat. He could tell she was sobbing, but before he could excuse himself to check on her, an anxious Ray Harvey appeared at his side.

"Sheriff, I done told her before not to be pickin up strangers. I dunno what she was thinkin, but she coulda been killed (pronounced *kilt* in his southern drawl). Says it was just a child, but weren't no normal one from the looks of things."

A retired farmer, Ray's accent was thicker than the pork chops down at the diner. Though he hadn't tended land in years, he was still dressed in a pair of denim overalls, worn work boots, and a faded John Deere cap, which sat cock-eyed atop tufts of uncombed, snow white hair. If there were ever a shortage of help for the harvest, Ray would have been ready to go at a moment's notice.

"Was she hurt, Ray?"

"None that I can tell. Them fellas in the ambalance say she's shaken up, mostly, and her blood pressure is outta whack. That an' she ain't lookin so good; all pale and jittery."

"Is she able to talk about it?"

"Don't think she's gonna say too much right now. They got one of them oxygen masks on her and gave her a shot of somethin to get her nerves calmed down. Got me so worked up I'm thinkin I may hafta join her."

Evan grinned a little at that and asked if there might be room for three. Ray turned his head, spat some chewing tobacco, and gave a hearty laugh through yellow stained teeth. Evan considered trying to talk to Miriam, anyway, but quickly discarded the idea. Even if she weren't already sedated, Ray had mentioned she wasn't looking too well. From what he knew of Miriam, she was a follower of Dorothy's mantra that a girl should always look her best, and it was a known fact that she wouldn't so much as step out of the house to check the mail without making sure her face was on. Under the circumstances, he decided he would respect her dignity and get whatever information he could from her husband instead, who, based on his appearance, subscribed to a different mantra entirely.

"I'm just glad she's alright," Evan said. "Do you have any idea what happened?"

"She come home from the store and I heard her screaming before she ever got inside. Kept goin on about how the person she picked up was dead in the backseat.

Said that somethin else got in the car too, somethin horrible, and that it killed the kid. I grabbed my shotgun and went outside, but they wasn't no one there. Only thing I saw was all the blood in the backseat. Looked like a deer was gutted back there."

Evan took a few steps toward the car and looked inside. "Dear God," he muttered.

The tanned leather of the seats was stained a dark inky red. It soaked the entire length of one seat before spidering out into a mass of spatters and sprays that painted the backs of the front seats and the rear windshield. It was just like Ray had said, only worse.

"What do you make of that, boss?" Dan asked.

Evan stood in silence for several moments before he was able to speak. "I've never seen anything like it. The amount of trauma a body would sustain to produce this much blood should have left behind tissue fragments as well. But there's not so much as a hair that I can see."

"Right. It's the damnedest thing, and no blood on the door handles, the jams, or outside of the car. Why would you kill someone in such a slovenly manner, and then take care not to get any blood on the doors when you hauled them out? And how do you do it in the time it took for Miriam to run inside and Ray to come back out? It's as if the kid just disappeared."

"Kid," Evan said, suddenly turning pale. "Ray, did Miriam tell you anything else? Did she say who was in the car? You mentioned something about a child."

"Yessir. Said she come across a young gal walking longside the road between here and town."

Evan breathed another sigh of relief. Dan had said Cody wasn't the victim, but without a body, how could he have known for sure? Unless, of course, he'd already questioned Ray and knew it had been a girl that Miriam had picked up. Either way, the certainty of it eased his mind. There was still the matter of dealing with what appeared to be the second murder in as many weeks, but at least Leslie wouldn't be burying her only son today.

"I asked her why she just didn't keep driving," Ray continued. "Nuthin odd 'bout some kid walkin alone. Then she says the girl only had a skirt and short-sleeves on, and that it was too cold to be out with no coat."

"Do you know if she recognized the girl?" Evan asked.

Ray shifted his gaze upwards and scratched his head, pushing the old ball cap further to one side until it appeared to defy the very laws of gravity. He contemplated for several seconds before answering. "No, but I'm thinking not. Said she looked weak and sick-like. Kinda dirty, too, but said she could see bruises though the muck. Runned away maybe?"

"Possible. She never gave a name then?"

"Nah, but Miriam said the girl kept askin for Charlie. Said over and over she needed to find him."

"Any idea who that might be?"

"Not round here. Been here my whole life, and no Charlies I know of. Lessin she meant ol' Charlie Peterson that used to live two houses down. Couldn't be him, though. Hell, he's older n' me. His family left town back in '50 after them killins. Scared a bunch off that did."

"Who was killed?"

"Kids. Three of 'em. Man named Walter snatched 'em up. Just went crazy, I s'pose. Lotta families took off afterwards, an' those that stuck around didn't talk about it none."

"And how does Charlie fit in?"

"He don't, other than he was the one that told the police. One of them kids that Walter got lived across the street, an' Charlie saw the whole thing happen."

Evan pulled a pad of paper out of his breast pocket, flipped it open, and began scribbling some notes. "I don't suppose you know what became of him? Charlie, I mean?"

"Well, last I knew, he was still up in Worthington. My brother an' his were buddies. Paul passed bout five years back, an' Charlie was at the funeral, but that's the last I seen him. You ain't thinkin he's the one this girl was lookin for, are ya?"

"I can't say either way, but do you happen to have a phone number for Charlie?"

"No, Charlie ain't got no phone. I don't recollect he ever has. Likes to keep to himself. But I can give you the address of that house in Worthington. Unless he done moved in the last few years, that's where you'd likely find him."

"That'll work," Evan said, jotting down the address and then slipping the pad back into his pocket. He thanked Ray for his help and told him to be sure and call if he remembered anything else. He said he would and sauntered off toward the ambulance. "And give Miriam my best will you?" Evan shouted after him.

Ray gave a tip of his hat, spit another wad of chewing tobacco, and disappeared behind the paramedics, where he would no doubt check in on his wife, and then perhaps inquire about a sedative of his own.

"How much did you get done?" Evan asked, turning his attention back to Dan.

"I got a recorded statement from Ray, photos of the scene, and was just collecting a sample of blood for analysis when you pulled up. As you observed, there isn't much of anything else back there. No hair, fingernails, or tissue that I can see. Still need to dust for prints, but the way this is playing out, I wouldn't be surprised if there aren't any. I wish someone could tell me what the hell is going on here lately."

"You and me both, but we're the ones who are supposed to find the answers." He paused, considering, and then went on with this next question. "Do you believe his story?"

Dan shrugged. "No reason not to. It's an unusual situation, but I don't think he and Miriam are killers, if that's what you mean."

"That's what everyone thought about Henry, too."

As soon as Evan spoke the words he regretted it. There was a flash of pain in Dan's eyes, and his face dropped. He looked like a kid who had just dropped his ice cream cone, albeit a very large kid. "Dan, I'm sorry. That was insensitive. I didn't mean ..."

"No, you're right. I've got to stay subjective, no matter how implausible it may seem. You think they could've done this?"

Evan gazed towards the ambulance and shook his head. "Honestly, I don't know what to think. You ever hear anything about the murders Ray mentioned?"

"No, but didn't he say that was in 1950? My mother wasn't even born until '51."

Evan chuckled a little. It didn't seem far-fetched that they wouldn't know about an event that occurred sixty years ago. After all, most of those old enough to remember had probably moved away or passed on. But still, something about it stuck in his mind. And one thing he knew about getting a hunch in his head was that if he didn't follow up on it, he'd never be able to let it go. "There's something I want to look into. It's probably nothing, but you think you can finish up here without me?"

"Have I ever let you down, boss?" Dan grinned.

"Right, stupid question."

Evan turned and headed down the drive. "I'll let you know if I find anything!" he called back.

"You gonna at least tell me where you're headed?" Dan asked.

"I'm going to find Charlie Peterson."

The first thing Evan did once he was back in the car was make sure Leslie was alright. Her eyes were still glassy, and the skin around them pink and puffy, but she assured him she was fine. He briefed her on what he'd learned from Ray, downplaying the condition of the back seat as much as possible. She, in turn, filled him in on the dreams that had plagued her sleep over the past couple weeks.

"I think it's the same girl, Evan. The dirty clothes, the bruises, and the name she tried to write on the wall. At first I thought it was Cody, but what if she was spelling Charlie?"

Evan studied her for a long moment. That the girl in Leslie's dreams could be the same one who seemingly vanished into thin air after leaving several quarts of blood in the backseat of the Harveys' Buick sounded preposterous on the surface, but it also intrigued him on some level. In fact, it only served to reinforce the nagging feeling in his gut that was telling him to follow up on the events of 1950. Why did it suddenly feel like he had been dropped into an episode of the *Twilight Zone*? "It seems like a stretch," he finally said, "but at this point I can't discount anything."

"Will you take me with you?" Leslie asked.

"Of course, but it's a little over two hours to Worthington. Assuming Charlie is even still there, and figuring at least an hour or two with him, that won't put us back here until after six or seven tonight. You okay with being away that long?"

"Not really. But if this girl is trying to tell me something, and if Charlie is the key, then I want to be there."

"Fair enough," Evan said, starting up the car and driving toward the railroad bridge leading out of town, the same one Leslie had driven under just a few short months ago while escaping her own past, yet unwittingly stumbling into a town with a more sinister story.

She glanced at the bridge, thinking those very thoughts, and then firmed her shoulders. If this town's past was going to chase her, then, by God, she would chase right back.

JIM MARTIN

CHAPTER 18

It was a quarter past three when Dan left the police station. He had returned there after finishing up at the Harvey residence, filled out a report on the incident, and bagged the blood sample he had so carefully collected. The last thing he wanted to do was contaminate the only shred of evidence that existed in this bizarre case. There was Ray's recorded statement, and the photos, of course, but the blood was the only thing that might provide a link to the killer, the victim, or both.

Once the sample was safe inside a tamper-resistant bag, he phoned the lab in Dallas and arranged for a courier to come by and pick it up the next morning. He then called the hospitals in the neighboring communities and inquired about any major traumas involving a child within the last twelve hours. There had been none. He informed them that a violent crime had been committed and to be on the lookout for the victim – a young girl between the ages of ten and fourteen - who had lost an awful lot of blood. He doubted he would hear anything back, and if he did, he assumed it would most likely be from the morgue rather than the hospital. After all, it seemed very improbable that anyone would survive such a vicious attack.

Stepping outside now, Dan twisted the key in the lock to the station doors, engaging the dead bolt with a heavy thunk. A low rumble erupted from the dark clouds overhead, and he hurried across the parking lot to his car. The wind had picked up considerably from a few hours before, sending leaves and debris scattering across the pavement and around his feet. There had been no time to check the forecast, but it didn't take a meteorologist to know that a storm was coming, and from the looks of it, quite a nasty one.

Not wanting to waste any time, he made his way to the diner. He hadn't eaten anything since the night before and was due for a good meal. His original plan was to spend some time in his favorite booth, but he now decided he would get the food to go. With any luck, he could make it to Leslie's place before the rain hit.

Evan had called a short time after he and Leslie left town and asked Dan if he would mind checking in on the house while they were gone. He had agreed, telling Evan he would stay until they got back, providing there were no further calls for police assistance.

"If there are, let's just hope it's Shelly over at the Hoot-n-Holler calling on a rowdy patron," Evan had replied.

Right, like the good old days before the townsfolk decided to dabble in homicide. Back when the worst I dealt with were a handful of domestics or disorderly conducts, Dan thought to himself.

He stepped into the diner a few minutes later and received a wave from Dorothy as she hustled by with several plates of food balanced across her forearm.

"Don't you ever take a day off?" Dan hollered after her.

"What? And miss a chance to see you?" she shouted back.

Dan smiled and made his way over to the counter, where a silver-haired woman he'd never seen before sat reading a magazine and eating lunch. She looked up over the brim of her glasses as he approached and passed him a menu.

"Oh, don't need one, thanks. Food has been the same here since I don't know when," Dan replied.

"Silly of me. It stands to reason the town sheriff would already know the menu by heart."

"Deputy sheriff. But, yes ma'am, I think I eat here more than I do my own home. Before I married, my wife used to say it wasn't other women she had to compete with, it was the blue plate specials."

The old woman laughed. She had a peculiar odor of butterscotch about her, with a hint of menthol, and wore a garish shade of lipstick that would have been the envy of strippers everywhere. She extended her hand and introduced herself as Harriet Vanderman.

"Dan Decker. Pleased to meet you, Ms. Vanderman. You have people here in town? Or just passing through?"

"Call me Harriet," she said. "I was just passing through, but now I think I may be staying a little while longer."

"You must have taken a shine to our town. Plenty of people do wax nostalgic and end up staying an extra day or two."

Harriet paused as she finished chewing a bite of her lunch. "It's a lovely town, no doubt about that. But the reason I'm staying is because I was summoned," she said, poking at the air with her fork.

"Summoned? You're not in some sort of legal trouble are you?"

"Oh, nothing like that, no," she chuckled. "It does concern you, however, as I believe you worked a most troubling scene today. But, I'm afraid you won't find the girl, Mr. Decker. I'm sorry to say, she's dead."

....

Steeped in history and unchanged in appearance, Millford Springs was one of those rare small towns that remained frozen in time. Its citizens still held fast to the values and ways of life that had fashioned the city, from its humble beginnings up to the prosperous and bustling mecca it had become in the mid-twentieth century. The city of Worthington wasn't so fortunate. Time hadn't been at all kind, its steady march aging her in the same manner it does all living things, leaving behind a tired and withered shell that would soon breathe its final breath, left alone to decompose and return to the dust from whence she came.

Leslie looked around at the ruined town as the police cruiser rolled past the city limits sign and turned onto the main road. The handful of residents occupying the barren stretch of city scape stared curiously, as if Evan and Leslie were the first visitors to this forsaken corner of the world in decades. From the looks of the place, Evan thought perhaps that wasn't too far off base.

"Not much here, is there?" Leslie asked.

"Casualty of the oil boom. This whole place sprung up around a pocket of crude. Once it dried up, so did the town."

"That's sad. Looks like it was a nice place once upon a time."

"I imagine it was. Millford had its fair share of growth from oil but, fortunately for us, there were the wheat and dairy farms to fall back on when the oil was gone. If it weren't for them, our town would probably look a lot like this one right now."

They passed a shuttered five and dime, the Woolworth's name still displayed prominently over the rusted metal awning. A faded advertisement was painted on the brick of the neighboring building, and depicted a soda jerk handing a bottled beverage to a patron on the other side of the counter. Both were grinning from ear to ear, with bold lettering above them reading:

Feel Alive with Bright Cola! Guaranteed To Add A Little Sunshine To Your Day

Leslie thought it a bold claim by today's standards, as any company using that slogan now would probably end up paying through the nose to some bitter sap claiming the soda hadn't adequately eased his miserable existence.

Evan pulled the car into the parking lot of a service station another block up. He pretended to need a pit stop, but Leslie thought it was more likely a ruse to get directions. When they had stopped outside of Baker's Grove earlier, Evan had keyed Charlie's address into the GPS unit on the dash and was unable to find a match. Leslie didn't find it all that surprising, since their destination was in a rural area, but she never understood what the deal was with men and directions. Was it really so emasculating to not know where you were going? She supposed Evan deserved some credit for his willingness to stop and ask, even if he weren't so eager to admit that it was what he was doing.

While she waited in the car for him to return, Leslie found herself staring at the remnants of an old theater across the street. Though it appeared to have once been as majestic as the Centennial back home, the projector here had long ago fallen silent. The numerous bulbs of the sign tower, which must have once danced against the night sky and blazed as bright as the very stars of Hollywood themselves, now lay extinguished and still. A large crack ran down the length of the box office window, and a door on one of the nearby poster cases screeched as it pitched back and forth with the wind.

She turned her attention to a handful of letters that still clung to the battered marquee of the cinema. Curious as to which piece of movie history was the last to be projected on the screen here, she tried to make out what the letters had spelled. It was a game she gave up in vain a moment later when Evan returned to the car.

"Well, the good news is that Charlie is alive and well, and lives about four miles down the road," he said, settling back in the driver's seat.

"Is there bad news?"

"Yeah, they were out of beef jerky," Evan grinned.

"Seriously?" Leslie asked, rolling her eyes. "You're as bad as Cody."

Evan laughed as he put the car in reverse and backed out of the lot. With arms folded, Leslie glanced back out of the corner of her eye. A second later, her mouth turned upwards and she began to laugh also. It was the first time Evan had seen her smile, much less laugh, in quite some time. He didn't say a word, but rather savored the moment and laughed right along with her.

....

Dan went rigid with shock at the old woman's answer. His mind spun out of control and an icy chill settled into his body, its needlelike tentacles jabbing him in a thousand places. "I beg your pardon?" he asked, wondering if perhaps he'd heard her incorrectly.

"The young lady from the car. She's already dead, and has been for quite some time, I might add."

"Ms. Vanderman, if you know something about this case, I think it would be in your best interest to tell me everything. Who is this girl? And how do you know her?"

"Oh, forgive me. I imagine what I've said seems quite shocking, and I apologize. I can be a bit direct, can't I? Please, do have a seat and let me explain."

Harriet gestured toward the seat next to her and Dan obliged by sliding over and resting his frame on the vinyl padding of the barstool. He moved as if he were in a trance, never taking his eyes off of the strange woman. She smiled as he sat, and despite the topic at hand, her demeanor never changed from the sweet, grandmotherly air she exuded. It was as if she were offering up homemade cookies rather than discussing a savage murder, and Dan found the whole thing more than a little disarming.

"To answer your question, I don't know who the girl is. In fact, I knew nothing of her until you shook my hand a moment ago. That's when I saw the car, and what happened. And, that's when she spoke to me."

"So, you're a medium? You talk to the dead, is that it?' Dan asked.

"In a manner of speaking, but not in the traditional sense of séances, tarot cards, and the like. I don't seek the dead, but I am tuned in to them. They talk and I listen. It's really as simple as that."

"Wait just a minute. Do you really expect me to buy into this?" Dan asked, raising his hands in protest. There was no denying that the circumstances of the case were strange, but ghosts? He considered himself a good Christian man, and believed in things of a spiritual nature, but he'd never subscribed to the theory of the dead hanging around after they passed on.

"I can't tell you what you should believe, Mr. Decker. I can only tell you what I know, based on what I've been shown. It's up to you what you wish to do with that information."

"So how does this work? You give me information and you get what in return? Money?"

"I understand you're skeptical. There are those out there that try to make a living by claiming to know the secrets of the dead, but that is not me. I don't offer false promises, and I've never taken a penny. Besides, it's not the living I typically assist, anyhow, but the dead."

If Harriet had an angle or a hidden agenda, some ploy to make a quick buck off of a tragic situation, it wasn't apparent thus far. Dan wondered how she could have known about the girl and the car to begin with. While he hadn't seen her standing around with the other onlookers at the scene, news traveled fast in this town. If she'd been in the diner for any length of time, wasn't it possible she overheard someone talking?

"So, you said the girl from the car spoke to you. What did she say exactly?" he asked suspiciously.

Harriet dabbed her mouth with a napkin as she finished eating, transferring a blotch of her bright red lipstick onto the stark white paper. It resembled blood, and Dan's stomach churned at the sight. He had seen more spilled blood over the past few weeks than he cared to, and though he didn't want to admit it, a part of him feared there was more to come.

"It all happened so fast, and there were so many thoughts and feelings, but she told the driver that she was looking for someone, somebody named Charlie. There is much sadness there, but also a sense of urgency. She needs something from him." Harriet paused and a horrified expression came over her face. "Now, she's afraid. Terrified of another presence in the car. He found her again. He's pulling her back to the dark place."

"Who found her, Harriet?" Dan asked.

"The man who murdered her. She's crying out but he's pulling her away. I can hear her screaming, *Save him. I have to save him.* And, then, she's gone."

"Save him? I don't understand. Why would she ask to save the man who murdered her?" Dan asked.

Harriet raised her mug and took a small sip, closing her eyes and taking a deep cleansing breath, as the warm liquid blanketed her insides. The cup clanked gently against the saucer as she sat it down with trembling hands, sloshing some of the coffee out onto the counter. She opened her eyes and placed a hand on the arm of Dan's jacket. What she said next nearly made him jump out of his own skin.

"No, it's not the man she wants to save. It's a boy. And he's very much alive. A boy named Cody."

CHAPTER 19

Fifteen minutes after leaving the service station, Evan and Leslie pulled up to a modest ranch-style home sitting at the end of an unmarked street. Chunks of rock crunched under the tires of the police cruiser as it came to a halt behind a late model Accord, which looked far better than it should at its age.

The same could also be said of the house itself which, outside of its dated architectural styling, looked as though it could have served as a model home. White paint appeared new against brown brick, and gleaming windows reflected the brilliant burnt oranges and reds of the sugar maples dotting the front yard. Rows of chrysanthemums in burgundy and gold were nestled in mounds of fresh mulch along the front of the house, while sweet autumn clematis grew thick around a trellis and archway off to the side. Beyond that le a cobblestone path flanked with lush purple Russian sage, and aster blooms of pink and white as far as the eye could see.

"Would you look at this? Not what I was expecting for a place out in the sticks. You think he did all of this himself?" Evan asked, making a wide sweeping gesture with his hand.

"Something tells me he did. It's lovely isn't it?" Leslie replied.

"Puts my yard to shame, that's for sure."

They walked up the path to the front door and rang the bell, waiting for several moments and then ringing again when no one answered.

"You think he's gone?" Leslie asked.

"There's a fire burning. I noticed the smoke coming from the chimney when we pulled in. You'd think someone would be around."

"Can I help you with something?" came a voice from behind them. Leslie and Evan turned to see a man holding an axe, standing at the end of the walk.

"Hi, we were looking for Charlie Peterson. Would you be him?" Evan asked.

"I am. And who might you be?"

Not only did the house and the car look well for their respective ages, but so did Charlie. Tall and lean, he was dressed in a green and white plaid flannel shirt and a pair of dark jeans. He had a full head of silver hair, neatly combed back, and a face that still possessed a boyish quality despite the light lines and wrinkles around his eyes and mouth.

"My name is Evan Reece. I'm the sheriff over in Millford Springs. And this is my friend Leslie Bradford."

"You a reporter?" Charlie asked, lifting the axe from his side and pointing it in Leslie's direction.

"No sir, I'm not. But we were hoping we might be able to ask you a few questions."

"About?" Charlie asked, eyeing them with suspicion.

"A man named Walter, and the girl he abducted. Something you witnessed, from what I understand," Evan said.

Charlie's shoulders dropped and he turned away. "There's a reason I moved out here away from everyone, Sheriff. Everything there is to tell should be in the archives of the town records. No disrespect to you, but I didn't particularly want to talk about it then, and I don't want to talk about it now, either. I just want to be left alone."

"I don't mean to make you dredge up bad memories. Believe me when I say I know where you're coming from. But there's a life at stake here, and I have reason to believe you may be the only one who can help," Evan replied.

Charlie looked confused. "Me?" he asked. "I think you're mistaken. I have no idea who you're referring to, or what it could possibly have to do with that God-forsaken day sixty years ago."

"The *who* would be my little boy, Cody. May we please have just a few minutes of your time, Mr. Peterson?' Leslie pleaded.

Charlie saw the quiet desperation in this woman, not unlike the sense of despair that had come to define his own life. But, even under that veil of sadness, her eyes radiated a genuine kindness. It was the same sweet gentleness he remembered in the eyes of another and, for one fleeting moment, it was not Leslie, but Ellie standing before him. He was a boy again, palms sweating and heart pounding just like they always had when she was near. But then the sinking reality that she was gone returned with a jolt, and the feelings faded as quickly as they had appeared.

He blinked, seeing Leslie again, and wondering how it was he could possibly be of any help to her. If there were a way, then he couldn't with a clear conscience allow her to suffer the same pain he'd lived with since that fateful day in May of 1950. He sighed, gave a slight nod, and in a soft voice said, "Come with me."

Evan and Leslie followed him around the side of the house and to the backyard, where he wedged the axe into a stump. A pile of logs, some of which had already been split for firewood, covered the ground nearby. They went inside the house through the back door and entered the kitchen, where Charlie opened up the refrigerator and grabbed two bottles of water, offering those to his guests before picking up another for himself. When each of them had a drink, he led them away to the living area.

The room was immaculate, without a speck of dust or clutter. While the furnishings appeared to be of the same era as the house, they were in pristine condition, looking like they'd been delivered just the day before. Based on this, and the fact that there were no family photos adorning the walls or perched on end tables, Evan considered it a safe bet that Charlie had been living alone for many years. A girlfriend or wife wasn't out of the question, but there were certainly no children or pets, which would have put a good deal of wear and tear on his otherwise untarnished belongings.

Evan and Leslie took a seat on the sofa, a vintage mid-century tufted single back, and Charlie sat down in a matching arm chair caddy corner from them.

"Forgive me if I came across the wrong way outside. It's just that, even after all this time, people still track me down and want an interview. They'll say it's for a book or some anniversary piece in the paper, but it makes no difference to me. I talked to one of them several years back because I was given the impression he wanted to write about the victims – about their lives, who they were, that sort of thing. It was supposed to be a tribute to their memory, but when the piece came out it was no different than anything else that had ever been written. Most of what I said regarding those kids was discarded, and it became more about the vile man who murdered them. They even went so far as to publish crime scene photos. I guess that's what sells papers these days," Charlie scoffed. "But I felt betrayed. They dishonored the memory of those children for a cheap piece of tabloid fodder. Since then I've refused to talk to anyone about that day."

"I'm very sorry. I know there are people out there who'll capitalize on anything, but I can assure you that isn't our intention. As someone who has suffered his own tragic loss, I have nothing but respect for you, and those who lost their lives," Evan said.

Charlie nodded, considering, and finally said, "So, how is it that I can be of help, Sheriff?"

"There was a murder committed by an upstanding resident of our town recently. Perhaps you heard?"

"No, sir. I don't talk to the media, and I don't listen to what they have to say anymore, either. I pick up a bit here and there when I talk to people in town, but the world is a much nicer place when you aren't constantly reading about all the bad things in it."

"Well, Henry was a charitable man, always doing good things in the community, active in his church, and well-liked by all who knew him. He never had so much as a parking ticket, yet, inexplicably stabbed a teenage boy to death with no apparent motive. According to my deputy, who had been good friends with the man, Henry acted like a stranger, like he had become someone altogether different, someone who didn't recognize his own friend standing before him, and who seemed to have lost his mind."

Charlie shook his head in dismay. His eyes softened into pools of sympathy and heartbreak as he glanced over at Leslie. "The boy who was killed. Was it ... your son?"

"No, it wasn't. We think, however, that Cody may have seen the whole thing. He was found unconscious several feet away. The doctor said he was in a state of shock. I got him home and in bed, and the next morning he was gone," Leslie replied.

"So, someone took him? This Henry fellow, perhaps?" Charlie asked.

"It couldn't have been Henry. He was shot and killed earlier in the evening," Evan said.

"Cody did tell me he had seen someone outside his room the night before, but I thought he'd been dreaming. The house was still locked up tight, and nothing had been disturbed," Leslie said. Her voice dropped to a register just above a whisper, and she lowered her gaze. "If only I had listened."

Empathizing with her pain, Charlie slowly shook his head and responded in a soft and sensitive tone. "I'm very sorry to hear about Cody, and I'm willing to help you in any way I can, but I'm still not sure how any of this relates to the past."

Evan sat forward on the couch and leaned in closer. "That's what we're trying to figure out, and where things get a bit stranger. I have to admit that until today, I knew nothing about the incident sixty years ago. I still don't know much, for that matter."

Charlie looked even more perplexed than he had just moments ago. As tragic as these recent events were, he couldn't fathom how there could be any connection between those and the events of 1950. Everyone that had been involved back then, with the exception of himself, had died. And while he didn't know how long Evan had been the sheriff of Millford Springs, his lack of knowledge surrounding the murders would seem to indicate that the town had long forgotten that dark day in its history, or had, at the very least, swept it under the rug.

That being the case, *something* had happened to bring Evan to his house, and it was that something which he now feared. A sense of foreboding stirred within him, a smoldering pit of trepidation that threatened to reignite every terrifying moment of that day in the cemetery. He closed his eyes and asked the question he was dreading. "So, then, what exactly led you to me?"

"A young girl, which in itself wouldn't normally strike me as unusual. It's the where and how of her appearances that have me baffled. I was hoping you might be able to offer some insight into her identity."

Charlie nodded. The anxiety within him continued to swell until it constricted around his neck like an invisible noose. He listened to the story of Tyler's encounter with the girl, Leslie's recent dreams, and Miriam Harvey's experience from earlier in the day. Then it happened. Evan said the one thing that kicked the chair out from under him, pulling the rope taut and sucking the air from his lungs.

"She kept asking for Charlie. Said over and over that she needed to find him."

Find him. The words hit like a shotgun blast to the chest. It was Ellie. There was no doubt in his mind about that. And she was looking for him. But, to acknowledge that fact meant that he also had to acknowledge the existence of ghosts, something he had never given any credibility to. He felt he was on the verge of hyperventilating. Closing his eyes, he sat back in his chair and sucked in a deep breath.

"Charlie, are you alright?" Evan asked, raising up from his seat and moving toward the man, who was now as white as a sheet.

"Fine, fine," Charlie wheezed. He motioned for Evan to sit and took a few more slow breaths, followed by a long swig from the bottle of water. The color returned to his face, little by little, and within a minute or two he spoke again. "Thank you, I'm alright now."

"You know who she is, don't you?" Leslie asked.

"Yes. Her name is Ellie Carmichael. But, how is it possible?" Charlie stammered. "She's been gone for a very long time now."

"I'm having a hard time with it myself, but there's no denying that something is going on in that town. Something none of us understands, at least not yet. Could you tell us what happened the day Ellie was taken?" Evan asked.

Charlie sighed and reached for the bottle of water again. His hands shook and the sorrow in his eyes deepened, the youthful glow he'd shown waning. Suddenly, he appeared haggard, and older by at least twenty years.

"I guess you would have to start with Walter. He was a very sick man. He'd always been eccentric, though nobody ever considered him dangerous. Had his wife and son not died in a car accident the year before, he might not have been. You see, it was his son's birthday the morning this all happened. William would have been turning ten had he still been alive. I'm not sure how long Walter had been spiraling into insanity, but he finally snapped that day.

"When Ellie and I came upon him in the cemetery, he was digging William up. We watched from a distance as he loaded the casket into the back end of his truck. We thought we were hidden, but then something happened which changed everything. He heard us, and I went to hide. Ellie, however, was too afraid to move. I started to go back for her, but Walter came around the corner. He never saw me, but Ellie..." Charlie paused. His face was red now with emotion, his eyes glazed over.

Leslie's heart ached and her eyes misted over as she watched the old man fumble with the water bottle in his hand. As he struggled for words, she tried to imagine what it must be like to have shouldered such an emotional burden for so long. He was just a child when these things occurred, and she saw flashes of that little boy before her now – a boy who was innocent, terrified, and heartbroken.

"He, um ... he took her. Choked the air out of her until she passed out, and then threw her into his truck. I ran as fast as I could into town and alerted the sheriff, but by the time they got to Walter's place it was too late, not just for Ellie, but for all of them. There were three all told - Ellie, Sandy Morgan, and Billy Watkins.

"Billy was a waif of a boy whose family was poor and lived in a shack of a place on the outskirts of town. He was made fun of and bullied at school quite a bit, mostly because of how skinny he was. That made him an easy target for anyone, but especially for someone as big as Walter. And he didn't have any friends, so there'd been no one to report him missing. Other than his family, who didn't seem to care much.

"Sandy was an easy target as well, because she lived directly behind Walter's house. She was always playing by herself in the yard. There must not have been anyone there to hear her scream when he took her. He had grabbed both of them earlier in the day, before going out to the cemetery. I doubt Ellie had been a part of his plan, but when we stumbled upon him, it made for another simple opportunity.

"The police believe Walter initially locked the children in the basement. Billy always carried a pocket full of green plastic army men with him, and they were found scattered in a corner down there. At some point, Walter took the children, including Ellie, upstairs and strapped them into chairs at the dining room table..."

He paused once more, and a single tear ran down his cheek. There was a tremble in his voice when he spoke again. "Nobody can say whether William's body was already propped up at the head of the table, or if he was brought in after the other children had been placed there, but when the police arrived it was quite apparent what Walter had been trying to do. There were balloons tied to the chairs, and a cake in the center of the table."

"Oh my God. He was throwing a birthday party," Leslie gasped.

"Yes. And when the children reacted with fear, Walter flew into a rage and bludgeoned them with a hammer. Billy struggled so hard to break free that he fractured the bones in one of his arms. Ellie managed to get loose, but the doors had been bolted shut. Her body was found in the bathroom where it appeared she had tried to hide.

"The officers had to kick down the front door to get inside, where they found Walter still screaming at the children, saying, "Look what you did. You ruined it. Ruined it all. " He came at one of the deputies with the hammer and was shot dead.

"After that, the town changed. People started locking their doors, and wouldn't let their kids out of their sight. There were many - my folks included - who moved away completely. But no matter how far from Millford Springs I went, that day followed. None of those kids should have suffered, but I always felt like I was the reason Ellie died. It was my idea to cut through the cemetery, my curiosity that led us to spy on Walter, and me who stood in silence while he took her. It should have been me. He should have taken me instead.

"Charlie, you were just a boy. If you'd tried to stop him, he would have just taken you both. If you hadn't alerted the police, who knows? Walter might have gone on to hurt others after you. You may have saved more lives than you know," Evan said.

"Maybe so, but it still should have been me. Ellie should have been the one to get away. All I'd ever wanted to be was her hero, and in my dreams I must have saved her a thousand times over, but when she actually needed me, I choked. Why? Why didn't I do something? I should have helped her." "

There was a long moment of silence in the room. While Evan understood the depth of Charlie's regrets, he wasn't quite sure how to offer consolation. He still struggled with his own guilt over Ryan's death, and in situations such as this, words only seemed empty and hollow.

"You must have really cared for her," Leslie finally said.

Charlie wiped his tears with the palms of his hands and cocked his head towards Leslie. His mouth turned up in a small grin and a bright twinkle reappeared in his eyes. "I know we were young, and people would say it's silly, but I loved her as much as I've ever loved anyone. I'm seventy-three years old and I never married. I had my fair share of relationships, of course, but there was no one quite like Ellie. Ever. None of them touched me the way she did. Before I retired, I was a commercial pilot and saw many wondrous things in my travels, but not a one of them ever moved me the way she could with just a simple smile. So, yes ma'am, I did, and do still, care for her very much. I would give anything I could, anything, to take back that awful day."

Leslie sighed, half at the romanticism and half at sorrow for this sensitive man who had lost so much. "That's very sweet. Some people go their whole lives and never find a love like that. Even if it was for a short time, and even if you were young, she was a lucky girl to have you."

"Thank you," Charlie said, smiling gently. "So, now that you know what happened all those years ago, what's next?"

"I don't know. But after listening to your story, I don't think Ellie is the only one who came back," Leslie said.

"Who else have you seen?" Evan asked, turning to her with a frown.

"Remember the thin boy with the crooked arm outside my door Halloween night?"

Evan sat upright. "Billy? You think it was him?"

"Yes. And it all makes sense. I had just seen a girl standing in the front yard moments before he appeared. I didn't get a good look at her, but I'm certain it was Ellie."

"Charlie, there's something I want you to look at," Evan said, jumping up from the couch and retrieving the envelope of photographs from his jacket. He found the one he had shown Leslie that morning and handed it to Charlie.

"If Ellie isn't the only one from the past that's been seen in Leslie's house, then maybe the woman in the window is someone who's returned as well. Do you happen to recognize her?"

Charlie looked at the photo and gasped. He knew who it was immediately, because he'd seen that face before. It had terrorized him then, and it frightened him now, for that was the face that used to stare down at him from the second story of Walter's house. Even as a grown man, the sight of her glaring back at him made his skin crawl. "I know this woman," he muttered hoarsely. "I never knew her name, but I know who she was. She was Walter's mother-in-law. An amputee who was confined to a wheelchair, and living in one of the upstairs bedrooms of the family house. Walter murdered her, too. Threw her down the stairs is what they said. They think he killed her prior to capturing the children."

Charlie glanced up at Leslie with a sudden look of alarm. "You don't live at 1401 Maple Ridge Lane, do you?"

"Yes," Leslie replied. "Could you tell that from the picture?"

"You have to get out of there, Ms. Bradford. That's *his* house. That's where it all happened. If the children and the old woman are back, then Walter might be as well."

Leslie's heart jumped into her throat, and she shivered violently. She closed her eyes and murmured something to herself, shaking her head in regret.

"Leslie, what is it?" Evan asked.

"The man on the stairs," she said weakly.

Charlie buried his face in his hands and shook his head. "Oh, mother of mercy, I don't know how this can be, but God help you, Ms. Bradford. If the man on the stairs is who I think he is, God help everyone in that town."

....

Dan sat the bowl of chili down in the passenger seat. It was still too hot to eat comfortably, so he reached into the sack and pulled out a slab of cornbread. The foil-wrapped hunk was approximately the size of his fist, and still nice and warm. Dorothy had basted it with an extra helping of honey butter before bagging it up and sending it on its way. Usually that would have made him as giddy as a girl standing in line for the latest *Twilight* movie, but not tonight. He tore off a piece of the bread and thumbed the business card that Harriet had written her phone number on.

He wasn't sure what to make of the woman's claims, but she seemed to know quite a lot for someone who'd only been in town a couple of hours. He tried to call Evan, but the line went straight to voice mail. Dan figured the cell coverage in Worthington was probably nonexistent, so he left a message and hung up.

The rain drummed louder against the roof of the car as Dan chewed another bite of cornbread. He was parked along the curb in front of Leslie's place. The house, which sat dark and silent, looked imposing at the moment, silhouetted against the bluish tinge of lightning rippling across the sky. Dan clicked on the radio and tuned into a ball game. It was the Cardinals vs. the Bulls, second quarter. The Cardinals were up by four, and Ian McGarvey had just scored a 40-yard field goal with a 1:30 left on the clock, bringing their lead up to seven. With two quarters left, it was still anyone's game at this point.

Leaning over the seat to pick up the bowl of chili, Dan caught a flash of something out of the corner of his eye. A light was on in one of the upstairs rooms now. Someone was inside the house.

....

"I can't believe no one told me about what happened in that house!" Leslie shrieked, throwing herself back in the seat of the car and balling up her fists. "I thought there were disclosure laws for that sort of thing!"

"There are. But in Texas you're only required to disclose any death that was directly caused by the house, like someone being electrocuted by faulty wiring, or a beam falling on them. Neighbors are more apt to divulge information about violent crimes to potential buyers but, as old as this one is, I doubt any of them are even aware of it," Evan replied.

"I just want my son! I want to find him and get as far away from that house as possible. But I don't know how to do that because none of this makes any sense."

"I know," Evan whispered. While the visit with Charlie had enlightened them as to who these ghosts of the past were, it hadn't answered the question about why they were back. He was up against something he couldn't understand, and the feeling of helplessness that came with that was disheartening. His gut still told him that it was all linked to Cody's disappearance, but the how of it was as elusive as ever. He could only hope that Ellie's presence would continue to guide them to the answers they needed. But what if there were none? What if she sought Charlie simply because of the bond she had shared with him before her death? What if she didn't lead them to Cody? Did she even know where Cody was?

A part of him couldn't believe he was even asking these questions, or taking them seriously, but at this point he couldn't see any other way forward.

He drove in silence, rolling back through the town of Worthington, trapped in his own thoughts. It looked ever more desolate now than it had during the day, a pale reflection of what it had once been. In a way, he thought it mirrored the condition of his own soul since Ryan's death.

Driving past the empty Woolworth's, Evan recalled the image of the smiling soda jerk painted on the side of the building.

Feel alive with Bright Cola! the ad promised.

If only it were that simple.

....

Dan used the key hidden under the mailbox to unlock the front door, easing it open and shining his flashlight across the entryway and up the first flight of stairs. He saw nothing. With one swift motion, he stepped inside and shut the door behind him. Save for the muffled sounds of the rain tapping against the windows, the house was quiet. He moved toward the stairs and was about to step up when he heard the slamming of a door. It had come from the first floor.

Dan popped the snap on his holster and slid the service pistol out of its resting place. Holding it close to his side, he stepped through the archway to his right and moved toward the back of the house, where he'd heard the sound. The beam of the flashlight danced about the room as he searched every dark corner. Passing the living area, and nearing the dining room, Dan noticed a glint of something on the hardwoods. He ducked down, examining them closely, then drawing back in disgust. Dark, wet smears of blood lined the floor, carving a wide path across the boards and ending at the doorway to his left.

He stepped cautiously around the blood trail and made his way to the door. There was a panel of switches on the wall, and Dan flipped them up, turning on the lights and scanning the room around him before putting his back against the wall and twisting the knob on the basement door. The hinges groaned and popped as the door opened. Dan peeked around the corner and saw a small light illuminating the top half of a staircase. A thick, musty odor leeched out of the damp abyss and stung his nostrils. He felt the food churn in his stomach and wished now that he hadn't just eaten.

The beam of the flashlight cut into the darkness below, but only a fraction of the basement was visible from this vantage point. He started to descend the stairs, the air becoming thinner and colder as he moved further down into the deep black void. He listened for movement, but the only sounds were those of water dripping and a distant roll of thunder from outside.

Reaching the bottom, Dan felt something brush the top of his head. Jumping back and ducking away, he pointed the flashlight in the direction of the cold object that had touched him. A lone incandescent bulb swayed on the end of a cord there, and he breathed a sigh of relief, then reached up and felt for a switch on the socket. There was none. He tapped the bulb and heard the tiny jingle of a metal filament resting at the bottom of the frosted glass. *Spent*, he though wryly. Wasn't that just his luck? Descending into a dark, creepy basement, convinced that there was something down here, and the light in the room wasn't working.

There was a sudden flutter to his left, and he spun in that direction, turning the beam of the flashlight in the direction of the sound. He saw only metal shelving and boxes of junk along the wall, but continued to probe the darkness until the light came to rest on a full-length mirror in one corner of the room. What startled him the most wasn't the initial glimpse of the reflection staring back, but the fact that it wasn't his own.

"Cody?" he whispered in disbelief.

He ran towards the mirror and called out again, but the boy only stood there, looking around but not seeing, as if he were on the other side of two way glass.

"What is this?" Dan asked, frantically touching the surface of the mirror. It felt like regular glass. He reached up and ran his hand around the frame and along the back, finding nothing out of the ordinary. He turned around and looked at the ceiling and the opposing wall for some sort of projector, but found none.

Turning back to the mirror, he saw Cody sitting down, pulling his knees up against his body, and looking around like he might cry. His mouth moved, but there was no audible sound. Dan knocked on the glass and yelled Cody's name. The boy didn't budge.

"He can't hear you," a voice whispered.

Dan whirled around and raised the gun from his side. "Who's there?"

The flashlight was dimming with the depleted charge of the batteries and, at first, he saw only blackness beyond the limited reach of the beam. But then, a pale white face emerged, followed by the vague outline of a body. It was a young girl. As she drew nearer, Dan noticed the bruises and the patch of blood on the side of her face.

"Who did that to you? And how did you get down here?" he asked, lowering his weapon.

"I'm Ellie. Walter brought us here. I need to find Charlie. Can you help me?"

"Wait. Are you ... the girl from the car today?"

He couldn't believe his eyes. Here in front of him was the girl Harriet had spoken of not more than a half hour ago. And the woman's statement about Cody may have been accurate as well. Even though the boy was ostensibly trapped inside of a mirror at the moment, he definitely appeared to be alive. While Dan couldn't quite wrap his head around everything, it would seem that Harriet had been telling the truth all along. But that meant that the girl in front of him was dead.

An abrupt thump from upstairs broke his train of thought. He listened for a moment, then heard another small knock.

"Don't go up there. It might be him," Ellie said. Her eyes grew wide and frightened, and her voice rose an octave.

"It'll be alright," Dan said, trotting back up the stairs. "Just stay here and I'll be back for you, okay?"

Back in the entryway, he stopped and listened. Outside, the wind pitched and howled, but the inside of the house remained silent. He slowed, reaching out with his senses. Someone other than the girl was lurking nearby. He may not have been able to see them, but they were there. And they were probably aware of his presence, lying in wait somewhere up there in the dark. Watchful eyes may already been fixed on him, he thought, as he ascended the first flight of stairs and stopped on the landing.

There was another soft thump, and then, a slow, steady squeak pierced the silent atmosphere. For a second, Dan thought the sound might be the result of the wind pushing through a crack on a loose window, but as the intensity of the gusts outside abated, the squeaking should have done the same. It did not. If anything, it was increasing.

Dan crept up the second flight, taking care to make as little noise as possible. When he reached the top, he turned left toward the noise. A thin sliver of light spilled out from under one of the bedroom doors, and the sound grew louder.

Squee-cha ... squee-cha ... squee

Something moved behind the bedroom door now, blotting out a section of the light, and Dan tightened the grip on his sidearm and lifted it in front of him. His heart raced with every passing second. The knob turned with a click and the door swung open, casting a tall shadow across the hall. Sheets of rain lashed against the window panes in frenetic bursts, and a fierce crack of thunder rattled the house. Then, the shape started to move and the lights in the room went out, leaving Dan standing in total darkness.

He depressed the button on his flashlight, desperately clicking it on and off, but it failed to light up. *Damnit, not now!* He banged the light against his thigh, and the bulb lit for a brief second before fading out again. He banged some more.

Nothing.

Squee-cha ... squee-cha

It was in the hall now, inching toward him. Dan took a step back toward the window and waited, feeling the hairs rise on the back of his neck. The squeaking stopped.

"Come on, come on," Dan muttered, beads of perspiration rolling heavy across his forehead. A moment later, he got what he had hoped for. Lightning flashed and flickered just long enough to illuminate an empty wheelchair sitting in the hallway outside the bedroom.

"Wha..?"

There was a bone chilling shriek and the chair catapulted itself towards the deputy.

Squee-squee-squee-squee; the wheels squealed faster, moving toward him, until the chirps became one long whistle.

Dan turned to run down the stairs, his left foot twisting underneath him at the sudden action. He fell to the side, slamming against the banister and tumbling hard and fast down the steps. He felt a bone shatter in his right arm, and tasted the warm saltiness of his own blood gushing from a busted nose, before finally coming to rest on the landing below. It took a minute for the disorientation to pass and the fullness of the pain to set in. He looked around, trying to get his bearings. He was lying on his side, with one leg turned up at a wrong angle, and the broken arm hanging limp in front of him. He tried to move, but that only intensified the agony. There was a burning in his back as the muscles began to spasm, causing him to cry out.

Above him, the lightning flashed again, and the wheelchair teetered on the top step, rocking back and forth. The last thing he recalled was the sound of metal scraping against wood as the chair began to topple down the stairs toward him. There was a burst of light, accompanied by a sharp stab of pain, and then Dan remembered no more.

CHAPTER 20

Evan leaned his head forward in the shower, letting the warm jets of water rinse thick pillows of lather from his hair. He listened to the splashes around him, felt the trickle of soap down his back, and watched as it all swirled down the drain. Scrubbing away the grit and perspiration from his body was simple enough, but cleansing his soul was a much more daunting task. A heavy scum of adversity had been building, and he wasn't sure how to get rid of it.

Twice today he'd watched as a member of his town had been carted away in an ambulance. But, while Miriam was simply recovering from a state of shock and may have already left the hospital, Dan was in much worse shape, and wouldn't be going home for quite some time, if ever.

"Hey, boss, I just had an enlightening conversation, and I think you'll be very interested in the details. Give me a shout when you return to civilization."

It was the last thing Dan had said when he left the message on Evan's phone. His voice had sounded calm;

no alarm, no sense of urgency, and nothing that had suggested a looming threat. Evan's curiosity was piqued, and still was for that matter, but he hadn't been too concerned when he tried to return the call and didn't get an answer.

Instead, he'd stopped at a barbecue joint in Baker's Grove and picked up some food – which neither he or Leslie ended up eating – and then made a detour to his house to pack an overnight bag. It wasn't until he pulled into the drive at 1401 Maple Ridge Lane that he knew something was wrong. The sight of Dan's empty squad car sitting in front of the dark house had unnerved him. And for good reason, as it turned out.

Evan flashed back to the image of Dan's twisted and broken body lying at the base of the stairs. Leslie's screams still echoed in his ears, along with the harsh raspy sound rising from the deputy's throat. He'd given his partner a couple light nudges to see if he could revive him, but was afraid to do anything more. For all he'd known, Dan had suffered a broken neck, and he hadn't wanted to move the man for fear of exasperating the situation, or worse yet, killing him.

He'd sat by Dan's side and talked, hoping that it would somehow help his friend hang on, while Leslie had frantically dialed 911. He'd noticed the pistol lying a few feet away, and wondered what Dan had seen that drew him into the house and up the stairs. Taking down a man the size of a grizzly bear should have left some sign of an altercation, but there was no indication of anyone else having been on the premises.

Based on the visible injuries Dan sustained, it looked as though he'd been beaten with a baseball bat. But Evan figured it would have taken a whole slew of men to get the drop on his deputy, and he doubted very much that a team of ball players had been waiting upstairs for someone to attack. Most people probably would have found that to be more believable than the truth of the matter however – that it was the dead who were responsible.

Shutting off the shower, Evan blotted himself dry with a towel and wrapped it around his waist before stepping out of the tub. Thick clouds of steam hung densely enough to nearly obscure the vanity area a few feet away. But that wasn't what stopped him in his tracks. There was something else wrapped in the fog; a figure moving slowly along the back wall.

Evan held his position and waited. There was no sound but that of water cascading down the drain. Whoever it was moved on silent feet. He was terrified, but also oddly fascinated by what he saw. Up to this point, the only thing he had to support his belief in the recent supernatural occurrences was the image of the woman in the photo and the eye-witness accounts of others. But now, it was his own eyes seeing something he'd never imagined possible.

A part of him wanted to move closer, but perhaps that had been Dan's downfall. He didn't know which spirit this was, or whether it intended him harm, and he surmised that a meeting with a ghost was a bit like swimming with sharks – you might get close enough to touch one and live to tell about it - but you could just as easily be ripped to shreds. He preferred the former, and decided that in this case caution was probably the better part of valor.

The figure swayed back and forth a few times in front of him, and then, in a blink, was gone. Evan took a few cautious steps forward and waited, making sure the specter was indeed gone. Once he was relatively sure he was alone again, he moved to the sink and wiped the haze from the vanity mirror, half expecting some ghoulish face to be staring back. But his own reflection looked back, pale and wide eyed.

He brushed his teeth and tugged on the pair of pajama bottoms and T-shirt he had set out earlier. Now that the adrenaline from his brief encounter had kicked in, he was ready to be out of the room. *Once you've seen the shark up close, it's time to get out of the water.*

He hated the idea of staying in this house, especially after what happened to Dan, but he hadn't wanted to press the issue with Leslie. It wasn't that she didn't realize the house was a dangerous place, but with so little sleep of late, he doubted she was thinking as clearly as she should. Being both mentally and physically exhausted, all she had wanted to do was get some rest.

He glanced in the direction of her room as he clicked off the bathroom light and walked into the upstairs hallway. With the pills Dr. Miller had given her, she should be fast asleep by now. Though he wished they were somewhere other than here, he was glad she had gone to the doctor that morning. Without the prescription, he doubted she would have been able to sleep at all, regardless of where they were staying.

After settling into his own bed a few minutes later, he wondered if he should have taken Leslie up on her offer of one of the sleeping pills. It had been tempting, for he'd had very little rest himself over the past couple of weeks, but, in the end, he knew he needed to remain alert in case something happened during the night. Whatever was in that house had blown through Dan like he were made of paper, and he wanted to be alert if it came around again. Even if it did, though, he wondered how much good he would be if Leslie *did* need him. After all, how does one fight what's already dead? Dan certainly hadn't been able to.

The phone on the night stand buzzed, momentarily startling Evan. He laughed in spite of himself. *Haven't even been here one night and I'm already this jumpy? What am I going to be like in a week?*

He snapped up the cell and answered the call, hoping it wasn't more bad news.

"Hello, Evan. It's Linda. I hope I'm not calling too late."

"No, not at all. How's Dan?"

"He's still unconscious. The neurologist just got the CT scans back and there's some swelling in the brain that he wants to keep a close eye on. He also said there were several broken bones but, thankfully, none involving the neck or back."

"Do they think he'll pull through okay?"

"They think so. The next twenty-four hours are the most critical. And until he's conscious it's hard to say how much the concussion has affected his memory or motor skills."

"God, I'm so sorry, Linda. You need anything?"

"Just prayers, Evan."

"Already said a few of those, but I'll be saying plenty more. Will you call me if you hear anything else?"

"Of course. Thank you."

"You're welcome. Dan's a fighter, certainly the toughest guy I know, and I don't think he'll give up and go down this easily. You know what I think he would say if he were telling me all of this himself?"

"No, what?"

"Besides the concussion and the broken bones, I'm just fine, boss."

Linda sniffled and he heard the smile in her voice when she replied. "Yes, that sounds just like him."

"I know it's probably going to be a long night, but try to get some rest. Leslie and I will come by tomorrow and check up on you both."

"I will. And thank you again. Good night," she said, and hung up the phone.

Evan lay back in bed and breathed a small sigh of relief. Dan was alive. Things sounded bad, of course, and he still worried about what kind of condition his friend would be in when he woke up, but he felt more confident now that Dan would be alright in the long run.

He closed his eyes and listened as soft curtains of rain began to fall outside. In time, the soothing rhythm calmed his anxious mind, gradually dissolving his thoughts into shallow pools of obscurity. Shifting into the peaceful space between wakefulness and slumber, he was suddenly aware of a new noise; a faint squeaking in the distance. He wasn't sure whether it was real or the onset of a dream, but the vagueness made it seem of little concern. As he slipped away into a deep sleep, the sound came once more.

Squee-cha.

CHAPTER 21

November 13, 2010

Leslie blinked several times as her eyes adjusted to the bright rays of light streaming through the curtains of the bedroom window. Her body was completely relaxed, and she lay in silence for several minutes. There was still a twinge of residual grogginess from the sleeping pill, but only a little. She couldn't remember the last time she felt this well rested. It was nice.

She had initially felt guilty about taking the medicine Dr. Miller had given her. The way she saw it, as long as Cody was still out there all alone, it somehow felt wrong to allow herself the luxury of a long and comfortable night's sleep. But the lack of rest had been taking its toll. Her thoughts had become muddied, and she was more sensitive than she should be. There was the old saying, *don't cry over spilled milk*, but that was precisely the sort of small and inconsequential thing which would have her bursting into tears for no good reason.

The revelation that she was living in the former home of a child killer had certainly done nothing to help her emotional state. And, returning to the house to find Dan on the verge of death had been more than she could take. She had never suffered a nervous breakdown, but was fairly certain she would have, if she'd gone another night without sleep. She owed Cody more than that. She owed *everyone* more than that.

Dan. I wonder how he's doing? Surely Evan's heard from the hospital by now. Come to think of it, what time is it? God knows how long I've been asleep.

Leslie rolled over to look at the clock on the night stand, and as she did so, her hand brushed against something unfamiliar. The small amount of lingering grogginess she felt disappeared in a flash, and the peaceful serenity in her waking mind was invaded by a rush of adrenaline and terror. An empty wheelchair sat at the side of her bed.

Bolting upright, she flung herself backwards to the far side of the mattress. Her heart pounded, and the sudden rush of blood sent tiny specks of light dancing across her field of vision. She closed her eyes and waited out a slight wave of disorientation, praying as hard as she could that the wheelchair would be gone when she looked again. But when she opened her eyes, it was still there.

There was an electrical tension in the air, the pulse and thrum of which quivered in her insides like jelly. The chair was angled, as if someone had been watching her while she slept. Though the seat was now vacant, the worn leather and cold steel seemed to stare back, as if the chair was cognizant of her every move.

Keeping her eyes on the chair, she eased out of bed, feeling the familiar icy sting from the hardwoods as her feet touched the ground. Taking a tentative step sideways, she felt the sensation of something moving across her ankle. A withered hand sprung out from under the bed, its bony fingers wrapping around her leg and clutching tight.

Leslie screamed and tried to run, but the creature held firm, causing her to tumble face-down onto the floor. She rose up on her arms and crawled forward, lifting and kicking as she tried to break free, but the hand only gripped harder. She turned to see a second arm emerge from underneath the bed, followed by a face – the face of the old woman from the window. Bones protruded sharply through her decayed flesh, while clumps of bloody, matted hair dotted the top of her skull; the thin, wet strands loosely shrouding a pair of cloudy white eyes that were void of pupils.

Leslie pivoted onto her elbows, drawing one leg back and thrusting it forward with a heavy kick, jamming her heel hard against the woman's mouth. The blow ripped through the layers of thin, papery skin and dislodged the jawbone, exposing a crooked, toothy grin.

The old woman let out a fierce shriek and loosened her grip, allowing Leslie to scurry backwards on hands and feet. Before she could stand and run, the cadaverous creature dug her long yellowed nails into the wood floor, scratching and clawing as her legless torso writhed back and forth, propelling her forward like a snake.

Leslie was cornered. She screamed again when one of the clammy, dead hands brushed her bare thigh. The old woman's teeth clacked together, she emitted another shrill screech, and then, latched onto Leslie's T-shirt and pulled herself up. The smell of death permeated the air, and Leslie's mouth hung open in paralyzed sobs as the woman closed in.

There was a sudden loud crash, and a pair of arms went around her like a vise. She cried out and thrashed violently against the attack.

"Whoa, Leslie. It's okay. It's me. It's Evan," a familiar voice said firmly.

Leslie stopped fighting and looked around. The woman and the wheelchair were gone. "Did you see her?" she asked, her voice shaking.

"I didn't see anyone. I heard you scream from downstairs. When I came through the door you were curled up on the floor in hysterics. Are you alright?"

Leslie nodded and brushed the tears back. "She was here, the old woman. She was right here. It wasn't a dream. I swear it wasn't."

"It's alright," Evan said gently, and with a touch that was as light as his voice, he lifted Leslie's chin with his finger and met her gaze. "I believe you."

She stared back at him with wide searching eyes, and wrapped her arms around him in a hug. "Thank you." she whispered in his ear. "I thought I was going to die."

"No, never. Whatever these things are, they'll have to take me first. I'm not about to let anything happen to you. I need you to promise me something, though. If they do get to me somehow, promise that you'll save yourself. Run, and don't look back."

"Evan, don't talk like that. I —"

"Please," he interrupted.

Leslie paused, and then nodded in agreement. They stood in the embrace for a long moment while she cleared her head, a rapid thump echoing in her ears. It took several seconds for her to discern that the heart she heard beating wildly was Evan's, rather than her own. While she had seen a terror in his eyes just now, she understood that it wasn't the ghosts of the house that had frightened him, but rather the fear of something happening to her. The realization made her hold on to him even tighter. "I want to get out of here," she finally said.

"Okay. Where to? You want to run by the diner before we go check in on Dan?"

Leslie let go and took a step back. "No, you don't understand. I'm going to get some things together and we're leaving. I can't stay in this house any longer."

Evan looked at her for several seconds. "You're certain that's what you want?"

"I am. There's been enough tragedy in this house, and I don't want to see anyone else get hurt, especially you."

"Alright, then," Evan replied without hesitation. "Give me a suitcase. I'll help you pack."

Forty-five minutes later, Leslie had most of the items she would need loaded in the back of her SUV. When she ran out of room there, she put the remainder of her things in Evan's trunk and prepared to follow him to his place. Before climbing into her vehicle, she took one last look at the house. Only two months ago this had been her dream, and now she would never spend another night here. How could it have come to this? Why now? And most of all, why Cody? A sharp stab of pain cut through her as she looked up at her son's room. She wondered if she would ever see him again.

Starting up the car and backing out of the drive, the tears began to fall harder than they ever had before. This time, it felt like all hope was lost. This time, she was saying goodbye.

....

With the exception of the maternity wing, a hospital just wasn't a happy place. You were either sick or dying, or knew someone who was sick or dying, and Evan couldn't imagine anyone actually liked coming here. He passed by waiting rooms filled with stoic faces. Most looked worn and tired as they waited anxiously for news of a loved one's condition, while others, having no doubt received a bad report, appeared to be grieving.

That would have been bad enough on its own merit, but then there was the unmistakable smell of the place. That cold, sterile odor that always twisted his stomach into knots and set his nerves on edge the second he detected it. Quite frankly, Evan hated hospitals, and right now, he imagined Linda hated them as well.

"Thank you for coming. Is Leslie with you?" she asked Evan, as he entered Dan's room in the ICU.

"No, she's on some medication now and is home resting," he lied.

He didn't like being dishonest, but what was he going to say? *She would have been here, but a ghost attacked her this morning, and now she's a little out of sorts. As a matter of fact, there's a good chance the very same ghost put your husband here.* That probably wouldn't have gone over so well.

"Good for her. That poor woman. I can't imagine being in her shoes right now."

"I don't imagine its easy being in yours, either. How is he?" Evan asked, nodding toward Dan.

His partner was lying in a bed a few feet away, a brace around his neck, and his eyes blackened from a busted nose. There was a cast on his right arm and left leg, and the tape around his ribs could be seen through a gap in the hospital gown. Wires and hoses ran from various places on his body to the IV bag and other assorted machines, which monitored his vitals.

"Better than yesterday. The brain swelling seems to have subsided a little, and he even woke up briefly early this morning."

"That's fantastic news. I knew that big oaf was a fighter," Evan grinned.

"The doctor said it was a very good sign, but I know he's got a long way to go. And, I'm not sure if he'd been dreaming, or if it was a result of the head injury, but when he came to, he was rambling on about Cody. Something about him being in the basement."

"That is a bit strange. Did he say anything else?"

"A woman's name – Harriet. He mentioned her several times as well."

"Probably just a dream. There are no Harriets in Millford Springs."

"That's what I thought, too. But he kept gesturing towards the closet. I really thought he was just disoriented, but after he fell back to sleep, I looked through his belongings and found this," Linda said, handing over a business card.

It was from the Red Wagon Inn. On the back, scrawled in black felt tip, was the name Harriet Vanderman, and a phone number. Evan scratched his head and stared at the card.

"I was hoping you might know something about her, but you look as confused as I am," Linda said.

"I'm afraid I am. Sorry to cut the visit short, but I'd like to find out what this is all about. I'll let you know what I come up with."

"Thank you, Evan. Tell Leslie I said hello, will you?"

"I'll do that. Will you let me know when he wakes up again?"

"You'll be the first person I call," Linda smiled.

Back outside, Evan glanced at the card again. *Who was this Harriet person?*

For one brief second, he wondered if it was one of those flirty twenty-something's that would sometimes breeze through town. The ones who said they loved a man in uniform and were more than willing to prove it. But he quickly discarded the thought. Dan was the last man who would agree to an extramarital tryst, and besides, the name Harriet didn't exactly scream sexy college student. Then he remembered the last message his friend had left him.

"Hey boss, I just had an enlightening conversation a bit ago, and I think you'll be very interested in the details ..."

Evan pulled out his cell and dialed the number on the card. The phone rang several times before he finally heard a sharp click, and then the voice of an elderly woman on the other end. What she said stunned him.

"Good afternoon, Sheriff. I've been expecting your call. We haven't any time to waste if we're going to find the boy. When can we meet?"

CHAPTER 22

It had been Leslie's intention to unpack while Evan was away at the hospital, but thus far, she had accomplished very little. Initially, she was too upset, which, of course, was the whole reason she had stayed behind in the first place. But her mood had changed after receiving the call about the woman named Harriet; a woman who just might have knowledge about Cody's whereabouts. And while Evan had warned against getting her hopes up just yet, for Leslie, that was easier said than done. After all, this was the only lead that had surfaced since her sons disappearance.

Evan had gone on to say he was remaining cautiously optimistic until his meeting with the woman was over, and that he would call the minute he had finished questioning her. That had been over an hour and a half ago, and Leslie found the waiting to be agonizing.

Every so often, the sound of a car coming up the road sent her racing to the window, but each time it had turned out to be one of the neighbors returning home. She paced the floor in a relentless fashion, stopping to check her cell phone every couple of minutes. *What could possibly be taking so long?* It stood to reason that a lengthy meeting with the woman was probably a good sign, but if she didn't hear something soon, Leslie felt certain she would burst from the mounting anxiety.

When the phone rang ten minutes later, she nearly knocked the lamp off the end table as she lunged to answer. There was no masking the urgency in her voice when she said hello.

"Hey, I've got Harriet with me and we're on our way to pick you up," Evan said. "I know it's probably the last place you want to go, but she's asking to see your house. Would you be okay with that?"

"I guess so, sure. I should be ready by the time you get here," Leslie replied.

She couldn't have been more ready. When Evan turned the car into the neighborhood, she was already halfway down the block and walking towards him.

So much for not getting your hopes up. Please, Lord, don't let it be in vain.

....

"It's a lovely home, Ms. Bradford. But the new paint can't hide the scars underneath. I can see them plain as day. Such a pity that you weren't aware of them before you bought the place," Harriet said, stepping up onto Leslie's front porch.

"I would have to agree with you. It's hard to believe that nobody seems to have any knowledge about what happened here."

"It's my experience that people often wish to bury the memory of such tragedies right along with their dead. But, they're naive. Had they been able to see what I do now, they would have done the smart thing, and burned this house to the ground. Only then could they have kept the evil from returning here."

Without skipping a beat, Harriet's tone, which had thus far been gravely serious, turned as cheerful and syrupy sweet as if she were Mary Poppins herself. "Shall we go inside now?" she asked with a smile.

As soon as the front door was opened, she disappeared inside, not waiting for an escort, but rather heading around toward the living area, as if she were the one who owned the place.

"Are you sure about her?" Leslie muttered to Evan.

"Too soon to tell, but unless Dan gave her the file on Cody, and the incident at the Harvey place, she knows things nobody else could."

"So, you're not skeptical anymore?"

"A little, but much less so. I'd like to see what else she knows."

Leslie nodded, and she and Evan made their way toward Harriet, who was standing at the back of the house with her hand on the dining room table. Her head was cocked to the side, and her expression was one of heavy concentration, as if there was something to be heard within the deep silence of the room.

"So much fear here ... and sadness. I can still hear the cries of the children. There are echoes of other voices, too – anger and madness. Your son encountered the source of that, Ms. Bradford. And it is he who holds him now," Harriet said.

Leslie knew what Walter was capable of, and a million terrifying images flashed through her mind, as she contemplated what kind of fear and pain could have befallen her little boy. The thought was gut-wrenching. She hated herself for not believing him that morning when he told her about the man on the stairs, and understood the depth of the guilt Evan wrestled with every day over the loss of Ryan. That mindset of, *if you had only done this or that, things could have turned out differently.*

"Where is he? Is he hurt?" she asked Harriet.

"He's alive. That I know. As for where, he's still in this house, more or less. But, getting to him will be a bit tricky, I'm afraid. He's where they are, Ms. Bradford."

"Which is where? We turned this house upside down when Cody disappeared," Evan said.

Harriet pulled a chair from the table and took a seat, motioning for Evan and Leslie to sit as well. She reached into her purse and pulled out a butterscotch hard candy, twisting the wrapper off and popping it in her mouth. "I can't seem to stay away from these things. Always have loved them. I've been told it's an addiction, but I suppose we all have our vices, don't we? But, a bag of candy is better than a bottle of gin, I always say," she chuckled.

She offered a piece to Evan and Leslie, who both politely declined. "Forgive me. I'm prattling on now, but you must allow an old woman her simple indulgences. At my age, it's about all I have left. Now, to answer your question, as I'm sure you're already aware, those who died in this house didn't move on, as most souls do after they pass away. They're trapped, so to speak. Stuck in a fourth dimension. You could think of it as a parallel existence, a shadow of this reality as we know it."

"If they're trapped there, then how is it they're *here*?" Leslie asked. "How do they cross over so we can see them?"

"Ever come across a building that was torn down and felt an unexplainable sense of loss, Ms. Bradford? Perhaps, like this, it was a house you lived in, or a school you went to, maybe just a place you used to frequent that held fond memories?"

"I suppose so, yes," Leslie replied.

"You feel that way because a small part of your soul has attached itself to that spot. There is truth in the phrase *you're leaving a piece of yourself behind*, because, quite literally, you are. It's the reason you feel at home when you return, and why there's sadness when the place no longer exists. Walter was an unstable man, and when he passed, his entire soul stayed locked in the one place he chose to remain."

"What about the others? Why didn't they move on? I can't imagine they would want to stay behind."

"Oh, my heavens, no. They can't, because he won't let them. They're afraid of him, and that very fear has become their prison."

"I feel for those poor children, but that old woman attacked me this morning. She's as crazy as Walter."

"She wasn't always that way. She harbors a lot of anger over what happened, and that rage has turned her bitter and vindictive, especially toward the living. From what I can tell, she always was a bit of a bitch, anyway. Probably best to stay out of her way," Harriet said with a wink.

"Why now, though?" Evan asked. "I mean, why didn't the previous owners of this house experience anything?"

"Like I said, their realm is separate from ours. I suspect that if we could see it, it might look a lot like this house, but it doesn't occupy the same physical space. They're only able to cross over now because a window has been opened, Mr. Reece; a portal between their world and ours."

"What opened the window?" Leslie asked.

"I'm afraid it's not *what*, but *who*. It was your son, my dear."

Leslie was speechless. She shot a glance at Evan, who merely shrugged, and shook his head to indicate he was equally confused.

Everything up to this point had made sense, providing you actually gave any credibility to the world of the supernatural. Had she listened to Harriet's explanation a month ago, she probably would have thought there was more than just butterscotch in the old woman's candies.

But this latest revelation gave her pause. How could her son have opened the door to this madness? There was no doubt Harriet would provide the answer, but would it be something she wanted to hear? If it involved Cody being the reincarnated, parallel version of Walter, or some equally bizarre twist, she wasn't sure she would believe, let alone be able to handle, such an explanation.

"I'm a little hesitant to ask, but how exactly did he do that?"

Harriet smiled as if she had sensed Leslie's apprehension, reaching across the table and taking her hand. "You look positively terrified, dear. But no need for alarm. I can assure you that Cody wasn't sitting around a Ouija board conjuring up spirits while you were away. It was no real fault of his, or yours for that matter."

"Then how?" Leslie whispered.

"To use another analogy, think of those times you've turned on the radio and come across a song you haven't heard in ages. All of a sudden, it's like you're transported back to an earlier time, remembering parts of your life long since forgotten. Your mind is like a picture show, and not only do you see those moments again, but you experience the sounds, smells, and even the emotions, suddenly there in the present, just as they were in the past."

"Yes, I've had that happen."

"In this instance, the song *was* your son, Ms. Bradford."

"I'm not sure I follow you. Cody had nothing to do with Walter's past."

"Not literally," Evan interjected. "I think I get it, though. I can't say for sure, but I'm willing to bet the previous owners didn't have kids, or at least not a son. When Cody got here, he was nine years old, same as Walter's boy. And then ..."

"The birthday party," Leslie finished.

"Precisely, dear," Harriet said. "He was the catalyst, or the song, if you will, that connected the two worlds. The window opened, Ms. Bradford, and the past came back to life."

"But what does he want with Cody? Why would he take him?"

"What's left of Walter is far from rational. Even in life, his refusal to accept William's death was what led to his undoing and, ultimately, the tragedy that followed. He doesn't see your son as Cody. He sees William. He sees *his* son."

"Oh my God," Leslie gasped.

"Maybe that's not entirely bad. I mean, if he thinks Cody is William, then surely he won't harm him," Evan said.

"I don't imagine so," Harriet said. "However, Cody is still human, and is only able to stay alive through the other children. They have been passing their energy on to him, but they're weakening now. While they can't die again, they will become dormant. And, in the time it would take for them to recover, the lack of food and water would likely kill your son."

"What do we do? You said we could get him back. How do we do that?" Leslie asked, panicking.

"First we find the portal, which should be easy enough for me to do. It's the other part that has me concerned," Harriet said.

"Which is?" Evan asked.

"You or I can only pass through in the presence of a spirit, and even then it's a one-way ticket. The only way to get in alone, and be able to return, is to have the key, Mr. Reece."

....

Charlie heard a noise, and his eyes snapped open. He tried to look around the room, but the dismal murkiness around him chased away all traces of light. The blackness that remained was stifling.

The distant sound he had heard came again, closer this time, the sharp tone resonating throughout his entire body. It was the distinct plunking chime of a music box. Each note faltered, as if the mechanism had wound down and now struggled to play. But the melody was unmistakable.

Hap-py birth-day, went the tune.

Charlie reached out, grasping for something, anything, but there was only an empty void around him. The temperature was sweltering, and the hot, thick air burned his lungs. He was overcome with a sense of panic and tried to run. But there was nowhere to go.

The revolving cylinder of the unseen music box chimed on relentlessly, its pins plucking the tuned teeth of the metal comb as the song became louder and louder.

Hap-py birth-day, dear ...

Charlie covered his ears and fell to his knees. There was another sound now. High-pitched wails and screams that cut through his soul and drove him to his knees. "Stop!" he yelled.

As if his cry had triggered a switch, the darkness disappeared and light flooded his eyes. Looking up, he saw a hammer and the bloodied hand that held it. He tried to turn his head, tried to holler out, but fear had seized him, rendering any form of movement impossible.

The hammer fell. His head snapped back on his shoulders and there was a sickening crunch of bone as his skull caved in under the weight of the blow.

Suddenly he woke, his body twitching from the quick change. He sat up and pulled a handkerchief from the breast pocket of his shirt, dabbing away the cold perspiration on his forehead. His heart was pounding, but

it had only been a dream. And not a new dream, either –
one he'd had before, though not often. And not for years.

Someone whispered his name.

He whirled around, searching the room with his eyes. It
was late afternoon, and there was still enough light
filtering through the windows to allow him to see clearly.
But, there was no one in the room with him. He was sure
of it.

Then he heard the voice again, faint but clear.

"Help us, Charlie."

It sounded like Ellie's voice. Probably just the remnants
of the nightmare echoing through his mind, but then
again, maybe it wasn't. Maybe, she had finally found him.
While most people would consider any ghostly encounter
a terrifying ordeal, he'd found the voice to be comforting
rather than frightening, and would have given anything to
see his friend just once more.

"Ellie?" he asked, voice cracking. "Are you there?"

He listened for several minutes, but heard nothing
more. Then he began to weep. He wept for a love lost and
for memories that could have been, but never were. He
wept for the brutality that befell Ellie, and the manner in
which she left this world. But most of all, he wept for the
innocent lives of all the children there that day – lives cut
short before they ever really began.

And now, there was Cody. Another blameless child.
Another family torn apart.

It was suddenly clear to Charlie what he needed to do.

"I'm coming, Ellie. I won't hide this time. I'm coming."

....

Harriet's fingers danced delicately across the face of the
mirror.

"I think we've found it," she said.

Finding the portal had taken less than five minutes. Leslie saw nothing out of the ordinary about the full length mirror in her basement, but the old woman had been drawn to it instantly.

"*That?*" Leslie asked, as if this were the only extraordinary thing the old woman had said since her arrival.

"Quite unassuming isn't it, dear? They always are," Harriet replied.

"But, you said something about a key. I thought it would be some sort of door."

"Not a key in the literal sense, no. This is why I said things could be tricky. It's a person we need to find. In the vision of the little girl, she was searching for someone ..."

"Charlie," Evan said.

"Why, yes. You know him?" Harriet asked.

"We do as of yesterday. I was able to track him down, and Leslie and I paid him a visit. He told us about the history of this house, and how he was involved with the murders, but it wasn't clear why Ellie was looking for him. At least, not then."

"You're very resourceful, Mr. Reece. I can see why you're the sheriff. I had hoped Charlie might still be living. Without him, any attempt at a rescue may have been impossible. How long would it take to get him here?"

"A couple hours there, and a couple hours back. How exactly is he the key?"

"We have no connection to what happened back then, but he was there, Mr. Reece. His bond with the girl makes him a link to the past. And, the fact that he still lives, roots him in the present. The portal will open for him, and he'll be able to bridge seamlessly between both worlds."

"Looks like I need to pay him another visit," Evan said.

Harriet nodded. "And quickly. Time is of the essence. I don't know how much longer we have. The children are able to keep Cody alive for the time being, but that's not our only problem," she said.

"What do you mean?" Leslie asked.

"The portal is closing for good. They don't stay open indefinitely, Ms. Bradford. If we don't get Cody out before it shuts, we will lose him forever."

JIM MARTIN

CHAPTER 23

November 14, 2010

It was just before 7:30 in the morning when Evan walked into the city hall building adjacent to the police station and greeted Francine Newman.

Franny, as everyone called her, was the weekend dispatcher. She hailed from the Houston police department, where she'd been employed for longer than most people had been living. Seven decades, to be precise. And, while Evan didn't know how many sheriffs had come and gone during her lengthy stint, he figured she could easily have diapered one or two of them before they were old enough to keep the peace.

Though she had officially retired and moved to Millford fifteen years ago, the weekend position, in her words, kept her from being idle too long. It also meant she could stay plugged into her soap operas during the week, and continue to support her two-packs-a-day habit without having to dip into retirement funds.

It seemed almost preposterous to Evan that the smoking hadn't either killed the woman or left her strapped to a tank of oxygen by now, but then again, he'd witnessed far more unbelievable things of late.

"Morning, Franny. What's going on?"

The woman stopped typing and slid her reading glasses off. The thick wire rims were attached to a mock pearl chain, which held the glasses at chest level when not in use. Though the oversized pearls were kitschy and bombastic in their own rite, they couldn't hold a candle to the garish pizzazz of the autumn-themed embroidered sweater draped over her thin frame. It may have been white at one time or another, but was now more of a cream color, with two large pumpkins on the front, nestled in a bed of orange and crimson leaves.

Evan briefly considered complimenting the old woman on her appearance, but then discarded the thought. While it might have started the conversation with the usually terse dispatcher off on the right foot, he didn't want to begin his day with a lie.

"Well, now, we both already know the answer to that," she barked. "If there was anything going on, you'd have already heard from me."

"Right. You'll have to forgive me. Haven't had my coffee yet this morning."

"So, what do you want, Sheriff? I've got a lot of work to do."

Based on Francine's disposition thus far -and knowing what a vibrant personality she possessed anyway - Evan suddenly wished he'd complimented the woman, after all. He wasn't in the mood for this kind of verbal fencing, and he was pressed for time. Taking a deep breath, he jumped into his request.

"Just wanted to let you know that the volunteer deputies are taking the calls today. I have to leave town this morning, and Dan was admitted to the hospital Thursday night, so –"

"What the hell happened to him?" Franny interrupted.

"He took a spill down some stairs. Suffered a concussion, and a few broken bones."

"Well, that had to hurt. He should be more careful, especially as big as he is."

"Room 402. In case you want to put that sentiment in a card and send it his way. I'm sure your concern would touch him deeply," Evan said with a note of sarcasm.

"Uh-huh. Anything else for you, Sheriff?" she asked, positioning the reading glasses back on her face and starting to type again.

"Yes, actually. I called yesterday and asked Nancy if she would check the archives for any files we might still have on a very old case. Did she happen to leave anything for me?"

Franny stood up and made her way to another desk a short distance away, where she retrieved a manila envelope and then hobbled back to the counter.

"Now that you mention it," she said, dropping the envelope and its hefty contents in front of Evan. "An awful day in history, Sheriff. Shook up all of Texas, it did. What in the world do you want with all this?"

"Just following up on a possible link to the Bradford boy."

Franny started to chuckle. Her laughter quickly dissolved into a series of dry hacks, which became so violent at one point, that it appeared she might shake the leaves right off her sweater.

"You alright, Fran? Can I get you some water?" *Or maybe an ambulance?*

The old woman waved him away and shook her head. A moment later, the coughing subsided and she settled back into her chair. "Nothing wrong with me," she wheezed. "I think you're the one that needs a drink.

There's not a thing in that file gonna help you with that missing kid. There ain't a soul around from that long ago."

"You are," Evan said, pulling the envelope open and peeking at the mound of reports and photographs inside. "And still quite spry, I might add."

"Humph!" Franny snorted. "Must be all those hours I spend at the gym. I'm a picture of health, can't you tell?"

"Yeah, but I think it's that sense of humor that makes you such a ray of sunshine."

At that, the old woman cracked a small grin, and then went back to typing.

"See you around, Franny," Evan said, tapping the envelope on the counter before turning and heading out through the swinging glass doors.

Crossing the parking lot, he noticed someone standing outside the front entrance to the station. It was impossible to tell just who it was in the dim early morning light, but as Evan walked closer, the visitor came into clear view. Evan's mouth dropped open in surprise.

"Morning, Sheriff. I was hoping I might find you here," Charlie Peterson said, strolling toward him.

"About twenty minutes more and you would have missed me. I was about to drive out to your neck of the woods and pay another visit. How are you?" Evan asked, giving Charlie a firm handshake.

"Fine, thank you. First time I've been back here since I was a kid. Doesn't look like much has changed."

"No, just the faces I would imagine. So, what brings you?"

"Well, it's about a dream I had last night. It made me think, Sheriff, about Ellie. Then, when I woke up, I heard her voice. She didn't tell me much, but I think she needs me. I think she needs me to do something for her. I don't know what exactly, but I thought if I came, maybe we could figure that out."

"Precisely why I was coming out to see you," Evan said, unlocking the station door. "Leslie and I have learned quite a bit since our visit. Why don't you come in and have a seat. I'll explain the whole thing."

....

Something was off. That was obvious the moment Leslie pulled up to the diner and saw the man standing outside, face pressed against the glass and hands cupped around his eyes to peer into the dim interior of the restaurant.

At this time of morning, when the first rays of dawn were still making their way over the horizon, the lights from within the diner typically cast a warm glow across Main Street, inviting early risers inside where, as Dorothy would say, "You can get your eggs any way you like, but the service only comes sunny side up."

But today, there were no lights. Only a dark, empty shell awaited those looking for a hot breakfast and an even hotter cup of coffee.

Leslie thumbed the button on the door panel of her SUV and rolled down the driver side window as she approached the man. It was Steve Holloway. She didn't know him well, but he was a weekend regular. Always ordered an Adam and Eve on a raft, a side of Zeppelin, and a coffee high and dry.

"Oh, hey," he said, approaching the window. "Where is everyone this morning?"

"I'm not sure. There was no note on the door?"

"Nah, nothing. Looks like coffee was made, and there's a light on in back. Didn't see anyone in there, though. "

Leslie wondered if something had happened to Dorothy, or more likely, Arthur. She recalled the day Dorothy had given him the once over about his cholesterol levels, and it crossed her mind that he could have suffered a heart attack. She certainly hoped not, but if that were the case, it seemed feasible that Dorothy would have opted to drive him to the hospital herself, rather than waiting for an ambulance to come all the way from Bakers Grove.

"Let me check around back and see if anyone's parked there. I'll try Dorothy on her cell as well, and let you know what I find out."

"Okay," Steve replied in a long Southern drawl. "Nowhere else I need to be for a while. Hope everything's alright."

"I'm sure it is," Leslie replied.

But, truth be told, she wasn't sure at all. In fact, she felt more ill at ease with each passing moment. It wasn't just the dark restaurant and her missing co-workers, either. There was more to it than that. There was a crackling energy in the air that buzzed through her body the way she imagined a jolt of 220 would if she were to grab hold of a live wire. It was that same sensation she felt yesterday morning when...

Oh my God!

Leslie raced around to the back of the building. As she feared, both Arthur and Dorothy's vehicles sat parked in their usual spots. She whipped her SUV into an empty space and jumped out of the car, fumbling through her purse for her cell, as she rushed toward the back entrance to the diner.

Finding her phone, she jammed Dorothy's number in on the keypad. There were several hollow rings on the other end, but no answer. After a few more seconds the line went to voicemail.

While she should have walked away then, or at the very least called for help, her concern for her friend was too great, overriding any misgivings she may have had otherwise. She threw open the back door and stepped inside, looking first to her left. At the end of the dark hall, the door to the office stood open, and a light shone from within.

"Dorothy?"

There was no response. Other than the distant peal of the air conditioning unit on the roof, all was still. She had never noticed the slight rattle in the fan before, but with all the hustle and bustle that was usually taking place, it was probably imperceptible.

Leslie started toward the office, and plugged Dorothy's number into her phone again. She stopped in her tracks when she heard ringing behind her. It was coming from the storage pantry near the kitchen. Turning around, she eased her way down the corridor.

Two rings. Three. Still no answer.

A part of her wanted to run toward the sound of her friend's phone, but the sense of fear that had eluded her up to this point began to creep into her bones, and she was afraid of what she might find at the end of the hall. She approached with slow calculated steps, watching for any movement.

When she reached the pantry and rounded the corner of the room, the shock of what she saw caused her body to go slack. She lost the grip on her phone, which clattered to the ground. Her purse followed, its contents spilling out into the hall. There in front of her, splayed out on the floor and face down in a pool of blood, was Dorothy.

Leslie threw her hands up over her mouth, stumbled backwards, and collapsed against the wall. Just an hour ago she had been buzzing with excitement over the promises the day held. The possibility that she could see her son by day's end was a thrilling prospect, and one she couldn't wait to share with Dorothy. Never did she imagine she would be walking into the nightmare which was before her now.

Had it been anyone else stumbling upon the scene, they probably would have thought this was the aftermath of a robbery that had taken a grisly turn. But Leslie knew better. It had to do with the odd charge in the air; that same strange feeling she had felt in her bedroom just before the encounter with the old woman. She'd felt it in the corn field the night of the festival, and again on Halloween, she realized, when the dead children were at her door. But none of those instances compared to the intensity she felt now. The atmosphere was alive and vibrating, each ebbing pulse of energy pounding between her temples.

She crawled over to where her phone lay and picked it up off the floor with trembling hands. As luck would have it, the plastic cover on the back had popped off, and the battery was missing. She let out a small whimper and began to scavenge the floor in search of it. That was when she noticed the movement from Dorothy's blouse. It was ever so slight, but the fabric rose and fell in shallow intervals. She was still alive.

Leslie dropped the phone, realizing there was no time to search for the battery. Turning and racing around the corner, she shrieked as she nearly collided with the man standing in the hallway. "Oh, you startled me! What happened here? Are you alright?"

"Oh, I'm quite fine," Arthur answered. There was an icy edge to his voice.

"Where have you been? We need to get help! Dorothy is hurt."

"I'm sure she'll die soon enough. She was lucky, though. Never saw it coming. Why, she didn't even have time to scream."

Leslie stood in stunned silence. She saw Arthur standing before her, only it *wasn't* Arthur. His whole demeanor was different – his expression, the way he stood, the manner in which he spoke and, most notably, the way he looked at her. It was a crazed and determined stare from pupils that were hollow, distant, and black as night.

"It wasn't like before. Not like it was with *her*," Arthur spat, his voice bitter and vindictive. "I made sure she screamed. Oh, yes, she screamed all the way down the stairs. And, when she pleaded for her life, I made her scream some more."

He began to laugh now, a deranged, maniacal howl that sent cold shudders down Leslie's spine. She took a couple steps backwards, and then froze when the man reached into the pocket of his apron and pulled out a butcher's knife. He eyed her with a wolfish grin, and held the blade out at his side, scraping along the metal paneling on the wall. The sharp point made a clicking sound as it fell in and out of the corrugated steel grooves.

Tick-tick-tick-tick

"The children screamed, too. I didn't want to hurt them, but they wouldn't stop. They ruined everything, and they made my boy angry. He told me they had to go. No cake for any of them."

Tick-tick-tick

"They had to die."

Tick-tick

"Just...like...you."

Tick

With teeth bared, and face twisted in a savage rage, Arthur raised the knife and lurched forward.

Leslie turned and ran toward the kitchen. She skidded around the corner and slammed through the swinging door that led to the front of the diner. Racing across the dining room, she threw herself against the front door. It didn't budge.

Stupid girl. You know the door deadbolts from the inside. How did you think you could get out this way?

But it was the only direction she could have run, at least at the moment Arthur gave chase. The only way out was to go back the way she came. It was either that, or break the glass, she realized, the thoughts rushing through her brain.

She glanced behind her, sure that Arthur would be standing there ready to strike, but saw with relief that he wasn't. The swinging metal door was just now opening again, the man emerging slowly from behind it. She had a few seconds at best.

The jukebox across the room fired up on its own, and began to belt out a big band tune. Arthur raised the knife and closed his eyes, waving the blade around as if he were conducting some sort of macabre orchestra. Leslie kicked at the front door, anxious to take advantage of his lack of attention. It rattled on its hinges, but the glass held steadfast. She tried kicking a few more times, but it seemed her legs would give out before the glass did.

"Going somewhere?" Arthur asked. His tone was deep and cryptic. "You can't leave. We haven't had our dance yet."

Leslie glanced back and saw that he was still standing at the edge of the counter, glaring at her with those soulless eyes. An abrupt pounding on the front door made her jump. She turned to see Steve standing on the other side. He pulled at the door, and then tried giving it a kick of his own. The glass still didn't give.

"Call for help!" Leslie shouted.

"What's going on in there?" Steve yelled back.

"Just go!"

Steve backed away from the door, his eyes wide with shock, and took off across the parking lot.

Leslie turned to see Arthur moving toward her again. She stepped quickly away from the door and eased further back into the dining room, trying to put more space between them. But she was cornered, and Arthur knew it. He didn't try to bridge the gap, but merely stood there, swaying left and right, not venturing far from the kitchen door.

Out of nowhere, a chair slammed into Leslie's right shoulder, and she stumbled forward. She turned in time to see another chair lift itself off the ground and hurl itself toward her. She tried to duck, but one of the legs clipped her across her brow, sending a warm gush of blood down her face.

She was going to have to make a run for it. Under normal circumstances, she figured she was quicker than the old man, and could easily outrun him. But this was hardly ordinary. And, if she were wrong, she'd be losing more than a first place ribbon. She'd be losing her life.

There was no time to think about that. Mustering her courage, she ran to her left, angled for the counter, and vaulted over, losing her footing as she attempted to land on the other side. Her shoulder slammed into a tray full of clean mugs, spilling cups and saucers over the floor around her. She picked herself up, breathing heavily, and glanced toward the kitchen door. Arthur was already rounding the corner, heading right for her at a fast clip. She stood up and grabbed a coffee pot from the warmer, swinging it sideways and hitting the man in the arm just as he brought the knife down. The glass urn exploded, sending a spray of hot coffee, and shards of glass, into the air. The knife skidded across the floor, and Arthur yelled out; an eerie cry that was more rage than it was pain.

Leslie kept hold of the handle of the coffee pot and used it as a set of faux brass knuckles, jabbing Arthur in the neck where it would hurt the most. The blow, and the sharp fragments of glass along the edge of the heavy plastic, pushed him back, a snarl on his face. It was all she'd needed. She pushed her way past him and darted into the kitchen.

As she came through the swinging door, she took two steps, before running full force into Steve, who'd come flying around the corner just in front of her.

"What are you doing?" Leslie sobbed. "I thought you went for help!"

"I called the police, but I wasn't about to wait for them to get here. What's wrong? Who's after you?" He glanced behind her, his eyes scanning the door and the room beyond.

Leslie pushed at him, trying to get him to turn around before it was too late. "Thank you, but we've got to –"

Before she could finish, the metal door swung open and Arthur charged forward, knife in hand. He plunged the blade deep into Steve's gut. The man reeled backwards into a work table, a look of shock and pain on his face. Leslie screamed, and tried to move around the men, but Arthur gave her a shove and she fell backwards, landing in a corner near the grill.

Steve shouted as Arthur moved in on him, throwing up his hands to ward off the attack. There was a brief struggle, but Arthur grabbed hold of the knife and gave it a twist, causing Steve to cry out and fall to his knees.

Arthur began to cackle with sick glee, dancing up and down. He reached over and pulled the blade out, and then jabbed it in and out once more. A heavy wet breath escaped Steve's lungs, and the man slumped over on the floor, his head hitting the tile with a dull thud.

Leslie sobbed, hunkered down in the corner between the grill and the fryer. She could hear sirens now in the distance, but she feared they would arrive too late. Arthur turned to face her now, his mouth twisted in a horrible grin. Death seemed only moments away.

"Arthur, please," she cried as the man drew nearer.

The man stopped and cocked his head to the side, as if what she said made him curious. For a brief moment, the darkness retreated from his eyes, revealing a flicker of recognition. "Leslie?"

Then, his eyes turned dark again, the man she knew as Arthur retreating into whatever had come over him. He drew his arm up and held the knife high in the air, his hand trembling, and took another step forward.

"Arthur! Don't!" Leslie pleaded.

Turning and seeing the knife, Arthur's expression turned confused once again. He saw the body on the floor and the blood on his apron. His right hand rose up with the knife, threatening to bring it down again, but was stopped by his left. The trembling in his limbs intensified, looking more like a seizure now than a case of the shakes. He was fighting against the madness that sought to control him.

Sweat poured down his brow and his jaw clenched, as he struggled to drop the knife. The entity that had possessed him fought back and swung, the blade coming down inches from Leslie's face. Arthur looked up at her, desperation in his eyes.

"Run!" he yelled, and with one last forceful grunt, swung himself onto the grill. The hot metal surface hissed as his hands and arms fell upon it. Wisps of steam rose from searing skin that bubbled and popped like bacon. The man let out a savage cry and fell backwards, the bottoms of his arms now a furious shade of red.

Leslie jumped up and ran hard and fast. She could feel the nausea building as she darted through the hallway, but knew she didn't have time to stop and be sick. By the time she reached the back door and launched herself outside, the queasiness was overwhelming. She steadied herself against the back of the building and closed her eyes. Blood-soaked images paraded through her head, and she fought the urge to throw up.

Emergency vehicles pulled into the parking lot with sirens blaring, and screeched to a halt. Car doors opened, voices shouted, and feet pounded the pavement, but the only thing Leslie could hear as she slumped to the ground were the haunting screams that still echoed from inside the diner.

CHAPTER 24

The darkness of early morning had finally retreated with the advance of daylight over the town of Millford Springs. Though the skies were overcast, as most November days are, the light had declared victory, having free reign until such time as the armies of night saw fit to march again. The annual Thanksgiving parade, and the start of the Christmas season, were less than three weeks away, and storefront windows were gushing with holiday decorations, while twinkling lights and tinsel gilded the wrought iron lamp posts along Main Street, adding an extra measure of cheer to an already charming vista.

It wasn't holiday shopping or parades that brought everyone outside on this day, however. The crowds gathered now to watch a different kind of spectacle; one in which peace and goodwill were conspicuously absent. And the flashing lights that caught their attention were not nestled amongst pine and evergreen, but rather belonged to the police cars and ambulances surrounding the Springs Diner.

Charlie Peterson approached the curbside where Leslie sat, and offered a blanket he'd retrieved from the backseat of his car.

"Here you go. You're shaking like a leaf."

"Thank you. That's very kind of you," Leslie replied. She accepted the blanket, draping it over her shoulders and cocooning herself within it.

Charlie took a seat on the curb beside her and they both sat in silence for a long moment, surveying the scene around them. "Your friends," Charlie said, nodding toward the diner, "they going to be okay?"

"I'm not sure. Dorothy was still breathing when I found her, so I think there's hope for her."

"And the others?"

"Steve I didn't know well, but I'm pretty sure he's gone. And Arthur ..." Leslie paused. Just speaking his name brought a wave of both fear and sorrow. "His arms are burned pretty badly, but I think he'll live."

"He's the one who did this?" Charlie asked, his voice low and gentle.

Leslie nodded. Her voice was thin and weak when she spoke. "Yes, but what I saw in there...it wasn't Arthur. It's like he was just a puppet for someone else. It was Walter. I'm sure of it. He spoke of the old woman, the children, the things he did to them. And the look in his eyes ... I've never seen anything like it. I'm terrified, Charlie. If Walter is possessing people, making them do things they don't want to do, are any of us safe? Are you? Is Evan? I know we need you to open the door to get Cody, but now I wonder if it's fair to even have you in this situation. What if you get hurt, too? Then what will we do?"

Charlie was quiet. He glanced back at the diner, a hard, reflective look in his eyes, and Leslie wondered if he might be having second thoughts. This wasn't the first time he'd witnessed the aftermath of one of Walter's killing sprees. It had to be bringing back some awful memories and emotions. And, agreeing to step into that mirror today would be like walking into a lion's den – a dangerous proposition, rife with uncertainty, and the very real possibility of death.

She'd always known there would be dangers, of course, but the prospect of getting Cody back had excited her so much that she'd pushed most of the fear aside. The incident in the diner changed all of that, and the risk she, and everyone going into that basement, would be taking was now clear. As much as she needed Charlie, could she really blame him if he wanted to walk away?

"You know, this was Ellie's favorite place," Charlie finally said. Though his eyes were on the diner, he seemed to see past the emergency vehicles, and beyond the shadow of death hovering over the scene. A nostalgic grin amplified the boyish quality of his face as he recalled happier days.

"I couldn't begin to count the number of times we came here together. She would always order a strawberry shake, and then plunk a nickel in the jukebox. There was one song in particular that she just loved. I can remember the way she would bob her head to the music, and how her ponytail would swish back and forth. Sometimes, she'd even try to get me to dance. I was always too shy, and she would say, *'Silly boy. Don't worry about the other people. Just have fun.'* Of course, we never had a shortage of that. She was so happy and full of life."

He paused, the bittersweet glimmer in his eye fading, as the past melted away and his thoughts returned to the here and now.

"That was so long ago that it seems like another lifetime. The boy I was then is a stranger to me now, as if it all happened to someone else. Sort of like a dream. That time period, the memories of Ellie, it's all just a dream now. And one I wish I never had to wake up from. You were right when you said Walter would have taken me if

I'd tried to stop him that day in the cemetery. I probably would have died along with the rest of the children. But, maybe there's a reason I lived. Maybe, it's so I could be here today. So I could put a stop to this madman. There was nothing I could do for Ellie, but there is something I can do for your son. And, I plan to do just that. I think it's high time to send Walter back to hell, where he belongs."

....

The old mirror sat in the corner of the room, under a thick blanket of dust. Who it had originally belonged to, and how long it had resided in the basement, was of no consequence. After all, it had been just a simple antique when it was purchased; an ordinary fixture made of wood and glass. It had only changed into something more – something much more – when Cody moved into the house.

Charlie stood in front of the forgotten relic, and stared at a hazy reflection of himself, wondering if, at that same moment, someone was staring back at him from the other side.

"Any questions, Mr. Peterson?" Harriet asked, tucking a butterscotch beneath her tongue as she spoke.

"Well ..." he hesitated. "I just wish I knew what exactly I was going to see when I crossed over."

"We're all afraid of the unknown, aren't we? I wish I could give you the answer to that question, but the truth is, I couldn't tell you without going in myself."

"So, you've never done this? How do you know it will work?"

"I know it works because, as they say around here, this isn't my first rodeo. I can tell you that, with each individual I've helped, the circumstances have been different. And the sights they reported on the other side were just as varied. You aren't walking into heaven or hell, but a spiritual in-between. However, there is usually some degree of mirroring. So if you were to go through a window in Central Park, you would get some interpretation of Central Park. Invariably, though, the end result of what you see will be determined by what the lost souls there have made of it."

"Then what you're saying is, I'll still be in this house when I step through?" Charlie asked.

"A variation of it. It would be much like going to an apartment building and walking from unit to unit. The floor plan remains constant, but in each, the furnishings and decor vary. Each one looks slightly different. But, be warned. Walter was a deeply troubled man, and it would be foolish to believe his world is exactly the same as this one. You could very well run into some, shall we say ... unexpected things."

"Like what?" Leslie asked, stopping her nervous pacing long enough to pose the question.

"Products of Walter's mind, Mrs. Bradford. The presence of strong spiritual energy, and a disturbed mind, can create all sorts of vile monstrosities. Things you would never want crossing over. Although, if they did, they wouldn't survive long. They are but extensions of him. And, as you've seen yourself, his strength is limited in our world."

"No offense, Harriet. But he seemed to be pretty capable this morning in the diner," Evan remarked.

"Yes, but he must inhabit another body to do so. Otherwise, the best he can do is become a bothersome ghost; toss some things around, push and shove, show up as an apparition, that sort of thing. Sure, it would be terrifying, but very unlikely to cause any permanent harm.

"Did you know, Mr. Reece, that most life threatening injuries sustained in a haunting are self-inflicted? People are irrational when they're afraid, and that's when accidents happen. It would surprise me none to find out that your deputy, Mr. Decker, simply saw something that frightened him and took a spill rather than being physically attacked.

"It's conceivable that an entity *could* give a nudge to someone already on the edge of stairs or hanging out a window, but they could not pick you up and throw you against your will. The notion that they can do such things comes from fiction. Why, I once saw a story where a spirit even caused someone to explode. Can you imagine? It's rubbish. You'd have a better chance at finding the Easter Bunny than having that sort of thing happen, Mr. Reece," Harriet finished, chuckling.

"Be that as it may, Walter has managed to hurt enough people, whether on his own, or through someone else. I can only imagine the greater danger on his side of the fence. Charlie may be the only one who can open that doorway, but that doesn't mean he has to be the one to go inside," Evan replied.

"What are you saying?" Leslie asked.

"I'll go. Charlie shouldn't have to be the one to do this. If he likes, he can stay just inside to guide us back out, but I'll take the risk of going further in. Besides, Cody knows who I am. He won't hesitate about coming with me."

"Whatever you need me to do, Sheriff. I'm here to help in every way I can," Charlie said, nodding.

Leslie walked over beside the mirror where Evan stood, her head shaking with a fierce determination. "No, Evan. You can't do this. I don't want you to do this. Suppose something goes wrong," she protested.

"But it's alright for Charlie to risk his life? Something could just as easily happen to him," Evan argued. "Which brings up another good point. If anything *were* to happen to him, then there's no longer a way to keep the portal open."

"I didn't mean it like that. You know I don't want anyone to get hurt. And for that reason, it should be *me* going in after Cody. I'm his mother. I can't ask either of you to put your lives on the line."

Evan shook his head stubbornly. "You don't have to ask. This is no different than if I'd found out that Cody was being kept in a house somewhere in Houston. I'd still be going to get him back."

"Evan, this isn't the same thing at all. You're not up against an ordinary man. If Walter comes after you in there, that weapon on your belt isn't going to save you!"

Evan stepped closer to Leslie and placed his hands on her shoulders. "No, but you were nearly killed this morning, and I'm not about to let that monster have another shot. If he were to take your life, *that* would kill me. I can't lose another person I love. Not this way. Not like this."

Leslie was taken aback by Evan's unexpected admission. More than that, she was moved to the brink of tears. Here was a man who had been promised nothing other than an offer of friendship. Now, it seemed that he was also a man who, after just a few short months of acquaintance, had become so attached to them, that he was ready to sacrifice his life, if need be, to save her and Cody. It was a far cry from the years of neglect she had experienced during her marriage to the self-obsessed John, and the feeling of having someone hold her in a higher regard than themselves was a new one. But, foreign as it was, it was also warm and uplifting. It caused her heart to swell. If there had been any doubt in her mind as to just how much Evan truly cared, there was absolutely none now.

She leaned in and touched her lips to his, lingering just long enough to detect a soft air of mint on his breath. Pulling back, she grabbed the front of his jacket and gave a light tug.

"Alright. Just, please, be careful in there. I need you to come back to me, okay?" Leslie whispered.

"You can count on it," he replied.

Leslie hoped she could. Standing there on the brink of this journey into the unknown, she was struggling with the nagging fear that she might never again see those she cared for. Having seen firsthand what Evan was going up against, and now with Harriet's warning of unexpected things, Leslie's anxiety had enlarged tenfold. But, hope wasn't lost yet, and she held on to it with everything she had left.

"And, Charlie, that goes for you too," Leslie added, turning and giving him a peck on the cheek. "I don't know how to thank you for doing this."

"Not necessary. Seeing you and your boy back together will be thanks enough."

"Are we all set, then?" Harriet asked. She stood with her hands folded together, her bright red lipstick framing a gracious smile, as if she were getting ready to preside over a joyous marriage ceremony rather than watch two men enter a living nightmare.

"I did wonder," Evan asked. "Once we're back out, what's to keep Walter from crossing over again? Coming after us?"

"Simple, Mr. Reece. We're not going to take any chances that he'll come through again. As long as you're back before the window closes on its own, we'll just destroy the mirror."

"What about Ellie and the other children? What happens to them?" Charlie asked.

"No need to fret over them, Mr. Peterson. These things have a way of working themselves out. But come now, we haven't much more time to waste. There's no way of knowing how deep inside Cody is, and I'm not sure how much longer this thing will remain open."

Charlie had hoped for a more direct answer to his question, but in the short time he'd been in Harriet's presence, he'd come to accept her eccentricities, and trust that she knew best, though her perpetual sunny disposition during matters of dire circumstance was a bit unnerving. He only hoped that was because experience had taught her that matters such as this turned out for the better more often than not.

"So, what do I need to do?" he asked.

"Just touch the mirror," Harriet replied.

Charlie reached up and placed his palm on the glass, wondering what exactly was meant to happen. He didn't have to wonder long. There was a quick flash of light, and the face of the mirror began to ripple like static waves across a television screen. The glass was no longer solid, instead feeling to Charlie more like lightning-charged gelatin. His hand dissolved out of sight as it pressed through to the other side. He quickly yanked it back, wiggling his fingers and balling them up into a fist.

"You alright? Does it hurt?" Leslie asked.

"No, just making sure it was still there," Charlie replied with an uneasy laugh. "A strange feeling, but it seems to work."

"You ready to do this, then?" Evan asked, giving the old man an encouraging pat on the back.

"I've been ready to nail this bastard to the wall for sixty years. Just been waiting on you," Charlie grinned.

With that, he took a step forward, the semi-solid glass parting to allow passage. Evan followed suit a moment later, the mirror closing behind him like a liquid curtain. And, just like that, the two men were gone.

CHAPTER 25

Harriet had been right. The other side was nothing more than a carbon copy of the original basement, right down to the boxes of old junk sitting on the shelves. That didn't surprise Evan. After all, it's what he was told to expect. What *was* a bit of a shock was how it all felt.

For some reason, he thought the physical sensations of this world would be different. Not that he expected to be in limbo, mind you, but because he'd assumed that the natural order of things would be altered in some fashion, this being a spiritual realm. He had considered the possibility that things which appeared tangible might turn out to be nothing more than hollow apparitions; mere shadows of the things they imitated, as with a mirage.

But, as he ran his hand along the bannister of the staircase, he found that it felt as genuine as its earthly equivalent. The space around him was cool and moist, possessing the same dank, musty odor he'd breathed just minutes ago, and, though there were no particular noises to be heard at the moment, the area still maintained a clear, audible presence. It was about as real as any place could be.

Charlie shuffled over to the base of the staircase and stood next to Evan. He was still rubbing his arms up and down, not because he was cold, but to alleviate the lingering effects of passing through the mirror.

"Still feeling it?" Evan asked.

Charlie nodded. "Let's just say I wouldn't want to have to take that ride on a regular basis."

Evan understood. Stepping through the glass had felt as if he'd been taken apart and deconstructed down to individual cells. It was like his entire physical being had been pumped full of Novocain and sent drifting, piece by piece, into a massive expanse, each numb particle floating in a sea of emptiness, while the conscious mind remained intact.

"Just once more to get back home, and then we shouldn't ever have to worry about it again," Evan replied.

"That's good, because my body isn't what it used to be. Too many trips like that and I'd be a ghost myself. Now, are you sure you want to go up there all alone?" Charlie asked, eyeing the doorway at the top of the staircase. "I'm not afraid to help you out. Until five minutes ago I thought this was a solo mission anyhow."

"Thanks, Charlie, but I'd prefer you stay, and be ready to get us the hell out of here when Cody and I get back. Don't want to risk anything happening to you."

"Well, alright. But don't hesitate to yell if you need me. I may be old, but I've still got a bit of fight left in me."

"I'll remember that. Hopefully, though, I can slip in and out without Walter even knowing I'm here."

Charlie had heard that before. He'd uttered more or less the same words to Ellie sixty years ago. And because of those words, she'd pushed aside her fears and followed him deeper into the cemetery. She'd believed him when he told her they would be alright, and trusted that he would keep her safe. He had given her a death sentence instead. The pangs of guilt, sorrow, and regret hit like a sucker punch, tearing open an old wound and ripping a hole through his chest all over again.

"I hope so, Sheriff. For all of our sakes," he replied.

Nodding, Evan plucked a flashlight from his belt and began to ease his way up the staircase. The wood groaned with each step, and Charlie wondered whether Walter already knew they were there. Perhaps, though, they would get lucky and Cody would be just on the other side of the door. Perhaps.

....

The first thing Evan noticed was the furniture. Coming out of the basement and peering into the dining room, he saw that the table and chairs were not the rich cherry wood Leslie had bought, but much cheaper ones made of Formica and chrome. The appliances were different, too. The white enameled Philco refrigerator, with its streamlined corners and thick steel door latch, wasn't the type one would find in any kitchen today. Like the table, the laminate flooring, and the turquoise cabinets, it was vintage. The layout of the room matched that of Leslie's, but the style was decidedly older. This was the house as it had looked when Walter lived in it.

It was a perfect throwback to an earlier decade, with one exception. Something was unusual about the wallpaper. Maybe it was just mimicking its age, but it had an odd texture, like that of shriveled fruit with rotted brown spots. Other sections seemed to be peeling away from the wall entirely.

Evan directed the beam of his flashlight to one such spot a few feet away, and stepped closer. The paper was pulled back to expose a long gash in the wall, which was crusted with something dark. This wasn't wallpaper, he realized, or even peeling paint. It was skin. Skin that was bruised, cut, and decomposing.

He drew back in shock. Ghostly apparitions, phantom footsteps, and the like, had been expected, but this? There was no doubt that Walter was crazy, but now Evan had a front row seat into the man's demented mind. He wondered what other disturbing sights awaited, and how much therapy one might require after spending too much time in a place such as this. The thought made him shudder. Doing his best to push the image aside, he made his way to the living area. He needed to get Cody out of here, and quickly.

Like the kitchen, the furniture in the living room was circa 1950s. A straight-back sofa covered in green damask, coffee and end tables in blond oak, and atomic-style lamps were arranged atop deep shag carpeting. Stark contrasts to the hardwood floors and modern styling of its counterpart. An easy chair sat in the far corner, and, though the winged high back was angled away, there was no mistaking the silhouetted shape of the person sitting in it.

Startled, Evan instinctively reached for the snap on his gun holster. He knew, of course, that bullets would be useless against anything not made of flesh and bone. But something about the feel of the cold steel on the palm of his hand offered a sense of security which, regardless of how false it may have been, still made him feel better.

Moving with a silent grace, he slid sideways, working his way around the room. The shape in the chair didn't budge. Evan's grip tightened around the handle of his weapon, and he stepped swiftly in front of the chair. With a sigh of relief, he pulled his hand away from his sidearm and relaxed. It wasn't a person sitting in the seat before him, but a mannequin.

The nude body sat upright, with its hands propped up on the arms of the chair. The head was positioned forward, but there were no eyes to stare back. There was no face at all, actually. Unlike some department store mannequins, which still, at the very least, possessed a nose, this one was nothing but a flat flesh colored mound of nothingness. Evan was grateful it hadn't been Walter in the chair, but still found the mannequin creepy as hell.

Adding to his sense of alarm, was the faint chorus of music filtering into the room, as if someone had just clicked on a radio. The song was old, one of those big band types from the 40s or 50s, with its raucous horns and jazzy tempo. Evan turned his light towards the front parlor, took a few steps, and listened. The music seemed to be coming from upstairs.

Another noise captured his attention, and he turned to look behind him. The mannequin still sat in the chair, but the head had turned to face him. The blank, expressionless gaze from eyes that weren't even there made Evan's skin crawl. He whipped the pistol from his belt and pointed it at the thing in the chair. Beads of sweat crawled across his brow, and the thumping in his chest grew loud enough to drown out the music from upstairs. The sudden laughter was much closer. It was a child's laugh.

Evan whirled around toward the front parlor, where the sound had come from.

Cody?

Long shadows were moving in the entry way. He took a couple cautious steps, and then turned back to make sure the mannequin wasn't somehow following him. It remained in the chair, locked in the same position from moments earlier.

Evan turned and moved across the room toward the foyer, accompanied by whispers and muffled voices. Rounding the corner with his weapon still positioned in front of him, he saw two children sitting near the bottom step. He was certain that the thin boy with the crooked arm was Billy Watkins, and the girl he guessed to be Sandy Morgan, given the fact that she didn't match the descriptions of Ellie. Their pale blue skin, and thin corpse-like bodies made them an alarming sight. But there was no malice in their expression. On the contrary, their eyes were filled with a deep sadness, which Evan found heartbreaking.

"Hi," he said, holstering his pistol. "Do you know why I'm here?"

The two children looked bewildered, as if they were the ones seeing a ghost. Billy began to fade away, but Sandy reached over and grabbed his arm. They looked at one another, and though nothing was spoken, Evan sensed that Billy was afraid. The girl turned back and nodded her head.

Something cold clutched the sheriff's hand. He jumped back and let out a yelp, which must have been too much for Billy. The boy vanished completely, leaving Sandy alone on the step. Evan looked down at the frigid object that had startled him. It was a hand belonging to another child, a girl who looked to be slightly older, and somehow more tortured, than the other two.

"Ellie?"

The girl nodded.

"You've been trying to get our attention haven't you? Do you know where Cody is? Can you take me to him?"

The girl nodded again, looking behind her, and then upstairs, as she clenched her hands together. She seemed worried and anxious.

"Is he up there?" Evan asked, stepping toward the staircase.

Ellie gripped his arm with a strength well beyond that of a girl her age, spinning him around, and shaking her head in a frantic motion. "No," she muttered, glancing up to where the music droned on. "Don't go up there. That's where *he* stays."

She gave Evan's arm a firm tug and pointed back the way he had just come. "This way," she said, leading him through the living room, and past the mannequin, which now faced forward again.

"What is that?" Evan asked.

"It won't hurt you. It's not like the things outside."

"What's outside?"

"Bad things," Ellie replied.

Like so many of Harriet's utterances, the answer was vague and arcane. Little cryptic pieces to a much bigger puzzle. Evan doubted the girl meant to sound enigmatic. Maybe the things to which she referred had no name. And even if they did, he was sure he would still be mystified as to what exactly *they* were. There was also the possibility that whatever she spoke of was too difficult to describe. Or, maybe just too horrible.

They came to a hallway at the far corner of the living room, which didn't exist in Leslie's version of the house, and made their way down the long corridor. At the end of the hall, a dim flicker of light cast a yellowish hue over a single wooden door. The source of the light wasn't an electric bulb, but something that looked to be physically alive. Whether it was organic, or supernatural in nature, was unclear. It existed as a luminous, pulsating mass, swirling around under a dome of murky glass affixed to the ceiling. Evan was intrigued, but maintained his distance.

Ellie placed her hands flat against the wood door and closed her eyes. Her breathing intensified, coming out in short, sporadic bursts, as she listened to something on the outside. An almost electric charge filled the air, and the slithering lump in the ceiling stopped moving, glowing brighter and emitting a high-pitched hum, as it fed off of the energy in the room.

Without warning, Ellie's eyes snapped open, and the labored breathing ceased. "They sleep," she said, reaching up and twisting the knob on the door.

As the door swung open, Evan saw what appeared to be an ordinary backyard, extending out about 30 yards. The caliginous landscape was ill-defined, but beyond the manicured lawn, he saw an endless stretch of dense fields overgrown with brush standing 10 feet tall, if not more. The sky, if that's what it was, was nothing but deep, empty space; a canvas of pitch black, void of stars or moon. At the farthest edge of the yard, tucked into the corner, sat a ramshackle wood shed. The shed's one window was dimly lit from within.

"He's there," Ellie said, pointing towards the structure, her voice low and tense. "Cody is in there. But you'll have to go alone. I cannot pass any further."

"Okay," Evan nodded. "But I thought you and the others were keeping Cody alive. How can that be if you can't go to him?"

"He wasn't always there. Walter put him there because of the old woman."

"I don't understand. You mean Harriet?"

Ellie nodded solemnly, never taking her eyes from the cabin. "He said she came to show the lady on the other side how to take the boy away. He said he had to make the lady in the house go away. Then, he put Cody out there with the bad things. So they could guard him. That's why I can't go out there."

"Who are *they*? What's out there, Ellie?" Evan asked, squinting across the yard in search of the things she kept mentioning.

"Cevoraks. That's what Walter calls them."

"And these things can hurt you? Even though you've already died?" he asked.

"The body I once had is gone, but the soul still lives. And spirits still feel pain," she replied, lowering her gaze.

"The pain of dying is better than what the cevorak can do. They latch on for eternity, and there is no rescue from their torment. Death will not find you again in this life. I cannot save you."

There was a deep sinking in Evan's chest. The sympathy he felt for these children was overwhelming. Was it not enough to die at the hands of a monster when your life had only just begun? But then, to be stuck with him beyond death, living in an eternal shadow of fear ... it was the most horrible thing he'd ever heard. Harriet had said this was not hell, but from what Evan had seen, he didn't imagine hell could be much worse. He had come here for Cody alone, but now he realized that he wanted to leave with all the children. He wasn't sure what he'd do with them afterward, but anything had to be better than this place. Surely, there was some way to save them all, including this girl who had worked so hard to bring them here.

Dropping down on one knee, Evan took the girl by the hand and spoke in the comforting manner of a father to his own daughter. "Ellie, listen to me. While I'm getting Cody, can you find Billy and Sandy, and then wait for us in the basement? When I get back, we're all going to get out of here, okay?"

She shook her head slowly, hopeless. "He'll come for us. Walter knows when we leave. He always finds us."

"Not this time. I'll make sure of it."

Ellie lifted her head and searched Evan's gaze. She knew he meant well, but how could he keep such a promise? Assuming he was even successful in saving Cody, he had no understanding of the things Walter could do. "We'll try," she finally said. "But don't wait for us. Just get the boy out."

Rising to his feet, Evan watched as the girl drifted back down the dark hallway. When she was out of sight, he swallowed heavily and stepped outside, pulling the door shut behind him.

The air was thick and heavy, without the slightest hint of a breeze. Evan thought the space around him felt constricted somehow, as if he were inside a hangar or soundstage, rather than the wide expanse of the outdoors. He wondered if there were boundaries to this universe; invisible walls that contained the house and its surroundings. It was a sound theory, but one he had no intention of testing.

This world certainly didn't include the traditional night time bodies of moon and stars. Without light from the sky above, Evan had to rely on the little bit of illumination provided by the window of the shed. It wasn't much, but he knew he would have to make the best of it. With those cevorak things lurking about, waving a flashlight around would be like turning on an attack beacon, and alerting them to fresh meat. Right now, darkness was his ally, and he would use it to his advantage.

He dodged to his left, moving through the shadow of night. Passing a rusty old swing set, he brushed against one of the seats, twisting the chain and causing the worn hinge above to creak. He grabbed the chain in a panic, silencing the sharp cry. Holding his breath, he listened and watched, praying that nothing would come charging out of the brush.

He waited for several more seconds, long enough to allow his eyes to fully adjust to his surroundings, but heard nothing. Once he could see that there were no more obstacles in his path, he stepped forward again.

That's when he noticed the scarecrows dotting the fields. There were at least twenty to thirty of them on this side alone. Unlike traditional scarecrows, which were suspended on cross-like beams, these had been impaled through their backs and stomachs on thick pointed stakes. Evan was unsure what purposed they served, as there were no crops, nor birds, for that matter, but they were gruesome. Were they intended to keep something away? Or were they just another fabrication of Walter's twisted mind?

The sight did little to strengthen his nerves. He picked up his pace, going from a slow step to a brisk walk. The shed was close now, maybe only thirty feet away. As he took another step toward it, he heard a quick rustling in the brush. Evan froze. He held fast, but there was no further movement. He took another step forward, then two. The brush was still. Whatever it was must not have seen him. He continued his steady march, keeping a close eye on the field, until he found himself at the entrance to the shed. Lifting the wood bar securing the entry, he pulled open the door and quickly slipped inside.

The interior of the shed was sparse. There were no tools hanging from pegboard, no lawnmowers, garden hoses, or any other items typically associated with such a structure. Several old oil lanterns, the source of the light seen from outside, sat on the ledge of the window to his right. At the far end of the room was another door, and next to it, an antique bird cage hung from the ceiling. Made of solid brass, with its stretched body and domed top, it was the type of cage Evan remembered seeing in the classic Looney Tunes cartoons he'd watched as a child. Judging from the size of this one, however, he doubted any cat would want to mess with the bird inside.

The cage appeared empty at first, but as he neared the door, he spied the creature inside. It hung from the brass bars with only its back side visible. The thing was anchored by six long spindly arms, which were hooked at the end, giving it an almost spider-like appearance. At around 2 feet in length, the body was split into two sections, the larger of which was roughly the size of a basketball. Apart from only having six legs, the biggest difference between the creature and an arachnid was the bony tail extending from the rear of its glossy black exoskeleton. It resembled a human spine more than anything else, each blocky section of the tail decreasing in size as it descended, coming to a serrated point at the tip.

As soon as Evan stepped up to the door and reached for the knob, the creature sprung to life, skittering around to the front of the cage. Evan jumped back, staring in horror. The color of the head matched that of the rest of the body, but the face was more human than insect. Its brow was furled, its triangular eyes black as coal. The mouth had both horizontal and vertical slits, allowing the folds of skin to flay open like a blooming flower, revealing very human upper and lower teeth, which opened and closed with the jaw. Underneath each flap of skin was a single row of pointed fangs, oozing a milky liquid. The creature started to emit a shrill chatter, its entire body shaking violently against the cage.

There was little time now, Evan realized. He'd been seen, and that creature was giving off some sort of alarm. He had to move fast before the escalating chirps of the cevorak caught Walter's attention, if it hadn't already. He twisted the knob, threw open the door, and burst into the room.

What he saw both shocked and relieved him at the same time. A dingy cot sat against the wall, with Cody lying in a fetal position on top of it. He faced the wall, as though he couldn't stand to look at the world around him. Evan rushed across the dirt floor and, as he did so, the boy curled up tighter and began to sob.

"Cody, it's alright. It's me," Evan whispered, reaching out for the small form.

The boy rolled over and his eyes fluttered open. "Evan?"

"Yeah, buddy. I'm here to take you home."

Cody jumped up and wrapped his arms around the sheriff's neck. When he pulled away, he stared in disbelief, the tears cutting clear pink tracks through the grime on his face. "How did you get here?" he asked.

"Your friend, Ellie, and a very nice man named Charlie," Evan smiled. "I can tell you more later, but right now we need to hurry."

"Okay," Cody said, hopping off of the cot.

Evan could see the shadow of the cage swaying on the wall behind Cody as the cevorak worked itself into a frenzy. Its cries had become louder, no longer angry chatter, but piercing screams. Beyond the walls of the shed, similar screams could be heard in the distance. It wouldn't be long before more arrived. They had to hurry.

"Cody, before we go, I just need to say one thing. If anything happens to me, I need you to get to the basement and find Charlie. He's waiting there to take you to your mom. Don't wait for me, just run."

Cody shook his head, in a panic. "Nothing can happen to you. You have to be okay. You have to come back with me."

"I'm going to try. But I might have to stay and fight while you go on ahead. Just get to your mom and make sure she stays safe. Can you do that for me?"

"Yes," Cody nodded, wiping his eyes with the back of his sleeve.

"Good man," Evan said. "Now let's get out of here."

He took Cody by the hand, and they made their way to the front of the shed. Cracking the door open, Evan peered outside. The fields swelled as the brush waved erratically back and forth. Thus far, the creatures hadn't breached the perimeter of the yard. They were safe, for the moment. With the path clear, Evan swung the door open and he and Cody sprinted across the lawn.

As they ran, he saw – to his surprise – an old black truck, parked near the back of the house. Its driver side door stood wide open. Had it been there all along, cloaked in the night? He certainly hadn't seen it on the way out.

Maybe, like the scarecrows, it had simply gone unnoticed. He hoped so. It would be a cruel twist of fate to outrun the cevorak, only to find someone else waiting just inside the back door.

There was a hard tug on his arm, as Cody tripped and stumbled forward. Evan yanked back to keep him from falling, but the slip slowed their momentum. The fields appeared to close in around them now, and thousands of cevorak began to flood out of the brush. They moved fast, closing the gap to mere feet. The ground shook as the beasts drew nearer, their high-pitched screams rising to earsplitting levels.

Evan and Cody pushed forward, using the last of their energy to reach the house, and bounded inside, pushing the door closed behind them. Like bugs pelting the windshield of a fast-moving car, the cevorak slammed into the other side of the door. They began to scratch, creating a wall of sound akin to rushing water, as hundreds of tiny claws dug at the wood simultaneously.

"Can they get through?" Cody asked.

"We're not going to stick around long enough to find out," Evan replied, taking the boy's hand again and starting down the hallway.

The big band music from upstairs still echoed, but only three notes played now, repeating themselves over and over.

Ba-da-da - *Thunk*. Ba-da-da - *Thunk*.

The source of the melody was likely a record spinning on an old phonograph. The needle must have become lodged within the vinyl grooves, causing the music to skip. But, who had set the record to play in the first place? And where were they now?

Half-way down the long corridor, Evan felt a drop of something wet hit his face. He dismissed it as perspiration and kept going, until another drop hit across the bridge of his nose. He reached up and felt a pool of something cool and tacky. His skin started to burn, and he came to a halt, pulling the tail of his shirt up and wiping across his face.

"What is it?" Cody asked.

"I don't know," Evan replied, pulling the flashlight off of his belt. "Something dripping from the ceiling, and it stings. Did it get on you?"

"No, I don't think so."

Evan clicked on the light and directed the beam above him. A lone cevorak hung upside down from the ceiling, the folds of skin around its mouth peeled back and quivering like the tail of a rattlesnake. Venom and saliva spewed from tooth and fang, as the creature let out a viperous hiss and hunched down on its legs.

Evan knew what was coming, but had no time to react, before the cevorak sprung from the ceiling and onto his back. He bucked and thrashed, but the creature held on. He tried slipping out of his jacket, but before he could, he felt the monster scamper down his leg. A series of barbed appendages projected from the bony vertebrae of the cevorak's tail, the spiky quills wrapping around Evan's thigh and clamping down tight. The mouth of the creature flayed open once more, the folds of skin flattening against the man's calf.

Evan cried out in pain, as the sharp fangs sank into his flesh. An icy sensation raced through his veins, and every nerve ending in his body was suddenly on fire. His knee buckled under and he fell to the ground, writhing in agony. Somewhere in the background, Cody cried out, but it was muffled, like he was lying at the bottom of a swimming pool. Evan tried to tell the boy to run, his eyes watering and jaw shaking, but the only things that came out of his mouth were short, heavy grunts.

He realized that he needed to go for his gun. It might be the only thing that worked against this creature. But he was on his side, with the weapon underneath him. He had another idea, but it wouldn't be easy. His arm twitched as he felt along the opposite side of his belt, using every ounce of his will power to keep his limbs moving. He felt as though white-hot lava was running through his veins, burning every inch of him. It was torturous to move his arm, but he kept at it, hoping for salvation. A moment later, he found what he was searching for. Sliding the Taser from its holster, he twisted around and pointed the stun gun in the vicinity of his leg. He didn't know whether the charge of the gun would even be effective, but it was the only option he had at the moment.

He blinked several times, trying to push away the heavy tears clouding his vision. Right now, the cevorak was a blur, melding seamlessly with his own leg. The last thing he needed was to miss and shoot himself. He paused, trying to focus, and took aim at the bulbous section of the creature. Then, he pulled the trigger.

The plastic blast doors flew open, and the two electrified probes fired, finding their mark. The creature reared its head back and let out a furious cry. Its body began to shake, and the thorny quills released from around Evan's leg. The thing tried to bend to Evan's leg again, but couldn't move against the stun gun's probes. It fell onto its backside and convulsed several times, finally dissolving into tiny sand-like particles, which dissipated into the air.

Evan dropped the gun and relaxed. His nerves still throbbed, but the pain was bearable. "It worked," he mumbled. "It actually worked."

The feeling of having cotton stuffed in his ears started to fade now, and he could hear the sound of the wavering music droning on.

Ba-da-da - *Thunk*. Ba-da-da - *Thunk*.

He felt Cody's small hands on his arm, and looked to see the boy kneeling down beside him. "Are you okay?" he cried.

"Yeah, I think so. But you should have run. We talked about this, remember? I need you to stay safe, Cody. We're almost there. Do you think you can make it the rest of the way?"

"But you have to come with me. You can't stay here. He'll hurt you."

Evan pushed himself up into a sitting position and placed his back against the wall. The pain in his body continued to subside, but his leg was still numb. He wouldn't be able to walk. At least not yet. "I just need a few minutes to recover. But I don't want you to wait. This is your chance to get home. Your mom is waiting for you."

"She's waiting for you, too! She'll be sad if you don't come back. And so will I!" the boy wailed.

Evan reached up and gave him a firm pat on the shoulder. "Okay, tell you what, I'll see if I can stand, but walking isn't going to be easy. You think you're strong enough to be my other leg?"

"Yeah, I can do that."

Evan leaned into the wall, and pushed up with his good leg, while Cody steadied him on the other side. "You ready?"

The boy nodded and Evan took a step. He kept one hand near the wall in case he fell, but Cody's timing was in perfect sync with his own, and the boy was providing as much support as he could. They began making their way slowly down the hall, increasing their pace as Evan's leg continued to hold him.

They were almost to the end of the hall when the music from upstairs came to an abrupt halt. Evan stiffened. There wasn't a single noise to be heard throughout the house now, as even the cevorak had ceased their incessant clawing at the back door. The resulting stillness set him on edge, for he sensed it was merely a precursor to the appearance of some other, more hostile, force. The sudden lack of music felt like the lull before the storm. He pushed on faster, urging Cody with his mind. They had to get to that basement, and fast.

A low hum broke the silence. It was the sound of the luminous mass Evan had seen earlier, that slithering chunk of plasma acting as an incandescent bulb. The thing was charging again, feeding off the tense current that rippled through the air. Shadows receded along the wall, as the buzzing intensified. The shimmering lump blazed brighter, and the hairs on Evan's neck stood on end. He realized that someone was behind them.

Cody must have felt it, too, for he swiveled around to look, and belted out a petrified scream. "It's him!" he clamored. "It's Walter!"

Evan turned to see the dark hulking figure of a man standing at the far end of the hall. The shape lifted its arms, which began to grow, elongating to twice the length of its body, while the hands transformed into razor-sharp talons. Lashing outwards, the tentacles gouged the wall, ripping through the fleshy exterior, and sinking in like a pair of grappling hooks. Walter's body leveraged itself into the air, suspended by the long arms. The legs followed suit and, like the arms, changed into protracted hooks that anchored into the wall. One by one, the limbs began to move, propelling the man along the wall like some giant insect.

"Cody, you have to go!" Evan screamed. "There's no way I can run, even with your help. You need to get to the basement!" Panicked, he turned and pushed the boy in that direction, hoping he would run for it.

Cody took a few steps backwards and started to cry again, his eyes pleading with Evan to come with him.

"I'll be fine. Just go. Run!"

Cody hesitated a second more, and then turned and ran for the basement door.

Walter's mouth opened, stretching ever wider, until it became a gaping hole as wide as the hallway itself. A serpentine tongue shot forth and wrapped around the sheriff's ankle, yanking him to the floor and pulling him backwards.

Opening the door to the basement, Cody took one last look behind him, and watched as Evan disappeared into a mouth of darkness. Turning away from the sight, he ran down the stairs to safety, all the while sobbing for the friend he was sure he would never see again.

CHAPTER 26

Leslie jumped up from the stair she was perched on and watched with bated breath. The surface of the mirror had illuminated, emitting several quick flashes, as the glass softened into a rippling pool of silver. Something was happening on the other side.

This was it, she realized. All the days and weeks of agonizing over the well-being of her son culminated in this one final moment. In the next second, she would either experience the most wonderful reunion of her life, or be dealt the worst heartache imaginable. The waiting was dizzying. And then, he was there, emerging from the mirror with rumpled clothes, grubby skin, and hair in disarray. Leslie had never seen a sweeter sight.

"Mom!" he yelled, running toward her.

Leslie knelt down and opened her arms wide, a flood of joyous tears streaming down her cheeks. When Cody reached her, the force of his eager embrace nearly knocked her off her feet. She laughed, and held him tighter than ever, kissing the top of his head over and over.

"Let me look at you," she said, pulling away and eyeing him up and down. "Are you okay? Were you hurt at all?"

No, I'm fine," Cody replied, shaking his head.

He was thinner, and covered in a good deal of filth, both of which gave him the appearance of an orphan who'd been living on the streets. It was nothing a hot bath and a couple of good meals couldn't fix though.

Leslie pulled him to her once more and squeezed tight. "I missed you so much," she said, nuzzling her cheek against his head. Her heart was aflutter, seeming to dance within her chest, while all of the pain and anxiety of the past few weeks melted away. Cody was home. She had dreamt of this moment every day since his disappearance, and had begun to fear it would never come. But now, here he was, unharmed and back in her arms. Never in her life had she been more grateful. And, though nothing could diminish the joy she felt at having her son back, the celebration itself was short lived.

Glancing up, she noticed Charlie standing near the mirror with his hands folded in front of him. There was a cautious grin on his face, as he delighted in the reunion, but Leslie could see that the smile masked a deeper and grimmer emotion.

"Evan," she whispered, realizing that he wasn't in the room. "Where's Evan? What happened to him? Are you going back?"

Cody looked up and uttered a single word, before his face turned flush with grief. "Walter," he said, burying his head against his mother's shoulder.

Leslie's eyes darted back to Charlie, and he met her stare, shaking his head as if to say he were sorry. She didn't need to ask what happened, for she already knew. Evan had kept his promise to her, though it meant sacrificing himself to do so. A wave of shock and sadness came crashing down, and Leslie dropped her head in mourning. Though she had tried hard to mentally prepare herself for the possibility he might not return from the journey through the mirror, there was no way to prepare her heart for such a loss. In that moment, she realized just how much she had grown to love this man, and now couldn't imagine having to live life without him. The agony seared her insides and she began to sob.

"I think we have some more company," Harriet said in a gentle manner.

Charlie turned to see shadows of his past reflected in the mirror; faces he hadn't seen since he was a boy. One by one, they stepped out from behind the glass and ambled past him. All but the last one who, upon entering the room, stood and eyed him with a mixture of curiosity and enchantment. Her head tilted to the side, and her bottom lip trembled when she spoke.

"Charlie?" Ellie asked.

Beyond the raven hollows surrounding her eyes, Charlie could see two soft pools of blue. They exuded a gentleness that even sixty years of being in Walter's prison hadn't erased. It had been ages since he'd been entranced by those eyes, yet still they had the power to hold him captive and make him weak in the knees.

"Yes," he replied, swallowing the lump in his throat. "Hello, Ellie. It really is you, isn't it? After all this time, you're still here."

Charlie had hoped he would see her during his time in the house, even if it were only a glimpse, just to confirm what he already knew deep down – that she was, in fact, the girl others had seen recently; the same one who had called out to him only yesterday. Now that she was standing in front of him, the sudden flood of emotion had him reeling.

He was euphoric at seeing her face again, but the dreamy elation was tempered by the guilt he felt over her death. Looking at her now, with her veil of bleak sorrow, he wondered what she was feeling. He couldn't help but think she had a very different view of him than she did prior to that day in the cemetery. It hurt to think it, but he wouldn't have been surprised if she hated him for what he had done. "Can you ever forgive me?" he asked.

Ellie started to extend a hand towards him and then stopped, turning to face the mirror. She stood in silence for several seconds, and then began to back away.

An ominous low rumble filled the room, followed moments later by a thunderous crack. The reverberation sounded like cannon shot, and created a shock wave that knocked Charlie to the ground. There was a flash of light, and the silvery tides of the mirror's surface pulled back as a figure stepped from behind the glass.

"Evan?" Leslie uttered in amazement. She cupped her hands over her mouth, half crying and half laughing from the sense of relief she felt at seeing him alive. He looked her direction and smiled. Then, she looked more closely, and her face drew down into a frown.

Cody began to bellow out in excitement and moved to run towards the Sheriff, but Leslie grabbed him by the arm and pulled him back. "Wait, Cody. Something's not right."

"What do you mean, Mom? It's just Evan. Aren't you glad to see him?"

"Yes," Evan replied. "Aren't you happy to see me? Why don't you let the boy come say hello?"

There was an odd inflection in his tone that sounded off kilter, but even if he hadn't spoken a word, Leslie would have known that it wasn't Evan standing in the basement. She had seen it the moment he looked her way. Brown eyes that were once warm and inviting had been displaced by cold, black pits. Though they hid beneath a different mask now, these were the same deviant eyes that had stared her down in the diner just hours ago. These were Walter's eyes.

Charlie must have known as well. Picking himself up off the floor, he shot a knowing glance in Leslie's direction and nodded toward the top of the staircase, inferring that she should go. She had no sooner reached for Cody's hand and risen to her feet, than Evan was on the move. He raised an arm to shove Charlie out of his path, but the old man held firm.

"No more. You can hide behind others all you want, but I know who you are, Walter."

The sheriff turned to study Charlie through narrow slits of eyes, and licked his lips, as if he were about to take a meal. He raised an eyebrow, and his mouth turned up in a wide devilish grin. "Hmm, and I know you. The little paperboy that used to come to my door. Did you come to collect?" he asked, cackling.

"That was me. But, I'm not a little boy anymore. And I'm not afraid of you."

"Oh, but you really should be."

"The boy stays with his mother, even if it takes every ounce of life in me to wrestle you back into that hell you crawled out of."

"You can't have what's mine, paperboy. I won't let you leave empty handed, though. I do have something to give you," Evan snarled, pressing the cold steel muzzle of his pistol into Charlie's abdomen, and pulling the trigger.

The blast shook the rafters, and the bullet tore through the old man, exiting his back in a crimson spray and lodging into the stone wall of the basement.

Charlie's insides felt as if someone had impaled him with a red hot poker. He stumbled backwards and clutched his stomach, feeling warm gushes of blood spurt from between his fingers. A woman's scream penetrated the ringing in his ears, but it sounded distant, and he was unsure who it had come from. The searing pain intensified and he fell back, knocking into the wall and sliding downwards, leaving a glistening red trail along the gray stone. He tried to look around him, but everything was a blur. "Leslie," he muttered through labored breaths. His voice was thin and barely audible. "Go now. Go."

The moment Evan had fired the shot, Leslie and Cody had already started running up the stairs. They were only two steps away from the door now, which suddenly flung itself shut. Leslie twisted the knob back and forth, to no avail. The latch wouldn't open. She rammed the door several times with her shoulder, using the full force of her body weight, but it still didn't budge. She turned to see Evan shaking his index finger at her in a back and forth motion, scolding her for running.

He turned his attention back to Charlie, walking over and placing a foot on the man's wound. Charlie cried out through clenched teeth, and Evan pulled back, bursting into a fit of maniacal laughter. "Oh, and by the way," he cooed. "That woman up there is not my boy's mother. No, his mother rots in the ground, and I use her skin to decorate my walls. I think I'm going to do the same with you."

The last thing Charlie heard was the click of the hammer being pulled back. Then, the gun fired, and the world around him disappeared.

Evan pulled the weapon away from the old man's limp body and turned his gaze toward Leslie. His smile broadened and he gave her a wink. "Oh, and the things I've got in store for you."

"I'm not so sure that's a good idea, Mr. Conley," Harriet said. The woman possessed a calm assurance and, despite the fact that someone had just been slaughtered a few feet from her, she seemed to have no fear. Her voice was as light and airy as ever.

Evan stopped and turned toward the woman. He didn't raise the weapon or move her direction, but stood with his gaze fixed. He studied her, as one might study the face of someone they recognized, but whose name could not be placed.

"You can't hurt the woman. Not hardly. You picked the wrong body for that. You didn't learn your lesson at the diner, did you?"

"What do you know?" Evan scoffed. "When I'm done with her I'll tear the lids from your eyes, flay the skin from your body, and hang you in my field to be feasted upon. You can watch while your bones are picked clean." He lifted his nose and sniffed at the air, taking in three long whiffs, and then nodding in approval. "Oh, yes, they'll like you for sure."

Harriet loosed a hearty chuckle, which shook her entire body from the waist up. It was the sort of whimsical laugh one might hear from a grandmother, whose grandchild had just said something amusing. "I'm afraid it's you who understands very little. Why do you think it is that you were unsuccessful in doing away with Ms. Bradford in the diner? Because Arthur cared for her like a daughter, and when she called to him, he fought to save her. His adoration made it impossible for you to carry out your will. And now, you're inside of a man who loves her deeper than anyone ever has. How much harder do you think he'll fight? You see, love is more powerful than you ever will be, Mr. Conley. In life *and* in death."

"Well, well, well. I guess I'll just free myself of this body and use yours instead then," the sheriff replied, raising the gun to his head.

"Evan, no!" Leslie cried.

He cocked the pistol and flashed a smug grin at her. "Bye-bye, lover," he crowed. "You–"

He stopped mid-sentence, and the smile disappeared from his face. The room had started to vibrate, and the air filled with a soft ringing, reminiscent of wind chimes. A delicate breeze stirred, and the ringing became louder, until the sound was that of hundreds of pairs of chimes playing in unison. Years' worth of old dirt and dust sifted through the slats of the wood decking above the room as the vibrations intensified.

"Whoever you are, old woman, you can spare me your tricks," the sheriff ground out, looking around.

"This is no magic show. You have done exactly what I expected you would, Mr. Conley, and now, the time of your reckoning has come."

The shaking stopped, and a wide beam of brilliant light filled the center of the room. A round luminous orb, the size of a baseball, floated out from within the bright rays, gliding through the air and zigzagging around the basement several times, before coming to a stop in front of Harriet.

"Is it an angel, Mom?" Cody asked.

"I...I don't know," Leslie stammered.

She was mesmerized, as the hovering orb started to twinkle and flash, becoming a dazzling show of light unlike anything she had ever seen.

Harriet lifted an arm, and the orb settled over the palm of her hand. The woman turned to the children, who had taken refuge behind her, and smiled a gracious smile. "It's time, children," she said warmly.

The orb moved from Harriet's palm and floated over to Ellie, where its glow increased tenfold, ablaze with shimmering pulses of light that were almost too bright to look at. The girl breathed in the life force emitted by the orb, and tears streamed down her bruised face.

"Charlie," she whispered.

For the first time in sixty years, tragedy's grip broke its hold on her, and she smiled, big and wide. The dark circles around her eyes started to fade, and skin that had been cold and blue, became vibrant and rosy. Clothes that were muddied and torn, became new again, the mask of brutality falling away to reveal the innocence and beauty of the child underneath.

Sandy and Billy followed, each transformed into souls that were as youthful, whole, and happy as they had been when they were alive. The shackles of fear, which had bound them for so long, were broken, allowing them to see that they were free, and possessed a power none previously knew they had; the power to rule over darkness.

Billy, who had been timid and scared in death, was the first to step forward. He looked the sheriff in the eye, seeing past Evan to the man who hid beneath, the one who had taken his life when he was but a boy. "You can't hurt me anymore," he said, bold and confident. "You'll never hurt anyone, ever again."

Evan's body flew back into the wall, back arched and limbs flailing. His mouth dropped open, and a black mist poured out, billowing like smoke from a coal-fired engine. Once the thick fog had emptied from the sheriff, he slumped forward, hitting the ground on all fours and gasping for fresh air.

The dense cloud funneled downward, stretching and changing, until it had formed the dark silhouette of an enormous gorilla-like man. The shape moved forward and belted out an angry feral roar, directed at the children trying to escape his grasp.

Billy was undeterred, pushing past Harriet to face the beast head on. He lit up, radiating with a bright orange glow. Lifting his hand, tiny balls of light emanated from his fingers and propelled themselves across the room into the massive black shape. The luminous spheres were like acid, burning holes through the inky mass.

Walter shrunk back, and doubled over in agony and rage. He regained his strength and charged forward in a furor. Ellie and Sandy moved to Billy's side and followed his lead, collectively sending thousands of starry spheres into the air. The light wrapped around Walter, stopping him in his tracks and lifting him off the ground, writhing and screaming.

Ellie pulled her arm back and thrust her hand forward. In one quick flash, Walter was catapulted through the portal behind him with a massive boom. The surface of the mirror erupted in a spray of shattering glass, while the frame buckled and splintered into pieces. The glowing light around the children ceased, as the last of the shards clinked to the ground, and the room went still.

Then, the orb brightened again, elongating and changing until it was no longer a circle of light, but a young boy.

"Charlie!" Ellie squealed, throwing her arms around his neck. "You came back for me!"

"Of course I did. I only wish it had been sooner. Ellie, I'm so sorry."

"For what?"

"That day back in the cemetery. I shouldn't have taken you through there, and I've never been able to forgive myself for what happened. I was sure that if I ever saw you again, you'd hate me."

Ellie grabbed Charlie's hands and gave them an affectionate squeeze. "It's not your fault. You didn't know. There's nothing to forgive."

"But, I should have saved you," Charlie replied, lowering his head.

Ellie placed a finger under his chin, rose up on her toes, and touched her lips to his. "Silly boy," she replied. "You just did."

Charlie looked into the eyes of the girl he had missed for so long, and smiled. He wasn't sure what waited in the afterlife, but it didn't matter. He had Ellie again, and whatever there was to see and experience, they would discover it together, which is exactly how he had always wanted it to be.

"Charlie?" Evan asked. He was still on his hands and knees a few feet away, coughing and trying to catch his breath.

"Hello, Sheriff. I'm glad to see you're alright."

"Yeah, I wish I could say the same to you," Evan replied, glancing quickly at the body lying against the back wall. "Charlie, I don't even know where to start. No apology could ever begin to be enough."

"It wasn't you who did it. Besides, I'm right where I want to be," Charlie said, glancing over at Ellie. "There will be questions about what happened here, though. I want you to tell people I'm the one who took Cody. Say I attacked, and you had to shoot me."

"Charlie, I can't do that. Your memory would be tarnished."

"What memory? I have no family left, nobody close that would be impacted. The only people who matter are in this room, and you'll always know the truth. What anyone else thinks is of no consequence. I have a new life now."

"Sure, but I mean —"

"You're an honorable man, Sheriff. Don't end up on trial for something you didn't do. You have Leslie and Cody to think about now. They need you more than you know."

"Okay, Charlie," Evan nodded. "Okay."

The beam in the center of the room amplified then, and the soft chimes played their graceful melody once more. As if called by the music, Billy and Sandy stepped into the light and were transformed into splendorous orbs, which danced and twirled about in a playful fashion before fading away.

"I think that's our cue. You ready to go home?" Charlie asked, extending his hand toward Ellie.

"I guess this is goodbye, then," Evan said.

"For now. Just for now," Charlie replied.

"Can I ask just one thing before you go? If either of you should see my son, if you see Ryan, would you tell him his dad said hello, and that I miss him?"

Ellie smiled and knelt down beside him, placing a hand on his cheek. Her touch radiated with warmth that spread through his body and calmed his spirit. Though she didn't speak a word, he found that she didn't have to. By some unseen connection, and the expression on her face, Evan knew that she had just seen inside his soul.

"You were a good dad," she said.

Evan knew there was power in words, but none had ever hit him with the force of these five. He had heard them countless times after Ryan's death. Even Leslie had said the same thing after she'd heard his story, and tried to comfort him. And, though he knew every one of those people had meant what they'd said, and that there was no lack of sincerity on their part, there was a raw honesty in the words of this little girl that was unmatched. She said what she did, not because she felt bad and wanted to make him feel better, but because she had looked into the very depths of who he was, had seen memories and quiet moments shared only between he and his son, and saw his thoughts, his worries, and even his very heart.

"I'll tell him. And, I'll tell him about everything you did for us as well."

"Thank you, Ellie."

The girl nodded and then stood, taking Charlie by the hand. "So, do you think there's ice cream where we're going?" she asked, smiling.

"I don't know," Charlie said, shrugging. "If not, I bet there's something even better. Why do you ask?"

"Because, you still owe me two scoops."

Evan watched as the two of them walked into the light and disappeared, the faint echo of their laughter lingering even after the bright beam faded away. His attention quickly turned to the staircase, where he saw Leslie running toward him with Cody close behind.

"Are you alright?" she gasped.

"I think so. A bit light headed, but I'm alive. Are you both okay?"

"Yeah. Yeah, we are," Leslie replied, wrapping her arms around him. "I thought I'd lost you."

"I thought so, too. But, I guess I'm a hard man to get rid of."

"That's good, because I was hoping you might stick around for a while."

"I think that could be arranged," Evan replied. He held her head in his hands, and they stared long and hard into each other's eyes.

"Are you two gonna kiss?" Cody asked with a heavy sigh.

"Cody Allen!" Leslie exclaimed, her face turning bright red.

"It's okay, Mom. That's what grown up people do. I just don't wanna watch."

"Alright," Evan chuckled. "If it looks like that's about to happen, I'll be sure and give you fair warning."

"Well, kissing aside, thank you, Evan. Thank you so much for bringing Cody back to me," Leslie said.

"You're more than welcome. I can't take all the credit, though. You've got Charlie, Ellie, and Harriet to thank as well."

"Oh, yes! I can't forget about you, Harriet," she said. She turned around to express her gratitude, but the old woman was gone. A quick check of the staircase and the surrounding basement turned up nothing. "That's really strange. She was just here a minute ago."

"Maybe she didn't want to be around when the kissing started, either," Evan grinned.

"Funny. But in all seriousness, where could she have gone?"

"I'm sure she didn't go too far. Probably had to run upstairs to the bathroom, or out to get some fresh air, both of which I could go for as well."

"Alright then, mister," Leslie said, putting her arm around her son. "You about ready to go home?"

"I don't know," he frowned. "I really think I need a vacation."

"You and me both, kiddo," Leslie laughed. "You and me both."

CHAPTER 27

November 18, 2010

They were serving lunch on Dan's floor when Evan arrived at the hospital. Roast turkey, from the smell of it. But, with the ever-present sterile odor in the building, it was hard to say with any real accuracy.

It dawned on Evan that the anxiety that usually greeted him when he entered the hospital wasn't present. Perhaps it was the food tempering the other aromas he so despised. Or, maybe, having gone to a pseudo-hell days ago made this place look like Disneyland in comparison. Either way, he was grateful.

Dan's door was open, and Evan popped his head inside. The deputy was sitting upright in bed, with a blanket up to his chest, while a soap opera blared from the television on the wall.

"Knock, knock," Evan said.

"Hey, there! Look who came to visit."

"Interesting choice. Franny would be proud," the sheriff remarked, gesturing toward the tube. "You two will have a lot more to talk about when you come back to work."

Dan shook his head ruefully. "There's not shit on this time of day. It's this, or stare at the walls, and the walls are starting to look mighty appealing. I don't know how that woman can like this stuff," he replied. He reached over and punched a button on the bed rail to turn off the television. "Good to see you, boss."

"How are you feeling, big man?"

"Oh, I'm a bit sore around the ribs, and my face looks like I went twenty rounds in the ring, but I'm doing alright. Could be the meds making me think that, though. I've got enough of those in me to stay pain free for the next 2 years," Dan jested.

"At least there's no permanent damage. And, from what you said earlier, no memory loss either?"

"None that I know of. Wouldn't mind forgetting a few things, though. Every time I see wheelchairs go down the hall, I about come unglued."

Evan laughed. "If it hadn't been for those stairs, and your big clumsy feet, I'm sure you'd have made that chair your bitch."

Dan threw his head back and roared with laughter, only to grab his side and wince in pain seconds later. "Oh, this sucks," he said, still chuckling. "I can't laugh, cough, or even crap, without feeling like someone is sticking a knife in me. So how are Leslie and Cody?"

"They're both well. To see Cody, you wouldn't even know he's been through such a traumatic event. It's remarkable, really. He remembers some things about Ellie and the other children, but the rest of the ordeal, it's like it never happened."

"That's not such a bad thing. You think he just repressed it all?"

"I don't know. Leslie considered talking to a therapist, but was afraid there might be too many questions. If the supernatural aspect came into play, she thought they might want to have her committed."

"But Cody isn't suffering any negative effects?"

"No, he's just as happy as can be."

"Glad to hear it. From what I saw before my fall, and from what you told me on the phone about your experience, it's probably better he doesn't remember."

The door to the room opened then, and a heavyset woman wearing purple scrubs entered with a tray of food. She set it on an adjustable lap table in front of Dan, replenished his water pitcher from a nearby tap, and returned to fill his plastic drinking cup. "You need anything else right now?" she asked.

"Actually, yes," Evan said, picking up a thermometer from the sink area and waving it in the air. "We need to check this patient's temperature rectally, but this just won't do. Could you please inform the doctor we're going to need something much larger?"

"Oh God, stop it!" Dan howled. His face turned a deep crimson shade from a mix of embarrassment, laughter, and pain.

The woman rolled her eyes and headed for the door. "You're gonna have to get someone else for that. I'm not a nurse, and I definitely do not work on that end."

As soon as the woman was out the door, Dan hurled an empty cup at Evan. The sheriff stepped to the side, dodging the projectile and laughing like a college kid who had just pulled the ultimate prank.

"Has Leslie seen this side of you yet?" Dan wheezed.

"Now that things have returned to normal, she's starting to. They say it's best to just be yourself, right?"

"That's good advice for everyone but you. But then, she's still around, so maybe it's love after all."

"So it would appear, my friend," Evan grinned.

Dan pulled the metal cover off of his plate and stared at the contents. Evan had been right about the roast turkey, though it looked far less appetizing than it smelled. It was joined by green beans, that were more olive than green, and mashed potatoes and gravy, which appeared stiffer and starchier than a shirt from the dry cleaner.

"Would you look at that? Is it any wonder I'm wasting away in here? I think the prisoners in county get better than this slop."

Evan agreed with Dan's assessment that hospital food was bad, but if the man had lost weight during his stay here, who could tell? "At least you'll be home in time for the holidays," he noted.

"Now there's something to be thankful for," Dan replied, forcing down a bite of potatoes. "So, on the phone, you said you had something you wanted me to see?"

"Right. How much did you learn about Harriet the night you met her?"

"Not much. She mentioned she was just passing through, but never did say where she was from, or where she was going, for that matter. I probably should have asked, but I was dumbstruck when she told me about the vision of Ellie and how it related to Cody."

"Did she mention where she was staying?"

"Sure. The Red Wagon Inn. Room 218."

"Yeah, that's what she wrote on the back of the card Linda gave me. When I got to the motel, Harriet was sitting on a bench outside. She got in the car and I interviewed her over coffee at the diner."

"That doesn't sound so unusual."

"No, but after her stealthy exit from the basement, I wanted to stop by and thank her before she left town. There was no one in room 218."

"Maybe she wrote down the wrong number."

"Possible. But when I went to the office and spoke with Rosalie, she said room 218 hadn't been used all week. In fact, only a handful of rooms had been rented during that time, and none of the guests matched Harriet's description. I checked the registry and compared the names against the tag numbers of the vehicles. They all checked out."

"Didn't Rosalie see you pull in the lot the day you picked Harriet up?"

"No, nor did she see a woman sitting on the bench. But, according to her, she stays in the back and watches television unless someone comes into the office."

"So, you're thinking that Harriet never stayed there. Why would she say she did?"

"I have no idea. But I'm certain she knew more about what happened in 1950 than she let on."

"How's that?"

Evan walked over to the counter, where he had set the manila envelope, and picked it up. "I had the old case files pulled from the archives, but hadn't had a chance to look through any of them until today. When I did, let's just say I got quite a shock."

He reached in and pulled a photo from the envelope and handed it to Dan. The deputy looked at the image for a second or two and shook his head. "Looks like the outside of Walter's house. I see bodies of the victims being wheeled out on gurneys."

"Keep looking," Evan said.

Dan saw an officer holding a lady back. The woman was crying, and looked like she was about to collapse. He guessed her to be the mother of one of the children. Beyond her, was a group of onlookers watching from behind a blockade. Of all the faces in the crowd, he recognized only one. It was Harriet.

"Dear God, how is that possible? How old should she have been back then?"

"I'm guessing between ten and sixteen, give or take, given her age now, " Evan replied.

"But, she's an old woman in this photo. She looks like she's the same age she was when I saw her in the diner." He stopped and looked up at Evan, his mouth hanging open. "Who is this woman?"

"Don't know. Whoever she is, I don't think she was here by accident. She knew all along what was going on."

Dan shook his head quietly, trying to take it all in. "So, what now, boss? You going to try to find her? Or at least find out who she really is?"

Evan walked over to the window and gazed outside, saying nothing for several long seconds.

"Boss? Something wrong?" Dan asked.

Evan shook his head. "No, Dan. On the contrary, everything is right. I think I'm going to leave well enough alone. File this away in the archive and pretend I never saw it. I don't have a clue who Harriet is, and quite frankly, I don't think I want to. What I do know, is that she's on our side and, in the end, that's all that really matters."

CHAPTER 28

December 25, 2010

Evan sat up in bed and looked around the room. The sun was just beginning to filter through the blinds, projecting thin strips of light across his lap. Outside the window, he heard a car pull up to his neighbor's house and someone shout, "Merry Christmas!" A door opened, and there was a jubilant mix of conversation and children's laughter.

A child's laugh.

Evan glanced over to the other side of the bed. It was empty.

Another dream. Of course it was. Just because it had ended differently than every other time didn't change the fact that it wasn't real. Ryan was still gone.

The vision had started out the same. He'd woken up in the middle of the night to a noise, and climbed out of bed to investigate. The bathroom door was ajar, a sliver of yellow light spilling from behind it. At first, he thought it might be Leslie or Cody, but he'd peered into their rooms as he made his way down the hall, and found them both fast asleep.

The sound of dripping water came from the bathroom ahead, and Evan had felt his breath catch in his throat. *Please, not again,* he thought. The nightmare hadn't haunted his sleep since the night of the Fall Festival, and he'd thought – hoped, actually – that it had gone for good.

Now it looked like it hadn't. A thin layer of perspiration coated his body as he neared the door. There was an awareness that he was walking through a dream, but, even so, he couldn't will himself awake. Something beyond his control always propelled him onward, forcing him to look upon the outcome of his carelessness a thousand times over.

The door swung open when he got to it, and he stepped inside the bathroom. The shower curtain was pulled closed. It seemed to taunt Evan, daring him to turn his back on the horror it concealed, yet knowing full well the man had no choice but to look.

Drip ... Drip

Evan walked forward and yanked the curtain back. The water in the tub rippled, and small streams snaked over the porcelain edge onto the floor. He expected to see his boy staring up at him from under the clear liquid, as he usually did, but outside of the water, the tub was empty.

What? This wasn't how it went. How could it be different?

He reached slowly into the tub and pulled the drain plug, wondering what this was about. The water level started to abate, and something stirred behind him on the other side of the room. He whipped around, and was stunned at what he saw.

Ryan stood in the doorway. Clad in pajamas, the boy held a picture book in one hand, and clutched a one-eared bunny with the other. "I'm sleepy, Daddy. Will you read me a book?" he murmured.

Evan's heart hammered, rendering him speechless. How long had it been since he'd heard those words? For a moment he questioned whether this was a dream or reality, but the memory of losing his son was still with him. It had to be a dream. Only this time, he was seeing Ryan the way he wanted to remember him. Not a lifeless body in the bottom of a tub, but the sweet, gentle soul he loved so much. "Hey, buddy, of course I will. Come on, let's go downstairs.'

Ryan opened his arms, and Evan scooped him up, planting a long kiss on his forehead. He could feel his son's little heartbeat strumming against him and was overcome with a rush of emotion. He hadn't felt this way since the day Ryan was born, the day he'd held his son for the very first time.

"You 'kay, Daddy? Why you crying?"

"Yeah, I'm okay. I'm just very glad to see you. These are happy tears."

Ryan smiled and held up his bunny. "Max, happy tears, too?"

"You bet," Evan replied. "It's always good to see Max. Does he want to hear a story also?"

"Uh-huh," Ryan nodded.

"Well, let's go."

After making their way downstairs, Ryan settled into his dad's lap and thrust his book forward. He had always been fond of Curious George, Dr. Suess, and the classic Richard Scarry picture books. Tonight was no exception. He had selected *How the Grinch Stole Christmas*, which Evan found fitting, given that it was Christmas Eve.

Evan began to read, and Ryan listened with rapt attention. It was customary for Evan to read in an animated fashion, crafting voices for each character and acting silly in order to bring the story to life. Ryan would light up and giggle with the best impersonations. "Say again," he'd remark, and then laugh even harder when Evan complied.

After the story was finished, Ryan asked to hear it twice more. It wasn't until the third round that his eyes grew heavy, and he started to yawn.

"Ready to get tucked in?" Evan asked.

The boy nodded, and hopped down from the couch. He bounced across the room towards the stairs, bare feet pattering against the wood floor, while Max swung to and fro from his one and only ear.

Evan followed, catching up to his son and carrying him to the bedroom, where he nestled him under the blankets and kissed him on the cheek.

"Max kiss," Ryan said, holding his rabbit up and laughing.

"Max, too?" Evan asked with mock surprise.

"Yes!"

Evan took the rabbit and gave it a kiss. "What's that, Max?" he asked, putting the bunny up to his ear, as if he were listening to something the animal had to say. "Ohh, you think I should give Ryan monster kisses?"

Ryan's eyes widened, and he threw the blankets over his head. Evan leaned in, giving exaggerated kisses all over the face and neck of the boy squirming underneath the covers. "Nom-nom-nom," he said, while his son squealed with laughter.

When Ryan poked his head out a moment later, his hair was a mess, and he wore a wide grin. He snatched Max back and coddled him in his arms, before reaching up and placing a hand on Evan's cheek. "I love you, Daddy."

Evan thought about the story he'd just read, and how the Grinch's heart had grown three sizes on Christmas Day. In that moment, he felt his had done the same. "I love you, too, buddy. You always remember that, okay?"

Ryan nodded his head and then rolled over on his side. Evan clicked off the lamp on the nightstand and lie in the dark, arm around his son, until they both drifted off to sleep.

Now, it was morning, and as Evan sat on the edge of the bed recalling every vivid moment of the dream, he smiled. He felt strangely liberated and, though he wished Ryan were still with him, he had a sense of peace for the first time since his son's death. In some small way, he had finally been able to say goodbye, and wherever Ryan was now, Evan knew Charlie and Ellie were there to watch over him.

He stood and walked to the window. The car he'd heard earlier was parked in his neighbor's driveway. An elderly woman stood with the trunk open while several children, their faces beaming with excitement, unloaded wrapped boxes and carried them inside the house.

He thought about his own Christmas memories as a child, and how he would wake his parents at the crack of dawn, often before the sun was even up, to remind them what day it was. Certainly, there was no time for sleeping when gifts were waiting to be opened.

The holiday always had a special magic when he was young, and while it was still his favorite day, the sense of wonder had faded as he got older. But, with Leslie and Cody in his life now, that had all changed. He found himself delighting in the sights and sounds of the holidays in much the same way he had as a child. Coming home each night to lights on the tree, the scent of pine lingering in the air, and age-old carols playing on the stereo always lifted his spirits. Best of all, though, was seeing the enthusiasm in Cody's eyes and spending time with the two people he cared most for.

Speaking of Cody, Evan wondered why the house was so quiet. A check of the boy's room revealed that he was still in bed. That shouldn't have come as much of a surprise. He was a late sleeper, just like his mother. Even the lure of Christmas morning wasn't enough to rouse him before he was good and ready.

Evan slipped downstairs and started a pot of coffee. He set out a couple of mugs, pulled some eggs from the refrigerator, and grabbed a loaf of bread from the pantry. Twenty minutes later, he popped a pan of cinnamon pecan French toast into the oven and hurried back upstairs. It was only 8:30, which meant he probably had time to shower before anyone else was up.

He collected a towel from the linen closet and returned to his room, tripping over something on the floor. Turning to see what was there, Evan came to an abrupt halt. He dropped the towel he was carrying, and crumbled to his knees. His body started to tremble and hot tears collected in the corners of his eyes. He blinked several times, thinking he must be seeing things. But, there on the floor in front of him, just as real as could be, was a gift — an object of a child's affection left behind to let his father know everything was alright. It was a worn, one-eared bunny named Max.

EPILOGUE

June 2011

Seven months after the autumn tragedies, the residents of Milford Springs still had questions. Questions for which there were no answers. By now, the population at large had resigned themselves to the fact that the events of October and November were an enigma, and doubted there would ever be an adequate explanation.

The media coverage surrounding the deaths and the kidnapping was less intrusive than Evan expected, lasting only a couple of weeks. A few of the more tenacious reporters hung around a little while longer, interviewing anyone old enough to talk, and hoping to find the one missing piece of information that would blow the case wide open. All went home without their exclusive.

Charlie had become the main target of the investigations, which inevitably brought the murders of 1950 back to light. Though there was nothing to indicate why he would have kidnapped Cody and returned later to attack Leslie, the correlations to the past didn't go unnoticed. Theories abounded as to how the original abductions, and that of the Bradford boy, were connected. Given that Charlie had been present when Ellie was taken, some speculated that he'd always been unstable, and may have assisted Walter in his crimes by baiting the other children. Others believed the memories of what he'd witnessed, and the subsequent guilt afterwards, were simply too much, chipping away at his psyche over the years until he snapped.

Regardless of which theory one chose to believe, few doubted that Charlie was responsible for Cody's kidnapping, including Mayor Bob Patterson. He accepted the account of Charlie attacking Leslie in the basement, and Evan saving the woman and her son, which allowed Evan to keep his job. Protocol dictated a short suspension while the state board investigated, but they concluded that the sheriff had acted in accordance with the law, and found the shooting to be justified.

The other question, and perhaps the bigger mystery, was what had driven Henry and Arthur to insanity, and led them to murder with no apparent motive. Even more frightening, was the fact that both instances had occurred only weeks apart. Some cried mad cow disease or rabies, despite the lack of evidence that either of those could lead to a sudden onset of homicidal tendencies. Others placed the blame on genetically modified foods or pesticides in the water - still a stretch for such extreme behavior.

Arthur himself shed little light on the situation, having passed away during a skin grafting operation. His last days leading up to the surgery were spent restrained in a hospital bed, staring out the window without ever speaking a single word. Doctors said his mind was gone, inexplicably short circuiting and leaving behind only a shell of the person he had been.

Only Leslie, Evan, Dan, and Dorothy knew the truth, and all mourned the loss of a good man and friend. Provisions were made for Dorothy to re-open the diner until such time as Arthur's will could be sorted out and she could purchase the restaurant. Leslie became co-owner, and on any given day, you could find both of them running about through a packed house, delivering food that was as good for the soul as it was for the taste buds.

Dan returned to work after four months. It was sooner than his physician would have liked, but the deputy argued that another day stuck at home watching daytime TV might induce irreversible brain damage. While the doctor dismissed the validity of his patient's self-diagnosis, he did take pity, and allowed Dan back on the job, with the stipulation that he perform only light duties for the first month. The deputy was more than happy to oblige.

Little by little, life returned to normal in Millford Springs, but the house at 1401 Maple Ridge Lane still sits empty. The murders, both present and past, have kept buyers at bay, and with each passing month, the tales of the place being haunted escalated.

Believers in the supernatural noted that, after Charlie's death and the house being vacated, the tragedies ceased. There were no more townspeople going mad, no more unexplainable deaths, and no missing persons. The same people also pointed to the story of the disappearing girl in the back seat of Miriam Harvey's car - something which has become legendary in its own rite - and claimed that as proof of an otherworldly connection to the horrific events. They even went so far as to presume the entire series of events had been orchestrated by Walter's vengeful spirit.

Even those who don't believe in the paranormal avoid walking directly in front of the house, and have warned their children to stay away from the place. But, kids being kids, it's not uncommon to see small groups of them clustered around the sun-faded For Sale sign on the lawn, daring one another to go inside. Some have come close, but none have ever made it beyond the front porch. They claim to see a face behind the door, or hear whispers or screams, at which point they always leave the property with due haste.

To this day, there are those in town who claim that late at night, when the moon slips behind the clouds, music can be heard emanating from within the house. Cynics scoff at the notion, asserting it is but a trick of the wind. But, those who have heard it for themselves say otherwise. They say you can make out each note of the phantom lullaby as it drifts beyond the dark house and breaks the stillness of the evening air. That it is a melody penned to lure unsuspecting souls into a hellish playground, where sanity and reason give way to deviant desires and murderous impulses.

They say, it is death's refrain.

They say, it is a madman's song.

A MADMAN'S SONG